UNBREAKABLE

GEORGIA COFFMAN

Cover Design:

Sommer Stein, Perfect Pear Creative Covers

Editing:

Marion Archer, Making Manuscripts

Proofreading:

Marla Selkow Esposito, Proofing with Style

LETTER TO THE READER

Dear Reader,

Thank you for picking up this book. It holds a special story that's been in my heart for years, and I'm still beside myself that I got to write it. On top of that, I got to write it in Corinne Michaels's Salvation series. And that is a dream come true.

If you enjoyed *Beloved* and *Beholden*, I hope you love the role Taylor plays in this story. I hope you smile when Catherine and Jackson make appearances too. This couple introduced me to Corinne's work, and they made me fall in love with her particular brand of drama, angst, and steam.

Unbreakable falls in those categories too. It's an emotional story of second chances, forgiveness, friendship, fighting for what you want out of life and relationships, and at its very core, there's love. Love is often difficult, sometimes painful, but it comes through for us in the end, even if it's years later. Aiden and Sage... their love isn't always easy or pretty, but it's *everything*.

Happy reading,
Georgia

"I like you."

I drop my hands to my lap and blink at him. The crowd and the music blaring through the speakers make the bar feel small.

It's hard to talk in here, and for a moment, I think I misheard him.

"I mean, I *really* like you." Aiden searches my gaze, looking for something, although I'm not sure what.

My body tenses.

My mind is blank. I should be thinking about all the reasons his confession is bad. *Wrong.*

Instead, I draw a blank.

The music is swiftly muffled by the blood rushing to my ears, like I'm hanging by a thread, ready to snap and fall on my face.

"I need air." I slide off my barstool and fight my

way through the crowd, bumping into sweaty bodies, my heart racing.

I sidestep the young bouncer and throw the door open. Emerging onto the sidewalk, I take a deep breath to try to steady my dizziness. I've had two drinks—*two*. And yet, it feels like I've had ten.

Aiden likes me?

He has feelings of more than friendship... for me?

It can't be.

"Jersey, wait." Aiden pulls me to the side.

The music is faint out here. The stars twinkle in the night sky. Giddy students sway past us, celebrating yet another week of finals behind us, which was what Aiden and I were doing. Celebrating before he goes off to law school in the fall, and I enter my senior year.

It's a normal Friday night, yet this moment feels life-changing.

"Please say something." He holds my hands in his, rubbing his thumbs over my knuckles. The moment I feel his warm touch, my shoulders sag.

I'm captivated by his liquid amber eyes.

It's always like this with Aiden. He makes me feel calm and comfortable and so many other things... but what do I do with his confession?

"Are you drunk?" I whisper, searching his eyes for a hazy layer, or any indication that he doesn't mean what he said. My heart is caught in my throat as I wait for an answer.

His lips twist. "No, I'm not drunk, Sage. I mean it."

I don't miss his use of my real name instead of the nickname he gave me two years ago.

It forms a knot in my stomach, but it's not the nauseating kind. It's the good kind. The terrifying yet liberating kind of excitement I felt when I drove a car for the first time.

But it only confuses me further—I've never thought of Aiden this way.

"I, um…"

He steps closer and cups my cheek. "I fought it. I fought my feelings for you as much as I could, but I can't do it anymore. You're not with him now."

Even though my thoughts and feelings are a mess, I tilt my face into his hand, loving the heat of it against my skin.

"Tell me what to do." He licks his lips, then leans closer still, so his lips are a mere inch from mine. "What do I do, Sage?" he rasps.

I don't have an answer, nor does he wait long for one. His lips brush against mine, so softly. Like a breeze rustling leaves, he peppers a light kiss across my tingling lips.

It lights something inside me that I haven't felt from a kiss in a long time. Simply put, it's exhilarating.

It takes everything in me to push him away. To take a step back. To think clearly.

"This isn't right." My chest heaves as pain flashes

across his expression. "I mean"—I gulp—"Dave… we just broke up. He and I were together for years. He deserves an explanation…" My voice trails off as guilt festers inside me.

Aiden runs both his hands through his hair, then down his cheeks, which makes his eyes frown even more. "Don't go back to him, Sage. Please don't."

"I need time to think." I choke on a sob that snuck its way up my throat.

He steps away like I rejected him.

"Aiden…" I reach for him, but he shrugs out of my hold. "I just need a little time. This isn't easy."

He remains silent as he stares at a spot on the sidewalk. *What is he thinking?*

Silently, he nods, his jaw set. He slinks away as if he's a martyr in this tense situation, and I'm left standing here with my emotions weighing heavily on my chest.

I want to yell and scream for him, but my words are lost in my shock.

Students bump into me, but I remain in place as he disappears around the corner without a backward glance.

And I know, in this moment, I lost my best friend.

Before I've had the chance to consider that I might want him to be more.

CHAPTER ONE

AIDEN

Eight years later…

"Tina's doing yoga in her underwear again."

I groan as I roll over and lay my arm across Raven's bare stomach. "Not exactly the first thing I want to hear this morning."

"She should really get some blinds. They're literally less than a dollar."

Sighing, I open my eyes. Raven's angled her neck toward the window where the curtains are parted just enough to view Tina's living room across the alleyway.

I prefer the floor-to-ceiling window behind the head of my bed. I purposely don't have a headboard. This way, I can lie down and fully appreciate the view of the Hudson River and Jersey City in the distance.

I keep my eyes firmly away from Tina's morning escapades. She's lived there longer than I have here, and after her husband died, she's had one man after another to cure the lonely nights.

And yoga. Enough yoga to resemble a pretzel by now.

"Stop watching her, you perv." I nuzzle Raven's neck, then trail kisses down her shoulder.

She turns her attention to me. "She's the one putting her business on display. Literally."

"She's a grown woman. Let her do what she wants," I murmur against her skin, distracting myself from the same conversation we have almost every morning.

She exhales and runs her fingers through my wavy hair. "You're only defending her because you like the cookies she drops off for you every week."

I stop kissing her and rake my gaze over the tattoo on her upper arm, up to her shoulder, until I reach her cheeks. "She makes damn good cookies."

"I better learn how to bake before she steals you away from me." She giggles. It's a feminine sound that doesn't seem like her, and it makes me think she's referring to more than Tina and her cookies alone.

As if any other woman would steal me away.

I hum, letting the scruff along my jaw tickle Raven's cheek. "I like the sound of more baked goods, but it's going to take a lot more than a few cookies to keep me from you." I kiss her lips, drinking her in like

I would expensive whiskey, liking that they're natural. Any minute she'll cover them in bright red, pink, or purple, depending on what kind of day this is for her.

"Aren't you meeting with the new PR firm this morning? You're going to be late if we keep this up." She nibbles on my bottom lip, then pulls back, her black lashes fluttering as she opens and closes her eyes.

I run my hands through my hair, sighing with exhaustion. I've worked long, nearly impossible hours to get our startup company rolling. We've created an app that allows users to buy and sell stocks in players of different sports, and their value is determined by an algorithm I carefully—and painstakingly—built over three years.

It's been five total years of grueling work, continual beta tests, and assembling the best team. Finding Jared, in particular, was a miracle. I did most of the heavy lifting, but he was a major help in perfecting the algorithm. Without him and his wizard skills, we wouldn't be where we are now.

We've had numerous meetings with investors too, although Westin has handled most of those. We learned after a few rejections that I don't belong in the spotlight. Westin's taken the lead on our funding and marketing, both of which are his strong suits, anyway.

But we've exhausted our connections over the last couple years as we tested the app in phases during every sports season, correcting bugs and faults in the sequencing and selection of the algorithm. Now, it's time for the official launch of Jock Stock, and we agreed a PR firm would be the most beneficial way to expand our reach.

This morning will be our first meeting since they took us on as clients, and we'll need to go over the campaign that will secure our place in the sports industry—our future.

Despite my excitement, my job and its long hours have taken a toll. *And at times, my sanity.*

Small business owners and entrepreneurs should receive daily medals for their dedication and drive to *not* stop. To motivate ourselves, especially when no one's watching. To reach for more and refuse to settle, or worse—give up.

"Go." Raven nods toward the bathroom.

Groaning, I toss the covers to the side. My body feels like it's made of cement as I drag myself to the shower. I rub shampoo into my hair, noticing how much longer it is than I normally keep it, but I haven't been able to make my last two haircut appointments. Between work, sleep, and sneaking in a date with Raven as often as I can, it's been hard to squeeze anything else into my schedule.

Thank fuck this is New York, though, and many places stay open past midnight. It opens so many more options for me, unlike my small hometown, where options are limited to begin with, and everything closes as early as eight o'clock.

I step out of the bathroom, a towel around my hips, when Raven says, "We should celebrate tonight."

"Maybe."

"You're going to have to take a break someday." She brushes past me into the bathroom, leaving the door ajar, and I catch small glimpses of her as she moves about.

Over the last few months, my loft has become basically hers too. More of her things litter this place than my own, and not only bathroom toiletries. She has throw pillows and rugs, canvases and paints, even tampons, which would have freaked me out if I didn't have two overly comfortable sisters. Mia and Avril share far too much about their personal lives with me.

But this is still my *home*.

Raven hasn't brought up the idea of moving in together, not since last month when I told her we should wait since her lease isn't up for another few months, after which we can revisit the topic.

What I didn't tell her is... I felt unsure when she asked, although I don't know why.

"Is that what you're wearing?" Raven twists her wet hair in a towel, wringing it out. "I thought Westin said business attire today because of the meeting."

I peer down at my jeans and plaid button-down

over a white tee. "But these are my good jeans. No holes or tattered cuffs."

She smiles, placing her hands on my upper arms. "You definitely should change, and we need to go shopping this weekend. You literally only have two pairs of slacks, A."

My jaw tics.

She's trying to help—I know and appreciate this—but having her tell me *we* need to go shopping makes me cringe, as if I can't take care of myself. Even Mia has never tried to take me shopping, and that's what she lives for.

"We're a casual office," I say, keeping my voice neutral.

"But you're on your way to making it big, so you'll need nicer clothes to impress people." She pats my shoulder, then kisses my cheek.

"That's another reason why I'm not the face of the company and Westin is. He's a lot prettier, and his closet is practically a J. Crew store."

She rolls her eyes. "Go."

Forcing a smile, I change into the nicest clothes I own—I haven't dressed up this much since I was in college interviewing for internships.

College.

It feels like another lifetime at this point, but the thought of that time in my life, when my world imploded, still makes me grimace.

I smooth my hair back into a low bun and leave the top two buttons of my shirt open, then grab a sports coat and assess myself in the mirror.

"It's perfect," Raven says from behind me.

I nod, then pull my leather messenger bag over my shoulder and kiss her once more before I head out into the fresh morning air.

We survived another brutal winter, and the smell of spring in the air gives us hope for relief—a new beginning.

On my way to the subway, I pass the bakery where Raven and I get coffees and pastries when we have a free morning. Past a small convenience store next to a dry cleaner. I move out of the way of a jogger and her St. Bernard, who's salivating and keeping pace next to her like she promised it a big steak later.

A taxi cuts off a minivan right as the light turns for us to cross. No one flinches. It's New York City, after all. I've lived here long enough not to be fazed by the chaos, either.

It's been almost eight years, but it seems like yesterday that I came here and met Westin at my last job. Our first conversation was over Fantasy Football and sports stats.

We sold IT equipment, and Westin outdid me every quarter. He has a way with words and natural charm that proved very helpful when we needed to secure startup funds. It's because of him that our app has become more than a simple idea.

It's a company.

I head down the stairs, disappearing into the dim light toward the subway. People run, walk, or idly stand to the side. One guy is hunched in the corner, and a couple guys use buckets as drums, an upturned hat in front of them with change.

Thirty minutes later, I get off the subway and walk a couple blocks to our new office in Midtown. We moved in a couple months ago, and I'm still getting used to the commute. It could be worse, though. It takes Jared an hour to get to work now, sometimes longer, which I'm sure he'll complain about as soon as he sees me. He complains about it every day.

The sun is high, reflecting off the windows of the buildings surrounding me. I maneuver around a few businessmen with briefcases like I'm switching lanes. When I find an opening, I race across to the sidewalk and stand in line for coffee from a small truck.

I take a deep breath, leaning my head back.

Back home in Virginia, I didn't have this bustle. I never walked to work, the grocery store, or the local coffee shop. Besides, the only coffee option was Randy's old café across town, which was mainly a donut shop with three coffee choices. He had three creamers in stock from the local Wal-Mart, and his version of a vanilla latte was stirring Coffee-Mate

French Vanilla creamer in a warm cup of medium roast.

I smile at the thought as I grab my coffee, welcoming the warmth of it in my hand. Randy's the reason I began drinking it black at such a young age. As he got older, he tended to forget the creamer altogether, and no one's had the heart to tell him—small-town family and all. Thankfully, from what Mia's told me, his daughter moved back to help him.

I take the elevator to the eighth floor of our building and get out. Our offices—more like cubicles—line the walls and have sliding glass doors, giving each of us a view of the elevators but little privacy. We aren't too concerned about it at this point, though. There are only ten total Jock Stock employees so far, and we're spread out. As we grow, we might discuss renovating the space to include more privacy.

A work in progress.

The second my ass hits the seat, Jared appears next to my desk. "Has an apartment become available in your building yet?"

"No, and before you ask, yes, Tina still lives in hers."

He groans. "I'm dying here. It's like waiting for the next *Star Wars* movie—torture."

"That's not what fans of *The Mandalorian* say." I pull my laptop out of my bag and set it on my desk, then hook it up to my monitor.

As Jared keeps on beside me, I pull up the reports from our quality assurance department. It's not really a department yet since there's only one person, but Westin says we should think big, so we call them all departments, no matter how few people are in each.

"Do you know what time I get up every morning?" Jared's eyes widen.

"I do know, because you tell me every morning."

"*Four*." He huffs. "Four o'clock a.m. Like I'm some kind of fitness fiend filled with self-loathing."

"Just think, now that you've created a habit of waking up early, you can start jogging in the mornings when you do find your new apartment." I point to his legs—his scrawny frame is that of a tall high schooler. "You should probably join Westin and me at the gym for leg day, though."

He rolls his eyes as Westin strolls in, briefcase in hand. He nods in our direction and makes his way to his office, which is next to mine. "You ready for our meeting this morning?" he calls over to me.

I drum my fingers on my desk. "All set."

He pops his head around the corner. "Jared, please tell me you're not complaining about your commute again."

Jared scoffs.

"You missed his riveting tale of how early he gets up." I laugh, swiveling in my chair to face them.

"It wouldn't be so bad if we didn't stay until ten or

later, most nights. I might as well bring an air mattress and camp out in my office."

"There's an idea." Westin snaps his fingers.

"Never." Jared shakes his head as he turns toward his own office.

We like to give him shit, but it's all in good fun. At the end of the day, we always have each other's backs. Which is why I've been trying so hard to keep an eye —and ear—out for any openings in my apartment building.

Once I'm alone in my office, I leave the lights off and pull up the reports. There's too much to squeeze into thirty minutes before our meeting, but I like to know what will be waiting for me afterward.

Once I print off the reports and prep for our development meeting, Westin buzzes me that it's time to meet with the PR firm.

I stop in my tracks by my office door as a slender woman with her hair pulled into a sleek ponytail walks in, a laptop bag and small purse slung over her shoulder. I instantly recognize her as Taylor from our previous meeting with CJJ Promotions when we hired her.

But the other woman stands directly behind Taylor, blocked from my view.

Nikki, our office manager and receptionist, greets them and offers them a beverage. After they politely decline, Nikki holds her hand out. "Right this way."

The mystery woman follows closely behind them, slowly coming into view the longer she walks. Unlike Taylor's heels, she's in flats, a pencil skirt, and a tucked-in blouse. Her shoulder-length hair flows in soft waves around her pink cheeks.

In a word, she looks natural, as if business attire is her second skin.

She walks like she belongs in an office. She's confident, but there's a comfortable air about her too. Stunning, and... *familiar*.

Those doe eyes.

High cheekbones and warm smile.

I stiffen, and my heart thunders in my ears like Mike Tyson's practicing his punches against the walls of my skull.

Her smile widens as Westin approaches them, and when her gaze drifts in my direction, her face pales.

What the fuck...

My heart is caught in my throat as I walk toward them.

What is she doing here?

Her sweet aroma consumes me, bringing back so many memories that I've long buried in the "Do Not Open" part of my brain.

She tucks her hair behind both ears as I'm taken back to college nights of video games and pizza. The grease glistening on her lips and how she would slowly, innocently, lick it off.

Afternoons in the park playing Frisbee and soccer. Sitting in her car while I introduced her to indie rock music.

And worse—I'm taken back to our night together when everything had been nothing short of blissful, but quickly turned into a nightmare.

I squeeze my eyes shut and run a hand over my hair, hoping she won't be here when I open my eyes again.

But sure enough, it's her.

Here.

It's been eight years since I last saw Sage Matthews. Since I heard her laugh. Since I admired the way her hair shined in the sun.

Eight years since I held her in my arms, before she rushed to another man.

She stands in front of me, looking beautiful —*breathtaking*.

Instantly, I panic as my gaze jumps from Taylor to Westin and back to Sage.

We're obviously supposed to work together.

For years, this company has been my whole life. How am I supposed to focus on bringing it home with Sage here?

Fuck me.

CHAPTER TWO

SAGE

I never thought I'd see him again.

I stare into his heated gaze now. His jaw is set. His hair is longer than it used to be. His short beard is also new.

But it's him.

Aiden Baxter.

His hazel eyes and slightly crooked tilt of his nose. He stands tall, grown up—a man.

"This is my new assistant, Sage." Taylor's introduction pulls me from my stupor.

"Hi," I manage, my voice raspy. The rest of my words are stolen from my throat, cast aside as memories play in my head like a movie reel.

All of Aiden.

From the sweet and carefree to the devastating and painful.

I blink at him, then turn to the other guy. He's taller but similarly built, as if he and Aiden are on the same fitness regimen. I shake myself out of this torturous twist of fate and try to focus.

This is my job.

My *new* job. I can't act ditzy on my first project.

"I'm Westin." The guy to our side offers his hand for me to shake. I stare at it for a beat, catching Taylor in my periphery, eyeing me curiously.

"Hi," I repeat and shake Westin's hand like I'm a robot. Stiff. Up. Down. Release.

He smiles kindly, his demeanor poised yet friendly. "This is my partner, Aiden Baxter. We started Jock Stock together a few years ago. He's our full-stack engineer and manages software development, while I handle more of the business and marketing side of things."

My eyes bulge, trying to comprehend what he's saying. He helped build this company? The one that created an app much like the stock market, but for sports—I find it hard to believe we're talking about the same Aiden.

What happened to becoming a lawyer? He's in sports now? Computer science?

I have so many questions.

Aiden shakes my hand in silence, seemingly as shocked to see me as I am him. Neither of us seems to have the capacity to mention that we know each other. That we have a history.

Instead, we remain silent as Westin shows us around their suite. "It's new, and we're still sprucing it up, but with a view like this, do we really need much décor inside?" He chuckles, and I know what he means.

The view of the city through the corner windows is magnificent. The river in the distance. The people milling below. It feels like we're kings of the world up here.

We end up in the conference room, where we take a seat at the long, wooden table. It's rustic but sleek, professional yet inviting, and the ceramic vase in the middle, filled with red gerberas, brightens the room.

It's welcoming, but I'm not comfortable. Far from it.

I feel Aiden's eyes on me throughout the meeting as we discuss their app's official launch. My mind races, but I try to focus instead on what Taylor needs. I watch her to learn about the firm and how she does things. What questions to ask. Her level of eye contact with clients.

I'm not new to business etiquette and customer relations, but this is New York. I'm currently in a tall office building between Times Square and the Empire State Building. In other words, it's all a whole new level for me, compared to my small hometown in North Carolina.

"We're looking at five months for the launch, so the end of July, correct?" Taylor asks. "At the start of football preseason?"

"Correct." Westin sits tall.

"Perfect." Taylor jots a few things down. "The contract we signed is for six months. We'll work with you to promote and execute the launch, then stay on for another month afterward to ensure you guys are set up for the future." Taylor grins at him like we're planning world domination—and in a way, it's accurate. After she makes another note, we move to the next item on our agenda. "In our pitch, we mentioned brand."

"Don't change a thing." Westin waves his hand. "What you said about our company being innovative, progressive, and advantageous for every sports enthusiast—it's spot-on. You nailed all that we're about, which is why we knew we had to hire you."

"Thank you." She nods. "With that said, let's talk social media strategies."

"Thus far, I've been handling all of our accounts," Westin says. "But I'd like to pawn the burden off to more capable hands."

Taylor smiles, then points to me. "Sage has a background in content creation as well, so she and I will tag team your social media platforms to maintain a consistently branded presence on your company's behalf."

"What a relief." Westin clutches his chest in exaggeration. "Now, I can spend more time babying the team." He rolls his eyes toward Aiden, his tone good-natured and fun. They seem more like brothers than business partners.

And given how far they've come, whatever they're doing is definitely working.

My gaze flickers to Aiden, who stares back at me, his eyebrows furrowed. He's curiously watching me like I grew three heads.

What is he thinking?

Years ago, I might've known, but he's a mystery now.

I shift in my seat.

The air between us is so thick. For me, our silence is worse than if we were yelling, and I hope Taylor can't sense my discomfort. If she does, maybe she'll chalk it up to be because this is my first outing with her to visit clients.

For the next hour, we go over possible media coverage, as well as podcasts and *YouTube* channels to schedule interviews with. Taylor pulls out a list of influencers to contact, as does Westin. He already has good relationships with several people in the industry, and they exchange those lists.

We talk press releases.

Email campaigns.

Ads.

At one point, I take a deep breath, overwhelmed. There's so much I need to learn. When I ran my small marketing firm in North Carolina, our target audience was narrow compared to what we're dealing with now. Helping Mrs. Meyers increase her quaint café's business was a fraction of Taylor's plan to catapult Jock Stock to the national stage.

But this is why I came to New York to begin with. For more than what my hometown could offer. And I'm confident I can do it.

First, though, I need to stop worrying about what it means to be working with Aiden.

Of all people, in all cities, Aiden Baxter is my first meeting—*how*?

I continue asking myself that very question for the rest of the hour, switching between denial, shock, and genuine confusion.

Once the meeting ends, Taylor and Westin make small talk, while I gather our things. As I do, a line of sweat travels down my spine, tickling me like the times an ant would run up my arm during my picnics with Aiden in college.

"I look forward to working together." Westin smiles, his teeth perfectly aligned and bright. I imagine it'll be on the covers of magazines someday.

I chance another peek at Aiden, who still watches me like he doesn't know what to do with me.

He hasn't said a word this entire time.

Westin nudges him, then leans back on his heels like he meant to get Aiden's attention more subtly. Aiden glances between us, first shaking Taylor's hand, then mine. "Yes. Thank you for coming by, and we look forward to working with you. What Westin said." Frowning, he turns around and heads to his office.

"We'll be in touch to go over progress soon," Taylor offers.

She and I wave one last time as we make our way to the elevator. Once the doors close, my shoulders sag.

"That was... interesting."

I squint at her through one opened eye. It's only my second week working for her, and I can't yet read her. If she's mad, she has every right to be. "I'm so sorry. I was flustered, and that was completely unprofessional. It wasn't like me, I promise. I'm better than that."

She studies me, and I wonder what she sees—the girl I was in college when Aiden and I were friends, the regretful divorcee, or the new and improved woman I'm trying to be?

The elevator doors open into the lobby, and we cross the marble floors, nodding to the security guard, and through the revolving doors.

"How do you know each other?" she asks as we step outside onto the sidewalk.

I tilt my head toward her.

"You and Aiden. He never took his eyes off you."

I blush. "It's a long story. I don't even know where—"

"Jersey!"

My heart lurches, and tears immediately sting the corners of my eyes. Before I can finish my sentence, I turn to find Aiden racing toward us.

I gulp, frozen in my spot on the sidewalk. Not even an angry pedestrian could move me.

"Are you okay?" Taylor gently touches my arm.

"Yeah," I rasp. "We're old friends."

"I'll give you a chance to catch up and meet you at the office."

"Are you sure?" I panic, worried that I appear too unreliable. I don't want my personal life to interfere with work. *Not again*.

"Of course. I'll start on research, but I'll save the *real* fun stuff for us to do together." She winks, then walks to the curb to hail a cab.

When I turn around, Aiden stands there, his hands in his pockets, shaking his head at me. There's a slight twinkle in his eyes too. One that reminds me of the times I played video games with him, and he'd let me win to make me feel better about being so bad at FIFA. He seems to have gotten over his shock from upstairs since he's here, which makes me relax a fraction.

"I can't believe you're here."

I laugh, glancing around as people skirt by.

He ushers me to the side, next to a food and coffee truck. Once we're out of the way, he doesn't let go. Instead, he wraps his arms around my neck, hugging me.

Letting out a weary exhale, I snake my arms around his waist and bury my face in his chest.

It's warm and familiar.

Like home.

My frail heart squeezes.

I never let myself think about him, given what happened with us, but hugging him now, I realize how much I truly missed him, especially the easy comfort and safety he once provided.

"I did not expect to see you this morning." Pulling back, I wipe a stray tear from my cheek, shaking my head. "What happened to law school? To taking down dirtbags and moving to Washington DC for a life in politics?"

He scratches his chin. "After I graduated, I spent the summer abroad, traveling Europe."

I instinctively tense.

"But when I got back, I couldn't bring myself to go to law school. It was like Europe opened my eyes to more possibilities. More *appealing* possibilities, anyway." He chuckles. "I took a few years off, and then, at my temporary job selling IT equipment, I met Westin. We were both pretty lost at the time." He shrugs. "Before I knew it, Jock Stock was born over beer at Hemingway House, and we never looked back."

Traveling Europe.

Appealing possibilities.

I almost don't catch the rest of what he says beyond that.

"That's amazing," I say, swallowing my emotions, trying to smile through them.

He nods. "The long days and even longer nights aren't always amazing, but with the launch coming, it's starting to feel like it's all worth it."

"From what Taylor's told me, you guys are impressive. She paused her own wedding plans to work on her pitch for your account—she had to have it."

"She's definitely meticulous and dedicated. We like that."

"I'll be sure to tell her. It'll make her feel better since her fiancé is getting agitated. Although, who could blame him? Their wedding is less than four months away." My lips curl.

He watches me with a special glimmer in his hazel eyes, but as the silence stretches between us, his light-hearted expression sobers. "How are you?"

I pause, considering his question. How much does

he know about my life during the last eight years? Does he know about my divorce? About my company?

How unhappy I've been?

I push through the knot in my stomach and straighten my posture. "I'm great. Just moved to the city a little over a month ago, so you'll have to show me all the hotspots sometime."

I freeze with my mouth agape, realizing what I've said. I still can't tell if he's happy to see me, or how I feel about seeing him again, either. I'm relieved, but the ache in my chest he caused all those years ago flares like an aggravated ulcer.

"I'm sorry." I bite my lip. "I know you're busy with the company and your life. You don't need me dragging you to all the tourist sights."

He clenches his jaw, and there's a familiar fire in his eyes that I haven't seen in years. It makes me squirm, shifting from one foot to the other.

I start to back away, waving my hands toward the street. "I better get back to the office. It's my second week, so I can't slack. Not that it's okay to ever slack, but—"

"Where's your phone?" He holds his hand out.

Confused, I give it to him, anyway, and our fingers accidentally brush.

He types on my phone, then hands it back to me. "You have my number. Call me anytime, Jersey," he says, his voice smooth and gentle.

I nod, my emotions clogging my throat as I stare at him.

Aiden Baxter.

Heartbreakingly handsome.

Ruthlessly evil underneath it all, yet the kind and caring Aiden I once knew is still somewhere in there.

Time has been good to him, to say the least. He's grown-up. More muscular and lean. He had trouble growing a mustache in college, but he has a beard now. It only adds to his physical appeal.

My heart races as I nod once more to him, then turn to find a taxi. I haven't perfected the art of hailing a cab yet, but I try to remember what Taylor showed me. Not to wave frantically—I'm not in need of an ambulance. Don't step off the curb until they come to a complete halt. Always sit in the back. And lastly, I don't have to make small talk. Most drivers prefer I don't, according to her.

Being from a small town without a cab service, I'm thankful for her easy guide.

I follow the steps, and once I'm settled into one, I peer out the window, losing myself in times long gone as the buildings blur. We stop every few seconds as traffic increases, and my breathing becomes rapid the longer I sit here.

Memories flood my brain like they're unearthed from a cemetery.

"This is Aiden from my college algebra class I told you

about." Dave high-fives a guy with dirty-blond hair that's trimmed on the sides. He's tan, and his deep amber-colored eyes remind me of summer nights when the sun sets.

When he greets me, his warmth reaches his eyes, which crinkle in the corners from his smile. "Sage, right?"

"Yeah." I dip my head, and his innocent use of my name makes my stomach flutter.

"Dave told me you want to move to New York City after college."

"Wouldn't that be awesome?" I fall in step with them as we walk to the student union. "I'd love to find a little apartment in Jersey City. I'd take the train across the river into Manhattan, where I'd work for a fancy company. I'd jog in Central Park. Get bagels and coffee every morning and be so in-tune with the city life that I wouldn't even need a subway map."

Dave wraps his arm around my shoulders, gripping my upper arm tighter than usual. Odd. "It's just a fantasy, like your poetry."

"My poetry?" I tense. "What's wrong with writing poetry?"

"I mean, it's great that you love it, but it's a hobby. What're you going to do—become a full-time poet? You can't make money doing that."

I sigh. He's right, but his mocking tone—how easily he dismisses my interests—makes my chest squeeze.

"Besides, do you know how expensive the city is? Even outside Manhattan. Even if we started saving the moment we

started dating four years ago, it still wouldn't cover one month's rent. And your poetry sure as hell wouldn't help." He chuckles while my stomach sinks further.

"Nothing's impossible," Aiden jumps in, but Dave doesn't seem to hear him as we enter the noisy cafeteria.

In line for our food, Aiden leans into me. "I like that you want to move to Jersey City and work in Manhattan. It's cool." He taps his chin in exaggeration. "I think I'll call you Jersey Girl from now on. Or maybe just Jersey."

"We're here."

I snap my attention to the driver, then fish my wallet out of my purse to pay with a card. Once it goes through, I get out and make my way into the building that houses CJJ Promotions.

Thankfully, Taylor puts me right to work, and I'm too distracted by numbers, account files, and social media for the next few hours to think about anything else.

I draft content, then re-draft.

Make coffee and lunch runs.

Schedule and confirm meetings.

And as the setting sun casts a soft glow over the city, I'm working with Taylor in her office. Our containers from a late lunch are stacked to the side. The only sound is soft music and shuffling of papers as we wind down from the day.

"Thanks for taking me with you today," I say, breaking our silence.

"Although most of your job will be done from here for a while, I want to eventually do outings with you like that." She leans back in her chair, her expression wistful. "When I was Catherine Pope's assistant, she gave me more and more responsibility, which gave me more experience and confidence to do this job."

"That must've been helpful."

"It was. She was amazing to work for—a brilliant mentor—and I admired her. She started here as an intern, worked her way up, and now runs her own branch of CJJ in LA." After a short pause, she meets my gaze. "I hope to do the same for you that she did for me."

"It means a lot. Thank you."

When I moved here, I didn't have a job lined up. It wasn't ideal, but I sold my business right before I moved. I had money to start my new life without the past holding me back.

Taylor took a chance on me, and I'll never forget the magnitude of that.

"Do you want to talk about Aiden yet?"

I grimace. How do I divulge my sordid past to my new boss without giving her the impression that he'll interfere with my work performance? "We met in college. He was, uh"—I clear my throat—"he was friends with my boyfriend at the time, and we hung out a lot. I hadn't seen him since he graduated and moved away."

She studies me, and I squirm like I'm in an interrogation room with a light shining on my forehead. She gives me a tight-lipped smile, then says, "I have a feeling there's more to the story, but I'll let you stop there until you're ready to share the rest."

I sigh with relief.

She intertwines her fingers on her desk in front of her and leans forward. "I know you're new and still getting used to things, but I'm always here if you need someone to talk to. Catherine and I had a great working relationship, but we were also friends. I'd like that with you too."

"I could really use a friend."

"I'm here when you're more comfortable."

"Thank you." I smile, genuinely grateful that I was lucky enough to find Taylor—a friend—in this sea of broken hopes and dreams that is New York.

I went on too many interviews to count the first few weeks of living here. I bounced from one company to the next, feeling more and more dejected every time someone asked me if I knew how to brew coffee and transfer a call. For weeks, I feared I was destined to remain behind a desk with a phone glued to my hand, warding off cold callers.

Then, I met with Taylor, and it was as if I was standing at the end of a rainbow next to a pot of gold. She saved my ass, to be frank.

Although I still make coffee and lunch runs and

deal with the occasional cold caller, there's more opportunity to grow at CJJ, a premier PR firm. She's already entrusted me with something as big as social media content. I have more responsibilities after two weeks here than I would've had at any of the other jobs I interviewed for.

"Don't forget that I'm from a small town too," Taylor says, a hint of her Midwestern accent in her voice. "I know what a shock it can be to move here, so let me know if you need any more guidance. We talked about taxis already. Maybe next week, we can discuss ordering food without holding up the line at delis."

"Perfect, because if I get yelled at one more time, I might cry." I giggle, recalling lunch the last couple of days at the crowded markets. "I'd stop going to the one around the corner, but it's too cheap and delicious."

We laugh together, then decide to pack up for the day.

"Nice job today," she says as I leave her office.

I thank her again, then follow her to the elevator, mentally composing a list of tasks I need to complete tomorrow.

Maybe I'll come in early.

"Listen," she starts as we ride to the bottom floor. "It's obvious you and Aiden Baxter have a history, but whatever he was to you before, just remember, he's a client now. We've been hired to do a job."

I gulp. "Understood."

Her expression softens. "My former boss I told you about? She fell for her client. They're living together in LA now and will probably get married soon, but their relationship was hard on her at first." She frowns as the elevator doors open, and we step off. "When secrets surfaced, it threatened her job and career—everything she'd worked hard for. You and I may not know each other well, *yet*"—she squeezes my arm—"but I can tell landing this job is important to you. So, I'm only offering you some friendly advice to be careful about crossing lines with him."

"I appreciate it," I whisper.

She pats my arm, then says, "See you tomorrow."

My body is tense as I walk toward the subway. It's like retracing my steps from the day I arrived at CJJ for my second interview.

I was scared and nervous, but Taylor was warm and made me feel like I could really have a place here.

After I accepted the job that day, I walked out on this very sidewalk, past the same buildings that stood tall and intimidating, yet they felt like friends rooting for me.

Because I'm doing it—the impossible.

I divorced Dave, and it was the first step to creating the life I always wanted but didn't think I could have.

I moved to New York.

Got a job at a top-tier firm.

Rented an apartment in Jersey City.

I sit on the subway, swaying with the train as it zips along the track. When we come to a stop to let people on and off, my phone vibrates, and I quickly check the text before it blurs once we start moving again.

Dave: Can we meet at the coffee shop? I want to talk.

I don't have to ask him which one he's referring to. It's the coffee shop he and I would always go to on Sundays. It was our weekly tradition, a routine much like our entire relationship.

As the subway jostles me side to side, I manage to type out that I can't meet him, swallowing down my urge to apologize to him. I'm done with that.

I also purposely leave out the fact that I don't live in North Carolina anymore. That I haven't been in town since our nasty run-in at the grocery store. I packed up my things the next day and headed north to move in with my cousin Naomi in Jersey City.

My phone vibrates again.

Dave: Why? What're you doing?

"I'm headed to my apartment hundreds of miles from you," I mutter under my breath. I would worry about seeming crazy to those around me, but during my short time in the city, I've seen much, much worse.

Me: I'm busy. Besides, you don't get to ask me those questions anymore.

Dave: I only want to apologize for what happened. I thought you'd at least give me the opportunity after all I did for you.

I scoff, then turn my phone off. I can't listen to any more of his guilt trips. Besides, I don't have to stand for his bullshit now, not since our divorce was finalized a few weeks ago.

I'm free of him.

When I'm alone on the train across the river, my mind drifts to Aiden.

To years of wondering what happened to him.

To my broken heart.

I thought I was free of the past altogether, but as fate would have it, Aiden and I now work together.

"Don't go to him." Aiden *tugs on my sleeve and pleads.* *"Stay with me."*

I sharply inhale, remembering our night together like it was yesterday.

Sweaty bodies tangled in the sheets.

Skin to skin.

Hot.

So much heat between us.

I inhale again to steady my racing heart.

I thought New York would be my fresh start, but how can it be? Working with Aiden, constantly facing the mistakes of my past, how can I start over here?

"So…" Westin leans against my door at the end of yet another dragging workday.

My office is dark, but the light from the main space behind him casts a freaky glow around him. It's quiet, aside from the buzzing noise coming from Jared's office. He's in the process of blowing up an air mattress—he changed his mind about sleeping here.

"Will today be the day you finally tell me about Sage, or do I have to wait until our next meeting to find out you two are secretly married or some shit?"

I keep my focus on the screen in front of me, avoiding his gaze. I can practically hear the burning questions inside his head. "Nothing like that."

It's been almost a week since she was here.

She hasn't taken me up on my offer to call me, and I haven't reached out, either.

Then again, what did I expect? We didn't leave college on speaking terms. Not a word since we went our separate ways.

Since she married Dave.

I haven't spoken to either of them since I crossed the state line into a new life. Changed my number.

Veered into a different career path.

Reinvented myself.

I've never spoken about them to anyone, but it's hard to keep Westin in the dark at this point.

We're not just business partners. We're friends. It's been easy to distract him with work this week, but there's nowhere to run now that we have a minute of downtime for once, especially since Taylor and Sage have taken some of our load. There were a few bugs I had to rework, but now, there's a pause in my hectic schedule as I wait for results.

"Must be something serious. You're not this silent about anything other than college. Are the two subjects related?" Westin pushes.

"Yes." I sigh, leaning back in my chair and turn toward him. I can hardly see his face, which makes it easier to spill at least one detail. "We were friends in college."

"*Just* friends?" Jared asks, appearing on the other side of Westin, seemingly out of nowhere.

I almost fall out of my chair. "Jesus Christ. A little warning next time, yeah?"

He rolls his eyes.

"Listen, Sage and I were friends in college. She was also my best friend's girlfriend at the time."

"Ouch," they say in unison, glancing at each other like they want to know more but don't know how far to push me.

They know my temper is that of a bear, so they tread lightly some days. Other days, they don't seem to care and make a game of teasing me over stupid shit like my love for Pop-Tarts.

Lila pops her head up from the desk in the far corner. "Westin, I have a question for you, please."

He eyes me as he walks backward, pointing from me to him. "This isn't over."

I shake my head, then unlock my phone. I check my message from Raven about drinks with her art friends. Exhaling, I respond that I'm still at work and won't be able to make it.

Before I click out of our thread, she replies back that I need a break. That I'm working too hard. That I'll be blinded from too many hours staring at a computer screen.

She's been concerned about the number of hours I put in at work, but she gets that this is important to me. She's been supportive, but lately... her concern has turned into something else.

Something I can't place.

I lean back, twirling the phone in my hands.

Against my better judgment, I click through my contacts until I get to Sage's name.

Jersey.

I rub my lip, then hover my thumb over her name.

"I think the name Jersey is growing on me," she says, eyeing me over her cheeseburger. She swipes a strand of hair from her forehead that the wind blew, then takes a big bite, half her face disappearing behind the burger.

When she pulls back, I stare at her lips. At her slender throat bobbing when she swallows. At her honey-colored hair that keeps blowing in her face.

I shift on the blanket we spread out for our picnic in the courtyard between our dorms. "Good, because that's your name from now on. I'm even sending weekly newsletters for others to make sure they call you that."

"Is that why Professor Adams wrote it on my essay?"

"Did she really?"

"No." She rolls her eyes.

"Damn. How dare she disobey my order? She's on my payroll."

Sage shakes her head, peering around us at the other students walking or studying at the wooden tables. She likes to people-watch. She once said it's where she gets her inspiration for poems, in the everyday, finding beauty in the mundane.

She turns her attention back to me. "You make it sound like you're corrupt. Like a drug dealer."

"Nah, I keep the drugs for myself. I don't like to sell."

She giggles, obviously aware that I'm kidding, then dips

her head and takes another bite of her burger. Again, I watch her every movement. Her curved jaw narrows as she chews. Her hair seems lighter out here.

I want to know everything about her.

What sports she plays, if any. Where she got the scar on her wrist. If she has any tattoos.

We've started these picnics a couple times a week, and I hope we continue because I can't stop myself from wanting to curb this aching—and highly inappropriate—curiosity.

She opens her mouth to say something—

"You started without me?" Dave plops down and gives her a kiss on the cheek. She blushes, and for reasons I can't admit out loud, I want to punch my friend in the mouth.

I swallow down the memory like I've been doing all week as new ones continue to surface. I click on her name, then open a new text before I change my mind.

Me: Are you settled in yet? You never told me where you're staying.

Westin calls out to me from the corner with Lila. "Aiden, we need your Einstein-sized brain over here, so we can finish up and go home."

"I'm not going anywhere," Jared's voice rings out as he audibly sighs over squeaking noises. He's obviously getting comfortable on his air mattress, having taken us up on our suggestion to sleep here. The last couple mornings have been more pleasant too, without his whining.

I set my phone next to my keyboard and stand, tapping my fingers against my leg as I make my way over.

And wait for Sage's response like I'm expecting an answer to a marriage proposal.

One I never had the chance to offer her before she accepted my friend's.

CHAPTER FOUR

SAGE

I shuffle boxes around my room and think up a plan for where it will all go. My first month here was spent interviewing for jobs—it was my priority. Now that I have one, I finally have free time to finish unpacking, but with so little space, it's hard to find room for everything.

Luckily, I don't have too many things.

I take in the few boxes littering the floor and the unmade bed—I need to organize and clean and settle in.

As I pick a box to open, I'm thankful again that Naomi let me move in here to begin with. I figured she was simply that desperate for help with rent after her last roommate moved out.

My relationship with Naomi became strained

during my marriage to Dave. But since our divorce, she's met me halfway to make amends.

And living with her, having someone who knows the city, has been a godsend.

I grab a few romance novels from inside the box. It's been years since I read a book, especially a love story. They kept me sane during college, giving me the occasional reprieve from studying, and I enjoyed them, once. I used to enjoy romance and all its wonder of happily ever afters. A wonder that has remained as such because I never experienced it myself, even though at one point, I thought I had.

Since Dave and Aiden, I'm questioning the notion of true love altogether.

I turn a couple books over in my hands and snicker.

"Fucking romance," I mumble, then organize them on my small shelf along with my limited collection of mysteries.

I jump when one lands with a thud on the floor, and a folded piece of paper falls out like a long-forgotten love note.

"What the…" I mutter, leaning down to pick them both up.

The book is a romance novel with a cover of a lone woman, and her head isn't showing. I tuck it under my shoulder, then unfold the piece of paper, and once I scan the writing there, my shoulders sag. My whole body deflates as I sink to the floor.

Sitting cross-legged by my bed, I recall the day I wrote this, saddened again that I spent so many years married to a man who didn't support me or my dreams.

Who didn't truly love me for who I was.

Smoothing the piece of paper on the scuffed floor, I run my shaking hand over the list as I read.

1. Go parasailing

2. Learn French

3. Go to a poetry festival

4. Live in New York

5. Take a cooking class

There are seven more items, but my eyes blur with unshed tears, feeling like I didn't write these things at all. The handwriting is mine, but I don't recognize it. I don't recognize these goals I once listed on a piece of paper like a grocery list. I was sure I'd tick off each item like I was buying bread and coffee. That they were as simple.

I laugh to myself in my empty bedroom, my tears still streaming.

I was in high school and naïve when I made this list.

It was about a month before Dave and I started dating.

Before I settled down with someone I believed to be my dream but turned out to be a nightmare.

I'd throw the list away or hide it back in the book, but it seems wrong to do so. Instead, I shove it in my pocket and get back to unpacking as my mind races.

Dave's brother stopped me at a gas station once and seemed stunned that we split up. "Sorry to hear about you and my brother," he said like he was offering his condolences—as if someone died.

And maybe part of me had.

Dave's yells echo through my head.

Whore.

Cheater.

Bitch.

Our hometown in North Carolina was too small for both of us. One run-in at the grocery store proved that much.

I was humiliated.

I lift my head when the front door lock jimmies open, and Naomi walks in, her arms full of groceries.

Standing from the floor, I waddle toward her, my legs wobbly from sitting too long. The apartment is so small, it's basically two steps from my room to her in the kitchen.

"Let me help." I grab a couple bags, but our fingers get intertwined, and one falls to the floor. "Oh! Sorry," I mumble. "Here, let me... get that..." On my hands and knees, I chase the stray fruit and boxes of noodles.

"Sage, it's fine. I'll get them." Naomi sets the bags on the counter and crouches down to help.

From this angle, I notice the spots on her scrubs. *What bodily liquids are they?* I fight my urge to dry heave.

"Gotcha," she whispers to the runaway orange, her tongue out as if she's a cat after a mouse.

"How was work?" I ask as we both stand.

Her brown hair is wild with naturally tight curls. She tucks one side behind her ear, but it doesn't stay. She smooths her top, running her hands over the stains without flinching. After all, it's her norm. She's been a nurse for several years now.

Which is also why she usually has dark circles under her eyes.

We unpack the groceries as she answers, "Fine. Had another twelve-hour shift, so I'm about to go pass the fuck out." She sounds like a zombie with her monotonous tone. "How's your week going?"

I bite my lip, focusing on unloading the bags. "It's been good so far, aside from this one girl at work—Piper. She's been difficult, but I try to avoid her. We don't work closely together, anyway, so it's been easy. Besides, there are plenty of others who have been amazing. Maya—she's another publicist at the firm—she says the funniest stuff."

Naomi nods, then opens the fridge to put away the cold items.

I sigh. "I'm still getting used to being a

contributing member of society again. A few short months without work felt like years."

She makes a noncommittal sound.

I hand her the carton of almond milk to put away and continue, "I miss being my own boss. Don't get me wrong, this new job is amazing with a lot of room for growth, and I knew I'd have to start at the bottom when I got here. I just... I don't know." I laugh under my breath, shaking my head. *How did my life get so messed up?*

"It'll take time, but you'll get used to it. Be patient. Besides, without Dave, you should have no problem moving up the corporate ladder. He's not here to screw it all up for you." She shuts the refrigerator door, all the groceries put away, and pats my hand. As she does, she gives me the look of pity I've been so desperately trying to escape. In a new city, where no one knows me, no one pities me.

I can just be me—whoever that is.

But with Naomi, I can't run away from what happened with my ex.

"Have you told him you moved yet?" she asks.

"No. He did text me the other day to meet for coffee, though. Said he wanted to apologize for what happened." I shrug. "I was vague and simply said I couldn't."

"Good for you. I mean, how do you apologize for

screaming at your ex in the middle of the coffee aisle?" She scoffs.

I wince. Dave's face was red. Angry. The specks of spit hit my cheek as he yelled in my face for being a cheater, even though I never cheated on him.

Still, he yelled like I was the gum beneath his shoe. While people pretended not to notice, he screamed and gripped my arm to keep me from running. Finally, the store manager had to ask us to leave. I dropped the bottled water and snacks I held and rushed out, my cheeks on fire from anger and humiliation.

I'd never felt so weak. I vowed that night to never let a man make me feel that way again.

Naomi squeezes my forearm—it's the best she can do. Even on great terms, she's not one to show too much emotion.

But we're still working on fixing our relationship, and it's getting better, which makes me feel less alone.

This situation is complicated, though.

She never liked Dave, so she's happy we're no longer married, but the *reason* she didn't like him is still an issue. He put distance between my family and me. Manipulated me, convincing me that he was the only one who cared about me, and as young and vulnerable as I was, I believed him.

I fought for him.

I took his side because I thought he was all I had.

All the while, he drove a wedge between Naomi and me.

In silence, she walks to the couch, and I survey the refrigerator for a few minutes. "What do you want for dinner?"

I peer over the refrigerator door to find her feet dangling off the end of the couch and her arms resting on top of her head.

"Naomi?"

A snore answers me, then silence.

She's asleep.

I shrug and grab a pack of raw chicken from the top shelf. "Chicken and rice it is," I whisper to myself and get to work.

As the chicken cooks and the night sky stretches across the city outside, I check the new message on my phone.

Aiden: Are you settled in yet? You never told me where you're staying.

I almost drop the phone.

I blink at the screen to make sure I'm reading it correctly, but sure enough, it's Aiden. His name hasn't popped up on my screen like this since we were in college, when it was an everyday occurrence.

I missed that... even though I shouldn't.

My thumbs tremble as I type out a response.

Me: I'm living in Jersey City.

I add a smiley face and hit send.

Aiden: Like you always wanted.

Tears well in my eyes again. He always supported me and my dreams, no matter how wild or seemingly asinine. We'd lie back, staring at the stars, sharing our hopes for the future as though if we told the sky, it would make them come true.

It was our thing. We'd spread a blanket out on the grass between our dorms, eat greasy fast food, and talk over soft music.

And each minute we spent together, no matter how simple, he made me feel invincible. It was one of the many things that drew me to him.

I flip the chicken, then chew on my fingernail, peering out the open window at the glistening river in the moonlight. Outside, even though it's late, car doors slam, horns echo, and muffled chatter from people on their balconies seep in through the cracks. New York City is a stark contrast from my hometown—a jungle to a meadow in comparison.

And I welcome the chaotic change. It's an adjustment, but the beginning of something special. I can feel it.

I flip the chicken again and turn back to my phone.

I want to ask Aiden why he moved here. He mentioned his temporary job, but why New York? That was always my fantasy, not his.

But I can't bring myself to ask him something so personal and intimate.

I don't even know him anymore, and I haven't in years.

Me: Do you like living here?

Aiden: I do. It's been a whirlwind since I got here, but all good things.

Me: It was nice to see you last week, and I'm happy for you.

Aiden: Let's meet for drinks tomorrow. No beer, though.

I giggle, relaxing my hip against the counter.

Me: LOL. Remember the Bud Lite I tried that ended up on my dress?

Aiden: You smelled like beer all night and then offended your roommate.

Me: She was offended by everything, even the

fact that I wore red lipstick. Said it was satanic.

Aiden: How dare you bring the devil into your dorm room.

*Me: Guess I was the wild child my mom always warned me against. *eye roll**

I gulp, standing upright. This is too natural. Too similar to the way we once were.

But I know better.

Aiden: Meet me for drinks.

I fish my bucket list out of my pocket. The sizzling chicken muffles the crinkles as I unfold the paper, but the list screams at me above it.

I could make something of myself here, where no one knows me.

He's a client now, Taylor's words echo in my head.

She was right when she said Aiden and I have a history, but she doesn't know the half of it.

How can I go to drinks with Aiden and not let it affect my work?

He was my best friend in college. *Dave's* best friend too.

And the aftermath…

"I like you. I fought it. I fought my feelings for you as much as I could, but I can't do it anymore."

I not only remember his confession but the pain and guilt in his voice too. If we would've gotten together, we would've risked our friendship, betrayed Dave, and never been the same. He put it all on the line, anyway.

But he thought I didn't return his affections. That I couldn't feel the same.

And he ran before I could explain.

He always ran.

It made me turn to the man who stayed. Who promised to love me forever.

Now, fate has brought Aiden and me together again, threatening my present.

But I'm determined to keep the past from ruining my future.

CHAPTER FIVE

SAGE

I said no.

I told Aiden I wouldn't meet him for drinks. Instead of being the adult I thought I was by now, I lied and told him I'd promised Naomi we'd do something since it's her only night off this week.

At least the last part is true.

At work, I organize Taylor's calendars, draft social media posts to run by her, and sort account files. They got sloppy before my arrival, during the time when Taylor was without an assistant, but they're organized now.

Exhaling, I sit at my desk to answer the phone—a client who wants to reschedule a meeting.

"Please hold while I check the calendar for her availability." I click to the right date and find that the time they've requested is open.

Once we confirm the change, I nod as if they're in front of me. "Thank you, and have a nice day."

I just hang the phone up when Piper seemingly appears out of nowhere and sits on the edge of my desk, pushing over my pen holder. "Oops," she says, her voice nasally and unapologetic. "How are you doing?"

"Fine. Thanks." I give her a tight-lipped smile as I gather the pens and set them in an upright holder.

"Must be hard, given your background."

I freeze. "What do you mean?"

"Working as someone's assistant? When you were your own boss once upon a time? How tragic to downgrade."

The hairs on my arms stand.

Her red lips twitch, obviously smug. "Word travels fast, as does this job. Even with your experience, it's not what you're used to, honey. Keep up."

"I'm right where I want to be, doing exactly as I'm supposed to and more." I grind my teeth.

She stands, tapping her long fingernails against my desk, then flips her dark hair over her shoulder. "If you ever need anything, let me know. I'm right over there"—she points to her office in the corner of the suite—"and I have more experience than *most* people here, so I can answer all of your questions." She winks, clearly making a dig at Taylor.

"Cute blue bra," Taylor mumbles sarcastically from behind me.

"Excuse me?" Piper spits.

Taylor pushes off her doorframe, pointing to her chest. "You missed a button."

"That's not an accident, darling." She rolls her eyes, but as she walks away, I catch her smoothing a hand over her chest like she's self-conscious.

"Rat," Taylor mutters.

I cover my laugh with my hand.

"If she starts bothering you, please let me know. She's been a real chore since she found out her boyfriend cheated on her."

"That's awful."

She scoffs. "I'd feel bad too if that boyfriend wasn't Catherine's ex-fiancé. She walked in on Piper screwing him a few months before his wedding to Catherine."

"Wow." I raise my eyebrows.

"She's always been a conniving bitch, but she's worse lately. Anyway, don't fall for her fake niceties." She stares after Piper's retreating form, even after she disappears into her office. "I've been itching to take her down. I promised Catherine I would, but I need to gather more ammo."

"Umm... your eye is twitching."

She shakes her head and peers down at me. "Never mind. Piper's downfall will be on next month's agenda.

Right now, I need the account file for Parker's Plaza. I have an idea."

"Of course." I stand, the key for the drawer in my hand, then pick up the note from my desk for her. "Your florist called while you were on the phone with Mr. Parker."

She groans, grabbing the note. "What does she want? I swear, if she asks me what shade of pink I want, I'll vomit. Did you know there are multiple options for *blush*? I thought it was its own single color." Her eyes are wide with disbelief.

Giggling, I nod. "Blush, dusty pink, pink, something called vintage pink, and more." I raise my finger. "Oh, and then there are so many different kinds of flowers that look similar too, but one is more expensive than the other. Be careful of that. Hydrangeas, for instance, are about three times the price of peonies. Peonies are pretty too, and you—I'm sorry. I'm blabbering on about flowers when you need a file. Be right back." I start to turn, but she stops me.

"Wait, how do you know so much about flowers? I don't remember reading you were a florist on your résumé." She raises her eyebrows.

"I was married." I shift from one foot to the other. "My divorce was actually finalized a little over a month ago. We were separated for a while, though, so it feels longer than that, to be honest."

Standing up straighter, her arms fall to her sides. "I

had no idea."

"Yes, well, it's not exactly the first thing I want to tell people about." I give her a warm smile. "Anyway, if you want, I'm more than happy to help you with wedding planning. Just because my marriage didn't work out doesn't mean I don't want the best for yours, so I'll do whatever I can to help."

"I appreciate it."

My chest is heavy as I unlock the drawer of files and pull the one I need out.

What I said to her is nice and optimistic, and I meant it.

But the whole idea seems to be a lie.

For the last year, I've started to think true love doesn't exist. That happily ever afters are saved for books and movies to exploit the idea and make money.

I wish I could believe otherwise, but after what happened with Dave and Aiden, it's impossible to.

Aiden.

After I declined his offer for drinks, he answered with a simple, "Maybe next time." My stomach fluttered—did he mean that? All night, I wondered if we might become friends again. If the universe throwing us together could be a second chance for us, but how?

So much happened between us. So much was left unsaid.

There's still so much we haven't shared.

By the time I finish everything on my list and get

home, I'm exhausted, but I have to unpack the rest of my stuff. I'm tired of skirting around the mess while trying to get dressed in the mornings. There are only a couple boxes left now, anyway, and I open one with torn corners. It looks older than the rest.

And when I peek inside, I find notebooks I haven't seen since college—I forgot I even had them.

My lips quiver as I run my fingers over the red cover of one.

I tentatively open the notebook like I'm opening the window to a messy past and flip to the first page of handwriting—*my* handwriting.

My head on the grass,

My heart in my throat,

The leaves of the trees stare back at me, yellow and orange for

the season,

And I wait for them to fall as I wait for you to come.

But the longer I lie still,

the more distant you become.

The leaves—crumpled, torn, fragile—they're my only

company,

along with the wind grazing my cheek.

Covered in swirling specks of yellow and orange, I lie still,

and wait for you to come.

I turn page after page of poems, long and short. Many lines are crossed out and re-written. There are highlighted notes in the margins to tweak certain poems, but it looks like I never did.

I haven't seen these in years. I haven't even written anything new in that time. These poems feel like another lifetime. As if another *me* wrote them.

I stare at the words as the memories and overwhelming emotions come rushing back. Each line is etched into my notebook with a pen, but as I slowly remember writing them, I realize they were written with my tears.

Most of these poems were written when Aiden left.

After that, I lost my desire to write as I lost pieces of myself.

Of my heart.

The day before marrying Dave, I thought about Aiden. I sifted through our memories together, searching for the signs. Searching for answers. Grappling with the truth.

But the truth, no matter how much I denied it, was that Aiden didn't want me—Dave did.

As for me, I... I was desperate.

I close the notebook and stare out the window. After all these years, all these forgotten moments, I've been forced to face the past more in the last couple weeks than I have since I married Dave.

The front door swings open, snapping me out of my trance, and I toss the book on my bed like it's a bomb.

"Sage?" Naomi calls out, kicking the door shut behind her.

I step out of my bedroom, taking in the numerous colorful bags in her hands, and quirk my eyebrow. "You went shopping?"

I wouldn't think it was weird, but Naomi isn't the type to go shopping for anything other than scrubs. She says it's a waste of time and money for her to buy street clothes since she rarely wears them.

She nods, setting the bags down with a thud like a few have bricks in them, which are probably only shoes. "I figured I should have other clothes in my closet in case we want to get drinks. Like tonight?"

"Tonight, what?"

"Maybe we can check out a cool bar?" One side of her lip barely tilts, and for her, that means she's excited.

I narrow my eyes at her. "You never want to go out. What's going on?"

She shrugs, dropping any hint of humor from her expression. "My last roommate always hung out with her boyfriend and never wanted to go out together, but you're here now... I mean, it's finally warming up enough to go outside without losing a toe to frostbite. You've been here for almost two months and haven't experienced the fun side of this city."

"I've done plenty of fun things."

She places her hands on her hips. "You went to

Central Park alone one afternoon and ate a hot dog. That doesn't count."

"It was a nice, cold day. I even got a hot coffee after." I giggle as she rolls her eyes like I told her my top goal in life is to own a red sweater—*boring*. "Besides, you never want to hang out with me."

She stands up straight, her teasing hint of a grin falling. "Sage, that's not because of you."

I bite my lip, fidgeting with my cuticles as the living room thickens with awkward tension. I didn't mean to say it, but we've been dancing around the subject for so long, something was bound to slip.

"I work a million hours a week. New Yorkers know how to trample each other, especially cyclists. I've seen far too many injured cyclists in my life." She sighs, lifting her neutral gaze to mine.

As an ER nurse, I'm sure she's seen her fair share of traumas of various levels. What she's saying sounds horrible and emotionally draining, but she's good at remaining detached—*too* good, if I'm honest. And because of her guarded nature, I can't read her to know where I stand.

"I'm sorry if it seems like I've been avoiding you. I'm really glad you're here."

I relax my shoulders. "Me too."

"So? You in for going out tonight?" she asks, and I'm not surprised by how quickly we moved on. "Please?"

I could use a night out.

Dave rarely ever wanted to. He used to joke that he wanted me all to himself at home. I thought it was sweet, until he had too many bourbons one night and confessed the real reason—he didn't like drunk guys flirting with me.

I don't have to think hard about Naomi's offer. We've barely done more than cook and watch Netflix since I got here, and I think going out together will help us grow closer too. "Let's do it. I think I know of a place too, but first"—I point to her bags—"you have to show me what you bought. I may need to borrow something."

Again, one side of her lip tilts upward, and I start to feel the lightness of us already. Our apartment. Our life here.

I'm more and more giddy with every piece of clothing she pulls out of the bag, one at a time, and holds each up over her scrubs.

"Wait, wait." I hold my hands up. "We need wine to do this fashion show right."

"I like the way you think."

With full wineglasses in our hands, she continues. I *ooh* and *aah* and laugh along to her story of the salesperson who insisted she buy a bright pink version of a dress because she bought so many in black or gray.

"Obviously, he didn't sense my tone or notice the

death glare I was giving him." She rolls her eyes, which makes me laugh harder.

She's always been the type to be on edge. Intense. Mysterious.

She'd be the perfect person to work for the police and go undercover—no one would ever catch on. I have yet to notice anything that excites her. Although, that's likely what makes her a great nurse. She's compassionate when needed, but she can also maintain a calm and detached façade under pressure.

She's a different Naomi than I once knew.

When we were young, she'd parade me around like I was her doll. She'd be thrilled to dress me up and paint my nails. It was easy to pull a full-on laugh from her.

She was the big sister I never had.

Until we grew up and grew apart.

She and her family moved away for a while, and then she moved to New York for college. When they first moved, we tried to stay in touch, but she's a few years older than I am. It was hard to keep track of thirteen-year-old me when Naomi was about to start college.

And being with Dave only added more tension to the mix.

But now, as two adults, we have the chance to redefine our relationship. The opportunity to become true friends.

"I think I'll wear this with my leather jacket." She holds up a black bodycon dress that reaches below her knees. "With my maroon booties."

"Damn. I'll be surprised if you come home alone tonight." I wiggle my eyebrows as the slight buzz from my second glass of wine settles in.

"Wouldn't that be a nice change of pace? For both of us." She snorts, then sips the last of her wine. She picks up a low-cut, A-line black dress and shoves it toward me. "Wear this tonight, and we need to change stat. I'm so ready for a night out. I need to feel like I'm part of the regular world—it's been too long."

After we're both changed, we reconvene in the living room. I hunch down as I run my hands down the sides of my dress. It's the sexiest thing I've put on since my honeymoon, and I don't feel like myself in it —it's too much.

Naomi briefly assesses me and purses her lips. "Don't try to hide. Wear that dress with the confidence I know you have. You look so great in it, I might even let you keep it. *Might*." She holds her finger up, then heads to our coat rack for her leather jacket.

She's stunning. Her hair is curly and loose, but she's given it more volume. Her light brown skin, thanks to her dad, appears silky smooth. Coupled with her poised gait, I have no doubt she'll make heads turn tonight.

Now, *she's* certainly confident.

I've always been self-assured when it comes to my career, but with Dave, our lack of sex life the last couple years of our marriage took a toll on me personally.

I haven't felt... *hot* in a while, but this bold dress is a good start to change that.

My chin high, I follow her out the door, grabbing my jacket on the way. In the cab ride to Hemingway House, she lends me her lipstick, and although it's a darker shade than I normally wear, I like it. Using her compact mirror, I happily apply it as best I can in this shaky taxi.

When we arrive, we maneuver around the small crowd outside the door. A small puff of smoke surrounds a couple as they take a drag of their cigarettes, and another couple nudges each other, laughing. I get lost in the picture in front of me, soaking it all in, internally stringing together a few words like I used to.

Clouds of smoke... we hide behind them... but reality remains... one we have to face with...

Naomi grabs my hand, shaking me out of my thoughts, and pulls me inside.

"How did you find this place?" she asks. As we sit at the bar, she signals the bartender and orders two red wines for us.

"One of our clients mentioned it, and I thought it sounded cool." I shrug, attempting to appear nonchalant and unaffected by the particular *client* I'm referring to.

Shifting in my seat, I drag my gaze over the brown leather booths along the wall, to the small wooden tables of two in perfect rows on either side of the bar, and finally to the far corner where a small stage is set up with speakers and a microphone. Karaoke is about to start.

"Before the quality entertainment begins," Naomi says with sarcasm and an eye roll, "I need to pee." She slides her glass of wine toward me. "Watch my drink, please."

Nodding, I slightly lift my leg to pull the flowy skirt of my dress down, then sip my wine. I swirl the liquid in my glass, watching the vortex it creates, letting it mesmerize me.

"Hey," I hear over my shoulder.

I stiffen in my seat.

That voice.

Strong, deep, and gruff.

He's the only person I know who can make a simple greeting sound so... powerful.

I may not know him anymore, but he has the same intensity about him that he used to.

Forcing the rich and oaky liquid down, I turn in my seat and find Aiden standing next to me. His hard, square jaw is clenched as he peers down at me.

"I thought you were hanging with your cousin tonight."

"I was... I *am*," I sputter, shocked to see him here.

Even though I heard about this bar from him, I didn't expect to run into him the first night I try it out. In New York City, I didn't think it was possible to run into the same person twice in so little time. I clear my throat and point to the two wineglasses in front of me. "Naomi's in the bathroom."

His shoulders visibly relax. "For a second, I thought you were avoiding me."

"Why would I do that?" I ask, straightening my posture.

He shrugs. "I expected you to call. To text. Something."

"I didn't want to intrude on your life."

The corners of his lips twitch. "You could never intrude."

Naomi returns, and I realize I have to introduce her to the one man I never expected to see again.

I clear my throat and point between them. "Naomi, this is Aiden. Aiden, Naomi."

She jerks his hand up and down in a firm shake. "How do you two know each other?"

"We work together, and we..." I open and close my mouth, meeting Aiden's gaze. Pain flits across his expression but quickly disappears. Before either of us can elaborate, Westin and another guy from their company walk up.

"Sage, hey. What a surprise." Westin puts his hand

out for me to shake. "You remember Jared? And Aiden said you two go way back."

Naomi eyes me, her thick eyebrows raised in question.

I tuck my hair behind my ears and nod. "Yes, hello. Nice to see you all again."

Westin signals for one of the two bartenders and orders beers for all three of them, then points to Naomi and me. "Next round for them is on me too." He hands him a credit card and raps his knuckles on the bar. "We'll start a tab, please."

"Oh, that's very generous, but you don't have to." I place my hand on his forearm to stop him.

Westin glances at me, his expression amused. "I know I don't *have* to, but I want to."

I drop my hand to my lap and settle back onto my barstool as he introduces himself to Naomi and shakes her hand as well.

I notice Aiden watching me, his lips twisted. His gaze is far away, like he's not here at all. And if I stare long enough into his darkening hazel eyes, I might let him take me away with him.

Like I would have all those years ago.

If he would've given me the chance.

Someone taps the microphone, pulling our attention in the direction of the stage.

"Who's ready for karaoke tonight?" A guy runs his hand over the side of his buzzed head, then waves from behind the microphone. He points to a girl standing in front of the stage and says, "We have our first volunteer. Everyone, give it up for Amy!"

I clap along with the rest of the crowd, my breath hitching as Aiden sidles up next to me. The first thing I notice is his radiating heat. The next is his minty breath on my cheek as he says, "You should sing Britney. For old time's sake." He smirks.

I shake my head, recalling our spring break trip my sophomore year. "I don't think so."

"Just as well. You probably don't have the skills anymore."

"Oh, I still have them. Don't you worry about that." I nudge his shoulder with mine.

"Prove it." His eyes dance as we fall into our old ways so effortlessly.

"When did you karaoke before?" Naomi asks.

I turn my attention to her, tightening my grip on the glass in my hand, and explain, "Spring break. I had one fun night with everyone, then sat the rest of the week out because of a severe cold."

"Bummer," Westin responds.

"You took two sips of NyQuil and acted drunk." Amused, Aiden's lips curl around his bottle of beer before he takes a sip.

"That stuff almost killed me." I stare at him wide-eyed.

"You're right. You did jump out of a moving

vehicle."

"It wasn't moving when I hopped out."

"We drove at least five feet when you thought it was a good idea to open the door and slide out. You couldn't even stand up straight." He chuckles. "We could've run you over."

He sobers when his eyes meet mine.

The humor in the air gets caught in my throat, almost choking me, and everyone's curious expressions blur.

All I can focus on is Aiden.

I take a sip of wine, watching him over the rim.

He stares back at me like he's mesmerized by the way I drink. As though it's more than merely tilting the glass back against my lips and swallowing the red liquid.

So, I keep drinking, intoxicated more by him than the alcohol.

Gulp.

His gaze flickers to mine, and for these brief few minutes, I remember who we used to be... before he broke my heart.

"You're just going to sleep, right? Get some rest?" Dave smooths my hair out of my face as I pull the covers up to my chin.

"Yes, but I'd like some company. If you leave, I'm going to sit here alone all day." I watch him expectantly, but he doesn't budge.

"What am I going to do while you sleep? My whole trip will be ruined."

"Well, it's not like I got sick on purpose. And I'm not going to sleep all damn day.*"*

"Don't curse at me. You know I've been excited about this trip for weeks."

"Just go." I sigh. "Have fun."

He kisses my hair, and I don't miss his cringe when he stands back up, like touching me right now is awful. Although it stings, I don't blame him, either, since my skin is rather clammy.

"I'll check in later. Get some sleep," he says as he leaves, shutting the door behind him with a resounding click that echoes throughout the room. On the other side, I hear him as he joins the rest of our friends for a day of water parks and drinking and fun—the makings of a memorable Spring Break.

While I sit with only my fuzzy head and sweaty palms.

And mindless reality TV.

As I reach for the remote to turn the TV on, the door to my room creaks open again, and Aiden steps inside.

"I thought you all left," I croak, my throat dry, and reach for my juice. "Did you forget something?"

"No, I just... didn't want to leave you alone." He shrugs.

I take a sip and cringe when I swallow. He pulls at the ends of his short hair and comes around the bed, where he sits on top of the covers. Grabbing the remote from me, he asks, "What're we watching?"

Aiden and I spend the day switching from reruns of

people completing obstacle courses—completing *being an operative term since many of them face plant, belly flop, and even trip over their own feet.*

But we laugh—a lot.

As the sun sets, I turn to him. "Thanks for staying with me, even though you didn't have to."

"Jersey, I would—"

The door to the condo opens, and a commotion follows. Our door is open, and Aiden kicks his feet over the edge of the bed, then stands, stuffing his hands in his pockets. "I'll see you."

My heart sinks when he turns his pained expression toward me. Thinking he's just worried about me, I say, "I'll be fine, you know. It's only a cold. I've had worse." My lips tilt.

He nods and steps into the hall where Dave's voice drifts into my room. "You feeling okay, man? I hope you don't have what Sage has."

"No, I think it was something I ate. Needed to sleep it off. I'm fine now."

"Been there, brother. Glad you're feeling better."

Confused, I lean up. Aiden wasn't feeling well? He didn't say anything.

Dave enters my room, a glass of water in his hand. He sets it on the nightstand and sits on the bed next to where I'm curled up. It's where Aiden was sitting moments ago, and for some reason, my chest squeezes that he's no longer here.

"How are you feeling?" Dave touches the back of his hand to my head. "Still warm. Not doing any better?"

I cough into my elbow. "Not really. When are you going out to dinner?"

"They're leaving here soon, but I'm going to stay with you. Maybe we can order in?" He smooths my hair down. "I missed you today."

"Me too," I say absentmindedly and snuggle into his side, repeating more firmly, "Me too."

"What do you say?" Aiden points, pulling me out of my long-forgotten memory.

I follow his finger in the direction of the stage, where a woman in sequined shorts bellows a Spice Girls song—*classic*. She dances along to it too, like she's performing a sold-out concert at Madison Square Garden.

I clap when she's done—she deserves it—and turn to the group. "I can't follow that act. I'll get *booed* off the stage."

The second I finish my wine, Westin waves to the bartender, then points to my empty glass.

Aiden tenses next to me, and I watch him in my periphery as I thank Westin for my new drink. *Odd.* "Aiden, why don't you get up there? If I remember correctly, you sound like Prince."

"No, no, no. You are not going to throw that in my face." Aiden chuckles, shuffling his feet.

"*Please* tell us the story. I need good ammo to hold over his head." Jared rubs his hands together.

"What were you drinking that night? Maker's

Mark? You won fifty dollars from a scratch-off and wanted, for once, to try an 'expensive' whiskey—that was your biggest goal in life." I roll my eyes, and Westin and Jared raise their beers to Aiden as I continue. "So, you bought a big bottle, drank most of it yourself, then begged us to go out, where you sang karaoke like an angel—in other words, Prince."

Aiden's eyes shine, his lips twitching. "You're leaving out the part where the ladies melted right at my feet."

I throw my head back and laugh, as do the others, especially when Jared fist-bumps Aiden. Even Naomi smiles widely, for once.

A lightness washes over me that I haven't felt in a long time.

The story I just told feels like it happened yesterday, before it all got complicated.

Right now, Aiden and I are simply old friends.

After a few more minutes of easy chatter, Aiden orders us a round of shots.

There's a pause from the stage as they switch singers, and Aiden sidles up to me again.

I shake my head as the bartender lines five shots in front of us. "No, no, no. I don't do shots."

"But you'll need it before you sing." Aiden nudges me.

"You insist on me singing as if I haven't embarrassed myself enough over the years."

"I need a reminder." He shrugs, his expression smug.

Naomi passes out the shots like they're our nightly tips. Once she's done, she holds her hands out, and in a voice louder than I've ever heard from her, says, "Wait! We need to toast first." She taps her chin, tilting her head back, then holds her shot up for us to follow suit. "To the strange workings of this crazy city." She eyes Aiden and me specifically. "And may all its angry drivers stop rear-ending each other. Anyone want to add anything?"

"To a successful launch," Westin offers.

Jared snorts. "I second that. We have a lot of investors who will hand us our asses if we fail."

Westin smacks the back of his head, to which Jared shrugs and peers at Aiden for help.

"I'm with Westin." He chuckles, and the sound travels down to my toes.

I gaze at Aiden's profile, studying the freckles on his bronzed skin. They're visible under the dim light from above the bar. Then at his slightly crooked nose —he once told me he broke it when he was a kid because he was running around the pool and slipped.

I only tear my gaze from him when Naomi yells, "Cheers!"

We clink our glasses, then toss back the shots like they're water, and I fight the urge to cough. *Fucking whiskey*, I grimace.

"Had to get you back for the whiskey-Prince story," Aiden whispers in my ear, his lips so close I can almost feel them. He takes the glass from my hand and sets it on the bar, putting distance between us for only a moment.

Grabbing my hand, he leads me to the stage as a female trio's rendition of "Friends in Low Places" comes to an end. They wave to the small crowd like they're celebrities, and it makes me laugh—these karaoke singers are so into this.

Once we reach the stage, Aiden yells to the deejay, "She'll sing anything by Britney Spears, especially 'Toxic.'"

"Do I have to?" I cover my face with my free hand.

"Yes. He's already trying to find your song."

My mouth hangs open as I blink at him. "You're insane."

There's a glimmer in his eyes. Mischievous. Like he has ulterior motives. And I'm too wrapped up in this strangely thrilling moment in a New York City bar with him to argue further.

Westin, Jared, and Naomi appear at our sides as I'm about to hoist myself onto the stage.

"Are you singing?" Naomi sputters, clutching her chest, and holds her drink up. She switched to vodka, which can only mean she's ready for a wild night. She once told me vodka is her party drink.

"Sing with me," I plead.

"No way." She pulls her phone out and holds it up. "I have a front-row spot and need to record every second."

Without thinking, I steal a sip of her drink, which I don't imagine she appreciates, and head onto the stage, where the deejay hands me the microphone.

Once the song begins, I let the buzz from the drinks and this night help me channel my inner popstar.

I move my hips to the rapid techno tune, walking the few feet from one side of the stage to the other like I'm on a runway. I hold Aiden's gaze as I transition to the next verse, singing at the highest pitch my voice can go, enjoying this carefree moment in this vibrant city.

Celebrating this new life of mine.

Because in my old life, I never felt this... *free*.

A small part of me admits that I'm also reveling in Aiden's stare. His eyes are bright, sparkling like stars in the dark sky. His hair is wild tonight, unlike the tamed bun he donned at our meeting, and his grin is infectious, like the first time we met. When he started calling me *Jersey*.

I throw my head back and sing the last note, holding it longer than is necessary, until the music cuts. "Whoo!" I yell into the microphone, then take a bow, and the room erupts with cheers.

Mostly, it's Naomi, Jared, Westin, and especially Aiden who cheer.

Shaking my head, I hop off the stage right into Aiden's arms as the next song comes on.

I'm flush against him, so close I can smell his deliciously heady cologne.

He licks his lips, and I can taste whiskey on mine.

The music echoes throughout the room, creating an exciting energy, one I feel in every part of my body the longer I stay in Aiden's arms.

Without words, he moves his hands to my hips and sways with me, dancing to the beat. The hairs on my neck stand as heat travels the length of my body, every sensitive nerve ending heightened.

Somewhere in the back of my mind, I know this is Aiden. The guy from my past who hurt me worse than anything else I've ever experienced. The one I once cursed and swore I'd never give a single moment to ever again, if by some miracle we'd be in the same room together again.

But here in the crowd, as he moves his body with mine, it feels different, like the years have forgiven us and made us new people.

Which they have—we're both new.

We've changed.

"You're glowing," he says into my hair, then spins me around, wrapping his arms around my waist from behind.

My back pressed against his chest, I let the wine wash over me like I'm being baptized and sway to the off-key, nasal tune of the next karaoke singer.

I dance with him, the rhythm coming naturally for both of us. We're in tune.

Hot.

I'm burning up, and my heart skips a beat when he spins me around to face him again, his lips close.

Enticing.

I remember what it feels like to be kissed by him as if it happened yesterday. To be consumed. To become drunk from the way his tongue sweeps over mine.

My eyes flutter closed, and I lean in...

"There you arc."

Aiden jumps back, putting space between us like we're at a middle school dance. He tears his focus from me, dropping his hands from my waist, and greets the woman next to us.

I blink, and every time he comes into view, the fire that was in his expression disappears until there's only shame.

"Raven, you made it." He hugs her, and when he lets go, she stays close.

"I got done with my class early and wanted to come hang. I haven't seen you all week." She kisses the side of his mouth—the same one I could almost feel on mine a few seconds ago—and my stomach sinks.

Emotions clog my throat.

The room spins.

"Who's this?" Raven waits for an introduction, both her arms wrapped around Aiden like he's going to run away.

She's claiming him and wants me to damn well know it.

I meet Aiden's regretful gaze. His eyes frown in the corners, remaining silent, and my stomach churns further that he can't even utter my name.

Clearing my throat, I find my voice. "I'm Sage."

"I'm Raven, A's girlfriend." Raven points between us. "How do you two know each other?" Her voice and stance are accusatory, tense, and on the offensive.

We were dancing closely, after all.

Our lips were close.

I even leaned in for him to kiss me—I was begging for it.

But it's a good thing we didn't, for more reasons than he has a girlfriend—*one who calls him* A.

And not because he's also a client, either.

But because I was stupid to forget, for even one night, what he did to me.

I can't get lost in him, not again. Not now, after all these years of putting him behind me.

The painful loss.

No, if I were to sink into the depths of Aiden Baxter again, I'd completely drown.

CHAPTER SIX

AIDEN

Shit.

What a clusterfuck.

Raven eyes me suspiciously. It's that look she gets while she studies her models, preparing to draw them —searching for any perfect flaws, as she calls them, and any secrets they hide in their eyes.

She's searching for the secrets I'm hiding about my relationship with Sage.

Westin claps me on the shoulder. "I got you another beer, and here's another wine for the lady." He hands Sage a glass, and their fingers brush when she accepts it.

The sight makes me see red.

What the hell?

But I'm also thankful that he interrupted us before

I could give Raven an explanation. Where would I even begin?

When it comes to Sage Matthews, I'd need a lifetime to describe our complicated and sordid time in college when I thought we could end up together.

When I thought she would choose me.

But she didn't, and I've been trying to live my life as though it didn't gut me.

"I'm going to find Naomi." She raises her glass toward Westin. "Thanks again."

"Sage—" My voice is lost in the music as she becomes another bobbing head in the crowd.

"You didn't answer my question. Who is she?" Raven drops her hold on me and crosses her arms.

"Someone I went to school with." I catch sight of straight honey-colored hair by the bar and head in that direction, calling over my shoulder to Raven, "I'll be right back."

I weave through the crowd, and as I near the bar, Jared stops me. "You have to help me, man. My ex-girlfriend is over there."

"Vanessa? The one who set your bed on fire?" My eyes widen, distracted by Sage's whereabouts. But Naomi is still here, dancing in the middle of a big group on the dance floor, and Sage wouldn't leave without her. *Is she in the bathroom? Outside?*

Fuck—where did she go?

"Yes," Jared hisses, peering over the bar, then grabs

both my shoulders. "She can't know I'm here, so you and Westin cannot, under any circumstances, get stuck alone with her. She will work her Wiccan magic on you and suck the truth, along with your soul, right out of your body."

"We won't talk to her."

He lets go of me and holds his hands up. "On second thought, why don't we just leave? We can get drinks elsewhere. Better yet, we can go to the office and take care of the two six-packs I put in the fridge yesterday."

When he starts to walk toward the door, I pull him back by his T-shirt. "Stay with Westin, and I'll be right back."

"Are you looking for Sage?" Naomi suddenly appears at our side like the crowd gave birth to her, making me jerk back. "What did you do to her?"

"Nothing," I say, my voice strained.

She purses her lips and twists her straw in her nearly empty drink as she studies me. "Who are you? That's what I can't figure out. She said you're a client, but you have stories from college together. Yet, I think there's even more to this mysterious tale."

Naomi narrows her dark gaze at me as she sips the rest of her drink, and a cold air surrounds us, causing a chill down my spine. *It's not Jared's ex I have to worry about—it's Sage's cousin.*

"I have to find her." I shake myself away from them

and rush through the group gathered at the bar. When I exit out the door onto the sidewalk, cold wind hits my face, stinging my cheeks like pricks of needles.

I turn to my left and right, but there's no sign of her.

My stomach rolls as I step around the corner of the bar to the alleyway. The balconies at the apartment building behind the bar each have potted plants on them, and the twinkling lights strung across one balcony to the other cast a dim glow, enough of one for me to recognize the woman underneath.

Sage leans her back against the wall, clutching her suede jacket around her. When she looks up at me, she's not the girl who was just singing "Toxic" at the top of her lungs for a crowded room.

She's vulnerable.

"You're not in a small town anymore. This is New York, and you have to be careful about running off by yourself." I lean against the wall beside her, and I feel her gaze on me like she's touching me.

My skin heats underneath my plaid shirt.

I grind my teeth to tamp down these overwhelming feelings. The ones I haven't let myself acknowledge since I saw her at our meeting, but they're taking over now.

"I needed some air." She clutches her jacket tighter, and my gaze falls on her bare ring finger.

Together, we stand in silence, admiring the starless

sky. It's the middle of March, and the nights are bitter, unlike the days when the sun usually shines and shares its warmth.

It's cold like the inside of my mouth, freezing the words on my tongue, and I practically choke on them when I do try to speak.

"I should've told you about Raven." I break the silence, my voice low.

"Don't." She pushes off the wall, her hands out. "You don't owe me an explanation. Not about her."

She whispers the last part so softly I almost miss it. *What else do I owe* her *an explanation for?*

"I'm going home."

"Wait." I instinctively grab her wrist, turning her hand into mine. Earlier tonight, I held her hand, my palm to hers, and it felt right.

Too right.

What the fuck?

"Aiden, let me go." Her bottom lip quivers, and my fucked-up heart splits further.

It's almost useless to me now, as the cracks in it aren't mendable, and it's because of her.

"Why did you choose him?" My gaze locks onto hers, finally asking her the question I've often wondered during these last eight years, and I hope she can see my pain. My despair.

I hope she can feel even a fraction of it, so she can

only begin to understand the agony she put me through.

The agony of believing for a few sultry hours that I had the girl I loved, but the truth was... she was never mine.

"I didn't," she says. Her gaze is unwavering and eerie, and it confuses me. "You chose him for me. When you left for Europe, you didn't just leave me. You took part of me with you and left the broken pieces behind. You have no idea what I went through."

I shake my head, remembering it very differently.

"I've thought about that night nonstop since I saw you."

My breaths become labored, knowing exactly the night she's referring to. The night that changed us. The night that's seared into my own brain.

How perfect we were together when we dropped our defenses and succumbed to the attraction between us. When she melted into me, and I wanted to keep her there forever.

"I thought you'd hesitate. That night, when I appeared at your doorstep, I figured you'd have thought it over and changed your mind. That you'd reject me after you thought I didn't feel the same as you. Instead, you took me in your arms, gripping me like I—"

"Like what?"

"Like I was always yours."

"You were never mine," I rasp. "It's why I had to let you go. Back then, I had to because of Dave. You and him... I couldn't compete." Halfway through, I know I should stop, but the words tumble out of my mouth. I pull her hand more tightly and bring her close.

Our quick breaths are visible in the frigid night and create a soft cloud around us.

"Things are different now." She searches my eyes, and all I can see in hers is devastation. She clears her throat, backing away. "You have a girlfriend, and you're a client. It's for the best that we keep things professional. There's no need for us to mention this again."

"Don't do that." I reach for her again, unable to stop myself.

"Bye, Aiden." She turns on her heel, and I stand in place, frozen.

I got to see a glimpse of the real Sage tonight—of Jersey. The one who dances like no one's watching. Who has a glint in her eye that lights up her entire presence.

She used to be so full of life, reaching for the stars like they were apples in a tree, hers for the picking.

Even though I couldn't have her, Sage was the love of my life. I never thought I'd get over her.

I never thought I'd see her again, and not only is she here now, but the feelings I thought were long gone are resurfacing, even though they have no place here in the present.

I should go after her and say... *do*... something.

But she looked at me like *I* hurt her. Like she's in pain because of me, when it's the other way around. Confused, I walk back inside the bar in a daze.

Back to Raven—*Raven*—she's the one I'm with. She's the one I love, *now*.

"It's for the best that we keep things professional."

I don't register the music or people. All I can think about is Sage and why her words make me feel defeated when she's not an option for me.

She never was.

But why can't I stop thinking about the fact that she's no longer *his*, either?

———

"We left the bar in a hurry." Raven slips out of her oversized wool coat and hangs it on the coat rack she found at a thrift store. Said it's the perfect rustic piece for my loft apartment.

It was the same day she showed me the new rug she picked out for the den.

Remaining quiet, I open the refrigerator, grab a beer, then walk to the couch where I take a seat. New York City blinks beyond the windows. Coming from a small town, I didn't know how I'd feel about the big city. If I would fit in. If I'd like it. If I'd eventually leave, but the longer I'm here, the more I feel at home.

At peace among the chaos of screeching tires on the road, people on their cell phones, blinding lights at night.

But right now, the chaos that stretches beyond my apartment is suffocating me.

Because this fucking city led me back to her.

"A?" Raven walks to me, her hips swaying. When she reaches me, she throws her legs up one at a time and straddles me. She leans in and whispers against my neck, "Want me to make it go away?"

"Make what go away?" Nausea builds as I taste acid in my mouth, mixed with beer and the small hint of whiskcy from before.

"Whatever's haunting you right now. You have that look." She wraps her arms around me and kisses along my neck, up to my ear.

I grip her hips and set her on the couch next to me. Running my hands down my face, my chest heavy, I sigh. "I need to sleep. We have a big few weeks ahead of us to prepare for the launch."

"Haven't you been preparing? What would one night of fun hurt?" She traces her fingers along my bearded jawline. "I'm not wearing anything underneath this dress..." She drops her voice to a seductive whisper that's proven to be effective in the past but does nothing to me now.

Except confuse me.

I walk to my bed, my back to her, when she says, "Who is she, Aiden?"

I hear her footsteps behind me, coming toward me with soft pats.

I'm a dick.

Why the fuck am I getting my head turned around because of Sage—*again?*

I'm not being fair to Raven. We've been together for nearly a year, and she's the one who's been there for me. The one who's made me believe I can fall in love again—I *have* fallen in love again.

And Sage? There's nothing there for me.

She wants to keep things professional, and that's what I'll do.

My shoulders sag, and I pull Raven toward me. I kiss her cheek, wanting to take away her concerns. "She and I went to the same college. I barely knew her."

I wait for her response. For her to push for more information and catch me in my lie. For her to see the resentment in my eyes.

But she only relaxes into me.

I expect it to make me feel better. For her peace to cure the turmoil inside me.

But I'm still on edge.

That night, I go to sleep with Raven in my arms, but I dream about Sage—*my Jersey.*

"You were never mine."

Our afternoons, our memories, even our night together—she was never mine to keep.

I toss and turn most of the night as small moments of my past with Sage haunt me.

Long hair blowing in the wind as we drove with the windows down.

A laugh full of life—the carefree kind that lifts you up.

Playing Frisbee when we were supposed to be studying.

Her back to me as she walked away when I begged her to stay.

CHAPTER SEVEN

SAGE

There's no sign of Naomi when I get home from work and plop down on the couch, my mind a blur from the day.

Thirty seconds after I get comfortable, basking in the quiet space, the lock on the door clicks. Naomi comes in, her ponytail lopsided and hands full of groceries.

"I thought it was my turn to do the grocery shopping." I meet her in the kitchen and grab a few bags.

"It's easier for me to do it."

"What? With all your free time?" I tease. "I'm starting to think you *like* the grocery store. Or is there a hot guy you keep going there to meet?" I waggle my eyebrows as we set everything on the small counter.

The paper bags crinkle as we empty them. We move through the kitchenette, stepping around each other as if we've rehearsed it, and in a way, we have, given how frequently we do this.

After a moment, Naomi eyes me. "Speaking of hot guys, what's the story with you and Aiden?"

I involuntarily cringe, missing a step in our routine, and bump into her. She steadies me, and I avert my gaze as I continue putting away the rest of the items. "There's no story other than we were friends in college. Haven't seen him in over eight years."

"Since before your wedding to Dave? Your *elopement*, I should say."

"It was a wedding," I correct her, pinning her with my stare. "We had a nice and intimate ceremony at a beautiful little lake, where he and his grandfather used to fish. He was really close with his grandpa before he passed, so the wedding there was special."

"Okay, but I wasn't there, and neither was your mom, so it was an elopement."

My heart cracks, remembering their absence from my big day. Naomi and I have made good progress the last couple months, especially since we went out last week. I've even talked with my aunt Ginger, Naomi's mother.

But the fact they weren't at my wedding continues to bother me, and I suspect it will for a long time to come.

Because I wanted them there, especially Naomi. Even though my family didn't approve of our hasty wedding or of Dave, I wanted them all there, but Dave convinced me it would be more romantic if it was just us.

The lake.

The sunset.

The flowers.

I was wooed by it, and it was what he wanted. I wanted to make him happy because of all he was doing for me, so we agreed to keep it small.

When Dave's brother and date showed up at the ceremony, I was shocked and disappointed, to put it mildly. I asked Dave about it, but he waved me off and justified his brother's attendance because we needed witnesses.

I didn't press him at the time because it was our wedding day. I wanted it to be special and memorable, even though nothing about it was as I imagined.

What I didn't realize at the time was how much I'd come to regret that my family wasn't there. That I would even resent Dave for the fact that I didn't have *my* closest circle in attendance.

Perhaps I wouldn't be as distant from my mom now.

Perhaps Naomi and I wouldn't have become estranged. Perhaps... a lot of things would be different, but there's no changing it now, no matter how badly I wish I could.

This is what I told Naomi when I first moved in.

We had a brief talk about it—mostly, I talked, anyway, while she quietly listened. Even so, I knew a quick explanation and apology weren't going to fix things, but over time, living here would.

Our little moments of progress prove it.

I sigh. "You didn't miss anything, anyway. It all went down in flames. We might as well have had our wedding at a courthouse alongside the hookers and drunk drivers."

She touches my shoulder, turning me to face her. "I'm sorry. I shouldn't have brought it up. There's no sense in talking about it again when it's in the past."

"As is Aiden." Frowning, I step around her to put the empty bags away.

When I turn around, she crosses her arms. "Is it? In the past? Because judging from the other night at the bar, there are still very real—and very current—feelings there."

"He has a girlfriend, Naomi."

"He didn't look at her like he looked at you, though."

I grip the bags in my hand, freezing by the trash can.

Suddenly, it's hard to breathe, like her statement wrapped itself around my lungs and squeezed. Because she's right. I noticed it too. He watched me like I was special.

The way he used to.

And if Raven hadn't shown up when she did, I would've fallen for it too.

"He hurt me worse than Dave ever did," I whisper.

"What happened between you two?" she presses, her expression one of genuine sadness and concern.

"He left." My tears build. Tears for Aiden Baxter well in my eyes for the first time in years as I relive the worst time in my life. Instinctively clutching my stomach, I let more of the weight of what happened slowly crush me. "He claimed to love me, but he ran when I needed him most and never came back."

My phone rings, interrupting us and shaking me out of the painful fog, but my stomach sinks when I check the caller ID.

"Speaking of the past..." I groan, letting the call go to voicemail as I wipe a stray tear. "It was Dave."

She grabs two glasses from the cabinet, asking over her shoulder, "What do you think he wants now?"

I exhale in frustration, taking a seat at the breakfast table, my emotions weighing on me. "One time it was to ask if I took the blender. Another time was a drunk call to yell at me for divorcing him. I never know."

He calls again, and I let my head fall forward on the table, exhausted from work.

And from Dave.

Naomi remains silent as she fills the glasses with water.

After the call ends, I get a new message.

Dave: Why aren't you answering my calls?

Then another.

Dave: Lee Ann said you moved. Where are you?

"He found out I moved." I click my phone off and rub my temples. "I expected news to travel faster around that town, to be honest."

"Does he know where you are?"

"Doesn't sound like it."

My phone vibrates again.

Dave: I can't believe you moved without telling me. I thought we could work this out.

I scoff. "He's acting like we merely broke up or separated. Like we have a chance of getting back together. It's why I got a divorce—to make sure that never happened." I shake my head, staring out the window. "He was a mistake," I whisper.

Naomi sits with me, setting a water in front of me, and sips on her own. Furrowing her eyebrows, she stares at the exposed brick wall next to us like there's a puzzle to solve.

"Naomi?" I place my hand on hers.

She shifts, then stands, asking, "What's for dinner? You already eat?"

"Are you okay?" I ask, unsure if it's me she's upset about or her work or something else entirely.

She's a closed book, and we've grown so far apart, I'm basically getting to know her all over again. I'm trying to, anyway, but she doesn't make it easy.

Offering me a small smile, she says, "I'm fine. It's you I'm thinking about."

"Thank you, but I'm okay." I rub my hands together and shake the sudden tension from my shoulders. "We can cook that chicken you bought. With zucchini?"

She nods and retrieves the food from the refrigerator as I grab the pans. We move in silence as my mind races, trying to figure out a way to get Dave to stop calling.

I've known him for almost half my life. He's persistent, even when he shouldn't be.

When we temporarily broke up in college, he fought for me when Aiden left. Dave vowed to always be there for me and try to make me happy.

I believed him. I needed something to put my faith in when my world was crumbling. Even though Dave didn't know what he was asking—he didn't know my secret—he offered me love and comfort and stability.

And at the start of our marriage, he tried to keep his promises. He tried to be a good man and a hard, dedicated worker because he was determined to make a good living for us.

But once his *why* changed, he gave up.

And part of me did too.

Because my heart had wanted someone else from the beginning—Aiden.

I'd yearned for Aiden, hoping he would stroll back into my life like he simply went to the post office and not around the world. But I couldn't have him.

I had to accept it then as I do now.

I know better than most that love only causes more heartbreak—Aiden taught me that.

And I have to see him in a couple days. I have to sit in a meeting with him less than a few feet away while I attempt to focus on my job.

On proving myself.

Instead of his eyes. His mouth. The way his jaw tics when he's deep in thought.

I have to pretend there's nothing more left for us than professionalism.

That's how it has to be.

"Hey, Mia." I switch the phone to my other ear as I wait in line for coffee outside our office building. "What's up?"

"What's up is that I've been trying to reach you for days," my sister whines on the other end.

"Are you hurt? Sick? Are Mom, Dad, and Avril okay?"

"We're all fine. Why?"

"Because you sound like it's been urgent to speak with me." I blink, tilting my head back toward the sky.

"This *is* urgent. I need to know when you're coming to visit. We haven't seen you in years."

"Not years, although that's also what Mom says."

I talked to my mom a couple weeks ago, and our call went about the same way as it always does—with thirty minutes of her asking when I'm coming to visit.

And it crushes me when I constantly have to say I'm working, but it's true. I can't take off to Virginia. We've been doing beta tests for ages, and we're nearing the end now.

I call and text as often as I can, but the truth is, I miss them too.

I move forward in line. "Mia, you know I'm busy with the launch."

"What about after that? We can do a Labor Day weekend getaway where we meet you halfway. You wouldn't have to travel all the way down to Virginia, and I'd be able to get a normal cup of coffee other than the sewage Randy serves."

The sound of something as familiar as Randy instantly warms my chest. Although I'm glad I moved away, my hometown will always hold a special part of me.

"What do you say?" Mia presses.

I pause, moving in line again. "I say... I'll do my best."

"That's what I like to hear, big brother. Talk soon." *Click*.

Once I grab two coffees, I head back toward our office building as Westin comes out. We meet on the sidewalk by the revolving door, and I hand him his black coffee.

"You were taking too long, so I thought I'd meet you out here. Everything okay?"

"Sure." I point behind me to the coffee truck. "Long line, and my sister Mia called."

He raises his eyebrows. "Asking you to come visit again?"

I nod as we turn toward the street for a taxi. Once inside, my shoulders grow more and more tense with every block we pass. We're meeting at CJJ instead of our offices this time.

I have to see Jersey today and pretend that I don't know her well enough to call her by a nickname. To pretend we can work smoothly together.

I inwardly laugh at my cursed fate.

When we enter, she's the first person who catches my eye.

She stands tall in a forest-green skirt that reaches her knees. Her hair is pulled back in a sleek ponytail, out of her face, and her eyes pop.

I bite back a curse.

It shouldn't be possible to be that devastatingly gorgeous. To have such natural beauty. I ball my fist at my side like I'm mad that she's so pretty, but I know the truth.

I'm mad that in a matter of a few interactions, she's managed to make me feel as hopeless as I did all those years ago when I pined for her—*pathetic*.

She said I forced her into Dave's arms, but I know the truth. There's no denying what I saw the summer after graduation, before I left for Europe.

She fucking married him.

It's too late now, anyway. I have Raven, who chooses to love me every day, when all Sage did was string me along like a damn puppy.

"Ease up," Westin whispers, squeezing my shoulder. "You look like you're ready to jump through that glass door."

"Can we just get this over with?" It comes out too harshly, and immediately, I regret it. It's not Westin's fault, after all.

"If it isn't the dream team." Taylor walks toward us with Sage on her heels. Pointing toward the conference room, Taylor says, "Right this way. Would you like anything to drink before we get started?"

Westin and I both ask for a water, and Sage nods, leaving us to grab a couple bottles.

She scurries away like she's running from me.

And I hate how much it pisses me off.

There was a time when we could spend hours together and not realize how long it had been. We'd get lost in conversation, a movie, music.

But that was *before*.

"How's Jock Stock doing since we last spoke? Any changes?" Taylor asks as we take our seats at the long table, facing a projector screen at the front of the room.

"We've been taking care of the snags, thanks to this guy." He lightly punches my arm. "We were also tweeted by Aaron Rogers, which was a nice boost." He shrugs, and I know him well enough to know he's downplaying it because he's modest.

It wasn't *nice*. It was huge.

"I saw that." Taylor beams, then jots something down. When she looks up again, a smile spreads across her face. "And I have more good news to go over with you."

Sage enters the room, tiptoeing inside like a mouse, and sets two water bottles in front of us and one in front of Taylor. Taking a seat next to Taylor across from us, she averts her gaze.

She doesn't look at me for the entire hour of our meeting as Taylor lists all the interviews she has set up for Westin and a few she's still waiting to confirm.

"Now, there is something I want to throw out there." Taylor glances between Westin and me. "I know you refused before, but I'd like you to reconsider having Aiden join you in the interviews. He can answer more of the specific questions regarding the app and the algorithm."

I shake my head before she even gets the statement out.

"Nothing good has come from me being in the spotlight," I say. "We've gotten this far because I stay behind-the-scenes. The only reason I attend these meetings is because... well, because CJJ doesn't harshly judge me on my background, or lack thereof."

"Jock Stock is doing well because of your contribution. I think you underestimate how much people care about your current success," Taylor challenges.

As brilliant as she is, she doesn't understand the position I've repeatedly been in before, none of which ended with me looking good.

Therefore, Jock Stock didn't look good.

"And you underestimate how much people care about your past." I instinctively focus on Sage, and she stares back for the first time since I walked in.

My gaze locks onto hers as Taylor says, "Please think about it because this next interview I scheduled will blow your minds, and I believe you'll be crucial." Taylor folds her hands on the table, building the anticipation. "Jenson Ross."

Even I sit up straighter, forgetting everything besides that name.

Westin pauses, and I know that blank look—he's trying to wrap his mind around the fact he'll be interviewed by Jenson Ross himself.

Sports mogul.

His podcast is in the top five on iTunes and has an enormous reach—direct to our audience.

In other words…

"This is huge." I slap Westin's back to snap him out of his trance. He's rarely speechless, but Taylor dropped a bomb to make Jock Stock explode like we've never even imagined.

"This... *this* is why we hired you." Westin slams his palms on the table. "Amazing. And now I need a year to prepare to speak to a man who's easily my top idol."

"You have two weeks," Taylor says.

Westin and I both just about fall out of our chairs. "I'm sorry, what? Two weeks to prepare? Two weeks until—"

She holds her hand up. "He is booked for the next several months, but he had a cancellation in two weeks. This will be fantastic publicity. Much better than if you went on his show right before the launch. This will also give us an *in* for connections to get the right people at the launch party. Trust me." She speaks with conviction, and it's hard not to believe in her. "I'll help you guys and coach you."

Westin and I look at each other, then nod.

"You're going to be huge." She and Sage both grin, and for a moment, I'm distracted by Sage.

By the need to reach across the table and squeeze her hand. To share this milestone with her—my best friend.

She hasn't been in my life for years, but right now, I want her to be.

Even though she doesn't.

Professional, I remind myself. She wants to keep things professional.

Taylor goes over the growing list of journalists and influencers for our launch party's guest list.

Toward the end of the meeting, Taylor moves to the last item on today's agenda—social media updates—and turns to Sage, who stands and uses a clicker to open a few slides on the screen.

"Here's where we are." She points to the slide using a laser. "Posts have been friendly but professional. Catchy, but not too much like a sales pitch. Your target audience is mostly male. According to a recent study, about eighty percent of fantasy sports users are male, white, and between the ages of eighteen and mid-thirties. We certainly want to capture their attention, which brings us to results."

She stands tall as she switches slides. Her voice is clear. Assertive. Confident.

She's breathtaking.

She continues with her presentation, and I tense as if she's talking dirty.

"By studying the analytics of each post on Facebook, we've seen a one percent increase in reach and a two percent increase in engagement. As you can see"—she moves the pointer over the numbers—"we've gotten slightly better results for Twitter. Instagram is still in progress. Overall, it's a small increase, but we're staying consistent with posts and interactions. We're optimistic that we'll report even better numbers at our next meeting."

We all nod along with her.

"Now, studies have also shown an increase in the

number of women playing fantasy sports. Almost twenty percent of the users are female, so we're targeting them as well. We're tweaking ads and mailers to better fit the target, but we're getting promising feedback on that front too." She glances between us, making eye contact as she speaks. "We'll send a follow-up email with this information as well, but this is to give you an update on our progress. If you see something you don't like, blame it on Facebook. Everyone else does." Sage smiles.

A joke.

She's direct, with the right mix of light-hearted.

She's meant for more than her current position. Last I heard, she opened her own marketing firm in her hometown.

This is New York City, but why is she starting at the bottom?

Westin and I exchange glances.

We're headed in the right direction.

This meeting has us fired up, and I'm sure neither of us will sleep for the next two weeks as we prepare for Jenson Ross and beyond.

Once we thank them for their work and meeting with us, Sage stands to show us out. No matter how buzzed I am over this meeting, the fact she's acting like we're strangers grates on my every nerve. Anyone else might consider it professional, pleasant even, but it only makes me grind my teeth harder.

Why does she get under my skin so fucking bad? Because I can't figure her out? I'm sick—it's the only explanation.

Westin walks ahead of me to answer his phone, taking it outside, and Taylor heads back to her office.

Everyone else bustles around the office, grabbing papers off the printer, while others are on the phone.

No one's paying us any attention, so I rush to Sage's side. "We need to talk," I whisper, then guide her out of the office suite until we reach the stairwell.

"What're you doing?" she hisses once we're out of sight, behind a closed door, but her voice echoes in the stairwell, magnifying her annoyance that much more.

"What're *you* doing? Why are you someone's assistant? *You* should be the publicist. You're qualified, educated, and perfect for it."

"While I appreciate the compliments, this is New York, Aiden." She laughs humorlessly. "Look around. The people here don't care that I graduated college with honors. That I ran a successful business in my hometown, where the population is less than one square inch of Manhattan." She steels herself, squaring her shoulders. "I sold my business, and it's helping me start over, even if it means beginning from the bottom."

"Just like that?"

"Just like that, so stop belittling me."

"That's not what I'm trying to do. I'm saying you deserve better, Jersey, but I'm not sure you agree."

"Don't pretend to know me, Aiden," she whispers. Her voice is eerie, so unlike her.

She returns my gaze head-on, and I can tell she's hiding something. She's not telling me the whole story, and I... I have to know.

"Why are you mad at me?" I ask, unable to stop myself from getting sucked into her vortex.

The more she talks and watches me with her wide eyes, the more I'm consumed by her and the need to figure this version of Jersey out.

"Aiden, this is my job. I told you I want to keep things between us professional, and you're doing the complete opposite." She pushes against my chest, but I don't budge.

Instead, I place my hand on the wall next to her head, and step closer, stealing the air she breathes like she's stealing my resolve. "I'll do what you want, if you answer my question."

"I'm not mad at you, Aiden."

"You are."

She squeezes her eyes closed, and I almost feel bad for this. But it's her. She's the one driving me to the brink of insanity, and I merely want to be put out of my misery.

"We may not have seen each other in years, but some things don't change." I run my thumb across her forehead. "Like this vein in your forehead when you're angry. And the way your lips part when I'm close."

Leaning in so that my trimmed beard brushes across her jawline, I whisper against her cheek, "I affect you."

Her shallow breaths are labored, and my whole body hardens.

Because as much of an effect as I have on her, she has more on me.

Pushing on my chest with both hands, she whispers, "And you're just as arrogant, infuriating, and impossible."

"To name a *few* of my many charming qualities." I pin her with my stare, unsure about what I expect her to say.

Unsure about what good an explanation from her will do at this point.

What do I want from her?

"Even if you're right about me, it doesn't change anything. Even if you weren't a client, you have a girlfriend and no right to do this to me." Her eyes are sad as she slides against the wall toward the door, away from me.

She touches the doorknob and pauses, making me think she'll say something else, but she doesn't. She walks through the door and shuts it behind her, closing herself off to me.

I start to go after her. The need to do so is like holding in a sneeze or being cut off mid-sentence, but she's right.

I have Raven.

All the times I stressed over not being good enough for Jock Stock, Raven was the one who supported and encouraged me. She listened when I expressed my concerns because... I don't have a background in computer science.

I didn't have any experience with computers and algorithms before my few online courses.

The information just clicked, though.

For me, sequencing, selection, and iteration all made sense as if it was simple addition or subtraction, so I messed around with different ideas until I felt confident in my ability. Which I do.

Aside from Westin's support, I've had Raven for the last year too. She understands it.

I *love* Raven.

Yet, being around Sage, I somehow forget anyone else outside the two of us.

And dangerously, I forget the reason Sage and I never worked out.

Shaking my head, I run down the stairs to the lobby to meet Westin and brace myself for his inquisition.

He's a prying dick.

I find him outside, still on the phone, pacing the sidewalk in front of the building. He doesn't seem to notice the dozens of other people milling around him.

I reach him as he hangs up. "Who was that? You looked pretty serious."

"Jared. He needs us back at the command center."

"Don't call it that."

"I thought you liked it when I used your lingo."

"It sounds nerdy coming out of your mouth."

"And you sound cool when you say it?" He smirks.

"Can we go before we get run over by the lady with the zoo on leashes?" I nod toward a woman walking five dogs, and they're coming right at us.

Westin waves for a taxi, and when we both get in, he rattles off our office's address and angles his body toward mine. "What's got your panties in a twist? Or should I say, *whom*?"

I ram my hands through my hair, taking a deep breath. "She drives me fucking insane."

"She didn't even say anything during the meeting, except at the end."

"That's what drove me to almost jamming a pen in my eye."

"Have you told Raven about her?"

"No. Why would I? It would only make her worried over nothing."

"Are you sure it's nothing? You got pretty worked up—"

"It's nothing of importance." I sigh. "Seeing Sage again brought the past back, reminding me I have so many unanswered questions. I thought I wanted answers, but I'm starting to think they wouldn't do me any good. It's best to leave it—and *her*—alone."

He remains silent as we turn onto our street, then says, "She has a unique beauty about her."

I whip my head toward him. "What's that supposed to mean?"

"What? She's beautiful." He shrugs, his back in the corner between the seat and door, as relaxed as if he said the sky is blue.

Which is accurate. Sage is pretty—it's a fact like the color of the sky—but coming from Westin, it feels like betrayal.

What the fuck?

He uses the card machine on the back of the passengers' seat to pay the cab, and we thank the driver as we get out onto the sidewalk.

"Want a coffee before we head up?" He points to the street cart with a blue sign on top.

I accept his offer, easing the tension in my posture, and walk beside him toward the cart.

Sage fucking Matthews is under my skin, and I need to stop this before it's too late.

I'm the one in a relationship now—our situations are reversed compared to the past.

I'm the one in love with someone else.

And Sage has no place in that—she can't change that.

I have the upper hand, the power, and I won't let her fuck my life up this time.

CHAPTER NINE

SAGE

"Where'd you go?" Taylor leans on the edge of my desk.

I look up from my computer, cringing. "Oh, Aiden wanted to talk about..." I lean back in my chair, biting my tongue from spilling the full truth. "My cousin and I ran into him, Westin, and Jared at a bar last week. It was interesting."

"Did you fall in his lap?" She giggles, straightening her skirt.

"What? No," I sputter.

"Don't look too surprised. It happens. My old boss, Catherine, I told you about? That's how she met her now-boyfriend. She fell in his lap, and the rest is history. Well, it wasn't that simple, but still." She winks.

"I have to meet this Catherine."

"You will. She's organizing my bachelorette party. I'll let you know when we have a plan. You have to join us."

"Of course." I nod, thankful for the invitation.

"Are you okay about..." She tilts her head.

"About Aiden?" I frown. "I'll be fine once he's done digging up the past. He's bringing up stuff he doesn't even want the answers to but doesn't know it yet."

"Sounds like you never got closure."

"What?" I blink at her like she turned a light switch on in my head, blinding me with her insight.

"Closure. Sounds like you two have unresolved issues you never dealt with. Maybe it would help you if you did."

"Maybe." *Or make it worse.* I worry my bottom lip, turning my attention to the calendar on my computer as Taylor walks back into her office.

How do I get closure from the person I once wanted *forever* from?

And why do I keep holding my breath like there's anything left for us?

He left then.

He has a girlfriend now.

That should be closure enough, right?

———

Like a bird with clipped wings, I have a heart

with no one to hold it.
A love for no one
to cherish.
But I loved you.
A love that was destined like water
sliding from a leaf.
Dripping from a faucet.
Falling from my eyes.
My heart beats with the hope of a new day.
That the water will find its way
from a puddle to an ocean.
Foolish, they say.
But I long for you.
In the night, I pray for you.
In my dreams, you loved me too.

I shut my notebook. I've been reading from it every day since I found it. This poem is one of the finished ones. Unlike the rest, I don't want to tweak the line breaks, the wording, or the rhythm in this one.

I remember the night I wrote it too. It was a couple months after Aiden left, right before Dave and I got back together and decided to get married. I was vulnerable and alone.

Terrified of the future.

I stare out my bedroom window, at the setting sun shining through, highlighting the dusty particles floating about the apartment. Like a bright future with a messy past.

That could be me.

If I refuse to let Aiden get to me—again.

Taylor's right—I never got closure.

I pick up my phone to text him to meet me this week to talk, but instead of clicking on my messages, I turn my phone off.

This nagging feeling stops me—this feeling that if we talk, if we get everything out in the open, it'll be over.

Really over with the one person I never let go. Part of my heart has always held on to him, even when I didn't want to or realize it.

The front door creaks open, and Naomi steps inside, hanging her coat up on the rack. "Sage? I'm home."

"In here." I stand from my bed and drop my tattered notebook on my nightstand.

"What's that?" Naomi points from the doorway, her scrubs a lighter shade of gray today than usual.

"Oh... I used to write poetry." I shrug, rounding my bed to nudge her out of here.

"Can I read them?" She doesn't move.

"Umm..."

"You've let people read them, haven't you?"

"Not exactly." I fidget with my fingers in front of me. "Aiden read some, once upon a time."

"I see." Her expression softens. "Well, if you feel comfortable down the road, I'd love to read them. I was an artist in my former life, after all. It was mostly paints, but art is art."

"Thanks, Naomi." I step toward the door, but then stop myself. "Wait, you were a painter?"

She gives me a sad smile. "I used to smoke too, but it's the one thing out of the two that I'm glad I quit."

My eyes widen.

"But yes. I was an art major when I first started college before I changed to nursing."

"What made you change?"

"Aside from wanting to help people, I needed something different." Her eyes darken before she hangs her head. "Some things, Sage... some tragedies are too much to handle, and you need a change of pace. Something to help you move on, and you can't do that—"

"—when it's staring you in the face," I finish for her with a whisper. "I know exactly what you mean."

I furrow my eyebrows. *What tragedy is she talking about?*

"Want to order in for dinner?" She walks to the refrigerator and pulls a menu from under a magnet, ending the conversation.

She puts her guard back up.

Why does she do that?

"I'm exhausted, and you've cooked every night this week," she calls out.

"Sure. That Chinese place you like so much?"

"And you don't like it?" She scoffs, moving toward the couch in the living room. "Their crab rangoon is the best I've ever had. And the sushi? *Orgasmic*."

"Wow," I say, sitting on the other end of the couch. "This place really has your heart. The only other time you're this animated is when you showed me what are very likely blood stains from a brutal murder." I point to the corner to a potted plant, under which are red splattered spots.

"You can't do New York without renting a creepy apartment." She shrugs. "I feel like I'm one of the city folk."

"You are one of them. Have been for a while."

"I've lived here for a while, yes. The city is definitely part of me, but you never forget your roots. No matter how long I live here or elsewhere, I'll always be a scared little girl from North Carolina."

"Must've been hard to move here all by yourself for college."

"It was, at first, but it made me seek out friends. I had a best friend." She visibly tenses and stops toying with the corner of a throw pillow.

"Naomi?"

She snaps her head up to me. "Do you know what you want for food?"

"Sure, but are you okay? You can talk to me."

"I'm fine," she says absentmindedly.

I can understand that—not wanting to go into detail—so I drop it. *For now*. After all, there's plenty I haven't told her myself.

She hands me the menu, and I ask for her order as I dial the number.

"Beef and broccoli please, and two orders of crab rangoon. I had one cracker and an apple all day, so I'm starving."

"On it."

"And afterward, maybe we tear into that ice cream in the freezer?"

"You know I never say no to ice cream."

Once our food is ordered, I get comfortable and turn Netflix on.

"Have you talked to your mom at all?"

I wince. "Once or twice since Christmas. I tried to call her a few times afterward to check in, but she only answered once." I exhale, recalling the long, awkward pauses in between a conversation that barely scratched the surface of our lives. "I thought we'd be doing better by now. I mean, I tell her I'm getting divorced, and all she says is, 'Good. I never liked him, anyway.' And that's that."

"Ouch." Naomi cringes.

"To be fair, she's right. Dave wasn't..." I twirl a

loose thread on the throw blanket around my finger. "He wasn't good for me."

"Shouldn't she want to be there for you, though? I mean, even if he wasn't good for you, divorce is still difficult."

"I wish I knew what she was thinking. Then again, it's probably a scary box to open." I laugh, but I don't feel it. It's only a sad attempt at lightening the situation.

"Give her time. She's probably hurt she wasn't at your wedding."

I remain silent for a moment, pretending to scroll through the new movies on Netflix.

After a short pause, I drop the remote and sigh, settling to tell Naomi the partial truth. "Dave and I... we got married because he was in love with me. I thought he was my chance at a better life. Our wedding was hurried, and my mother was so opposed, she thought if she didn't show up, that we wouldn't go through with it." I give her a tight-lipped smile. "It was her way of teaching me a lesson, like she's done all my life. It's why I was packing my own lunch at six years old."

She purses her lips. "Maybe my mom can talk to yours? She might listen to her big sister, for once?"

"Maybe, but we both know how that'll turn out." I smile. "Somehow, they'll end up arguing about something completely irrelevant, like who stole whose boyfriend in high school and who gave whose stuff to the Goodwill without their knowledge."

Naomi cracks a smile too. Our moms don't have much of a relationship anymore, partially because Naomi's mom moved away, and the distance put a strain on them.

But mostly, it's because they fight about everything.

Besides, even if they did get along, my mom rarely makes time for anything or anyone outside her work as an interior designer. She's branched out to all of the surrounding towns, taking on more clients than she can handle, which means she lives on coffee and stress, detached from any personal relationships.

I used to admire her work ethic. She even inspired me to open my own business and be an entrepreneur as well, and that's about the only thing I have to thank her for.

Even so, I often wondered if she was different before my father died. He passed away when I was only four years old, and I don't remember much from that time. I got used to her absence as I grew up, but sometimes, when I need to feel close to a mother figure, I imagine she was different with my father around. That she was warm and loving and generous.

Because the fantasy is more comforting than reality.

"I'm sorry, Sage. That must've been difficult not

having your mom in your corner when you needed her." Her voice is pained.

"It was." I gulp, turning my attention back to the screen. "It was another lifetime ago, though. A distant memory now," I whisper.

She squeezes my shoulder, and the small contact is surprisingly consoling.

Deeply inhaling, I shake my head. "Now, what movie are we watching? Something happy and fun, hopefully?"

"Not exactly my strong suits." She sets the pillow to the side and stands. "But you can pick whatever you want. I'm going to change before the food gets here."

As she walks to her room, I flip through the movies until they blur.

The guilt eats at me.

The guilt of not being completely forthcoming with my cousin—the one I'm trying to build a solid relationship with.

But I can't tell her, not yet.

Not until I tell the one person who's also involved in my past. In my memories. The one who broke me eight years ago and didn't have any intention of putting me back together.

"I think I should take the meeting alone." Westin leans against my door.

"Why?" I sit back in my chair, crossing my arms.

He tilts his head to the side, his eyes a mix of guilt and sympathy. "Because you turn into this crazy Aiden whenever Sage is involved, and we need to focus. They're squeezing us in to go over our interview with Jenson Ross. It's in one week. *Jenson Ross*, man."

"Yeah, I know who he is." I glare at him.

"This isn't the time to get our heads stuck in our asses about a girl, no matter how great or beautiful she is, and—"

"What the fuck is this?" I stand, my temper rising.

He points at me. "This is what I'm talking about. You lose your head when it comes to her."

I blow out a frustrated breath, gripping the back of my neck. "I'm sorry." I put my hands up in surrender.

He nods, silently accepting my apology, and after a short pause, he says, "I don't get it, man. You're not dating her. You're with Raven. Right?"

"Yes." I rub both eyes with my palms. "Yes, I'm with Raven. There's nothing between Sage and me, and I won't let her distract me. Okay? I'm good." I lower my voice to assure him my head is on straight like my mother taught me.

I don't admit that the silence from her for a week has been torture.

That researching athletes and stats, meeting with the team, and long hours haven't been enough to distract me.

That I haven't seen Raven much the last few weeks, and there's obvious tension between us when we do hang out.

I'm wound up.

"Listen, it's not only Sage. It's the stress of all this." I wave around my office toward the rest of the space. "It's a lot of pressure, and it's growing every day. We'll be appointing board members soon, and it's all coming to life, you know?"

"I know." He stands tall and comfortable like we're talking about sports—our specialty. But when we started down this road to build Jock Stock, we had no idea what we were in for.

We've had a lot of good days and just as many bad.

"It's what we've worked so hard for, Aiden." He squints at me.

I smile, easing the tension out of my shoulders and the room. "I'll behave, you'll see."

His frown turns into a grin as he sticks his hand out for me to shake. "That's the Aiden I recognize."

I drop his hand and put my arms out wide, emphasizing how relaxed I am. How evolved. How over the whole thing with Sage I am.

"Then you won't mind if I ask her out?"

My smile falls.

"What?" I blink like I don't recognize him.

"Since there's nothing between you two, I was thinking of asking Sage to dinner."

"You want to take out Sage? On a date?" I stiffen and hold my breath like I'm going under water and don't know when I'll breathe again.

He shrugs. "Yeah. I think there could be something between us."

"With Jers—*Sage*?" I work my jaw back and forth. "She's recently divorced, you know. I don't think it's such a good idea for you to take her out and—"

"Who are you taking out?" Jared interrupts, making me jump back, bumping into my chair.

"We should really put a bell around you. What, are you walking around barefoot?" I peer down at his feet, but he's wearing shoes. *How does he do that?*

Jared pops a chip in his mouth, and the bag wrinkles in his hands. "So?" he says between chews. "Who are you going out with?"

"Sage."

I cringe at the sound of her name coming from Westin's mouth.

The thought of her with him makes bile build in my throat.

"The hot assistant from CJJ?" Jared quirks an eyebrow and slows his chewing as he eyes me.

I'm stock-still, paralyzed by the idea of another man getting his chance with Sage. The woman who's had her claws around my heart for years, without me even knowing it.

But she shouldn't.

I shouldn't have my balls tied up over her, not after what she did. Not after I've moved on. I'm with someone real. Someone who doesn't make me want to punch a wall.

"Forget I said anything." Westin throws his hands up in surrender. "Obviously, you're having a moment, and I don't want to make things weird."

Before he finishes his sentence, I shake my head. "You're not. She's not mine." I clap him on the shoulder and head for the door, calling over my shoulder, "Let's go."

"Right behind you."

Westin grabs his briefcase on the way to the door,

and I grind my teeth, fighting the urge inside me to jog.

To scream.

To tell Westin he can't take Sage out, even though I have no right.

But the words are on the tip of my tongue the entire ride to CJJ.

When we arrive at their suite, I take one look at Sage, her hair down and wavy like she used to wear it, and I'm on the verge of exploding.

But as promised, I manage to make it through the meeting while Taylor coaches us, mainly Westin, with mock interview questions. I jump in when necessary, but mostly I stay quiet and attempt to ignore the way Sage's cleavage is emphasized over her blouse every time she bends to set our coffees in front of us or reaches across the table for papers.

It's torture.

And I don't miss the way Westin eyes her, either, as if he's never seen a beautiful woman before.

Like she won't rip his heart out the way she did mine.

But even so, I can admit there's something special about Sage. About her smile and the way it reaches her eyes.

Those damn eyes.

They're soft and kind, and does she still narrow them—do they still darken—when she's turned on?

I squirm in my seat, then stand as we end the meeting. Westin rounds the table to shake both Taylor and Sage's hands, but he lingers with Sage's, engulfing her petite hand in his bearish claws.

I sigh—I need to get the fuck out of here.

But I'm frozen in my spot, and their laughs are muffled by the blood rushing to my ears.

The minutes tick by.

My chest squeezes.

And Westin is *still* shaking her hand.

Balling my hands into fists at my sides, I round the table and thank them for their time. I told him I'd be professional, right? It has nothing to do with forcing him to let go of Sage's hand and step aside.

Her eyes flicker up to mine as I shake her hand, and her annoyance is obvious, which makes me smirk.

"Thank you so much for the coffee and everything, *Sage*." I purposely emphasize her real name instead of using her nickname to see if—and how—she reacts.

I have every right to be mad at her, but my tone is demeaning and harsher than I intended.

For one brief moment, hurt crosses her features, and she doesn't say anything. She merely nods and turns around, her files clutched to her chest.

I'm such an asshole.

Westin and I head out of the conference room together, when Taylor pops back up. "There's one more talking point I think will help. We need to hit your brand more on the head…"

The rest of what she says is muffled as Sage moves in my periphery toward the hallway.

"I need to run to the restroom," I say to them, inching toward the direction where Sage disappeared, then point to Westin. "Fill me in on the way back to the office."

I exit the suite and reach the hallway, but it's empty. I have half a mind to barge into the ladies' room for her, but I wait, running my hands through my hair.

I peer around the corner toward the suite. It's quiet and empty out here.

I should go.

I can escape without anyone seeing me.

This is her workplace, and I'm chasing her down like an immature teen. I'm an adult, and this isn't cool.

But I don't move. My feet remain planted.

I know it's wrong to confront her here, but the urge to clear the air is too strong. I can't make myself walk out of here without at least asking her to meet me later—anything to move past this tension that seems to only grow stronger every time we see each other.

I lean against the wall, exhaling as I tilt my head toward the ceiling. After a moment, Jersey emerges, stopping in her tracks when she sees me. "What?" She puts her hands on her hips.

"It's cute when you're mad. Your cheeks blush like you're shy when I know you're anything but, and"—my gaze flicks to her forehead—"there's the angry vein."

She lets out a humorless laugh and tries to side-step me, but I block her way out.

I want to pin her to the wall, hold her to me, be close to her.

But *fuck*... I can't.

I'm caught in limbo. Trapped in a constant loop of mixed emotions, and I'm losing my grip on reality.

"What the hell is this?" she asks, peering behind me for onlookers, I assume. "Another secret meeting? This is my work, Aiden. Any of my colleagues could see me. Perhaps you should book a meeting next time."

"Don't be sarcastic. You said to keep things—"

"Professional? Yes, that's what I want. I love this job and don't want to lose it."

I grind my teeth, then bite out, "You're the one who's making this more difficult than it has to be."

"No, *you're* the one being an ass, so excuse me for not wanting any part of it." She slips past me, her back hunched as she slinks away.

I am being an ass.

How the fuck does she keep doing this to me?

I work my jaw back and forth, slowly deflating.

"He's going to ask you out." My voice is barely above a whisper as I turn to face her and become even more defeated.

She visibly stiffens, then faces me too. "What're you talking about?"

"Westin." I stuff my shaking hands in my pockets, keeping my voice low. "He wants to take you to dinner. Will you say yes?"

"He hasn't asked, and I doubt he will."

"When he does, will you say yes?"

She takes a purposeful step toward me, her eyes on fire. "I told you I'm none of your business. We're not even friends, let alone anything else."

"We are friends."

"No, we aren't, Aiden." She throws her hands up. "Friends don't ask each other not to date other people."

"That's not what I'm asking. I'm not fu—" I exhale with frustration, spinning in place. "I'm not jealous."

"It sure sounds like you are, and it's not fair." When I face her again, she visibly steels herself, and it's like a punch to my dick. "You have no right to ask me about Westin. No right to pretend like you're mad if I do say yes. You have a *girlfriend*."

"This isn't about me."

"It's always about you."

"What is that supposed to mean?" I grab her arm

to keep her from walking away, finding it hard to keep whispering. "Unless..."

"What?"

I search her eyes for any indication that I misunderstood. Does she still have feelings for me? Is she not over what happened between us, either? Is that why she's mad at me?

That can't be right, but even if it is...

"It's too late." I let go of her. "Too late for us."

"Good thing I don't want you," she says, but her voice is weak.

"Keep telling yourself whatever lies you need to in order to sleep at night." I step toward her, then lean down to whisper, "I have."

The last thing I hear is her gasp before I walk away.

I leave her behind me, without looking back, like the time I told her I had feelings for her, and she put Dave before me.

Will she chase me now? Show up on my doorstep to tell me she needs me?

Do I even want her to?

Before I round the corner, Westin appears.

"Hey..." His voice trails off as his gaze falls from me to Sage behind me. "Everything okay here?"

Forcing a smile, she nods. "Just fine." As she passes us, she glares at me.

How the hell did we get here?

All I did was try to be there for her all those years ago. To win her over as her friend and more. I fought for her love, while Dave merely demanded it.

He never deserved her.

Yet, somehow I'm the one being punished now.

"Ready?" Westin asks me.

"Yeah. Let's get out of here," I grumble.

In the cab back to our office, Westin remains silent. It's not until the elevator drops us off upstairs to our cubicles, where Jared is surely hiding, that Westin finally speaks.

And I wish he hadn't.

"I was never going to ask her out."

I snap my head at him.

"Sage. I was never going to ask her out because even though you say you're with Raven, part of you is stuck in the past. With Sage."

"That was a dick move," I say, purposely ignoring the end of his statement.

"Maybe, but it's not worse than what you're doing. Even though you and Raven haven't seemed to be on the same page lately, she doesn't deserve this."

"It's not what you think."

"It is, though." He tilts his head, peering at me like he pities me, and it pisses me off. "You've been different since the first time you saw her. More on edge. Tense. Not as focused."

I hang my head, disappointed in myself.

"In all the years I've known you, nothing, not even when you started dating Raven, took your focus. We need you, man. Jock Stock is so close to making it big. *We're* so close." He's pleading again.

Westin doesn't plead. His mere presence exudes dominance—the kind that urges those around him to put their best efforts forward without him having to beg—and I'm letting him down.

I'm letting our team down.

"Take the rest of the afternoon off. Get your head together. Be ready for our future because, Aiden, it's going to be difficult, and we need you."

I nod, then grab my bag. I don't want to leave them hanging, but I'm no good to them like this. Wound up. Broody.

A mess.

I need to get my shit together, starting with Jersey.

There's so much left unsaid and unexplained between us, and no matter how badly I want to avoid the mess we made all those years ago, I have to face it. I have to face her.

My heart races merely at the thought.

I need a fucking drink first.

CHAPTER ELEVEN
SAGE

"Westin said you'd be here."

"Why arc you talking to Westin?" he growls.

"I was looking for you." I sit on the barstool next to him and glance around Hemingway House. "I didn't realize this was your regular hangout spot."

"It serves the best beer. And the company is all right." He raises his mug toward the bartender. "Thanks, Joey."

Joey turns to me. "What can I get you?"

"She's not staying," Aiden says at the same time I ask for a glass of Merlot.

"Merlot, please," I repeat, then glare at Aiden. "We need to talk."

He sighs, his shoulders slumped. "What about? Work? God forbid we talk about anything else."

"Would you stop being an ass for one second?"

"Can't. This is my fourth beer, around about the time the asshole in me comes out."

"How many times a day do you drink your fourth beer then?" I counter as Joey sets my red wine in front of me. Thanking him, I cringe when Aiden laughs humorlessly. The sound is cruel, and my stomach hurts like he punched me there. Ignoring him, I say, "I think we need closure. If we're going to continue working together and be successful, we need to get over the past. No more secret confrontations after meetings. No more snarky comments. Closure."

He turns to me as if in slow motion, as if I told him someone died, and he's so anguished he doesn't believe me.

"Aiden, please..."

His frown is so pronounced, it seems painful. "Stop. Just... stop."

"We can't continue like this—"

He shakes his head. "It's been a long fucking week. I know we need to talk, but can we please... sit here and enjoy our drinks first? The music? And the fact that Joey's had a receipt stuck to his shoe for the last half hour?"

Joey's stops in his tracks and lifts his shoe. "Shithead. Why didn't you tell me?" He stares at Aiden, who shrugs.

"Easy. That's all I want for us for a few minutes." Aiden turns his pleading gaze to me. It makes him seem young. Innocent. Fragile. He doesn't appear to be the Aiden I know. "Please."

I nod and sip my wine, accepting that this is what he needs.

When I first stepped in here, I was ready for a fight. Ready to unleash my pent-up tension on him. After all these years, I was finally ready to use my truth as punches, kicks, and blows. For him to feel half as broken as he's made me.

But seeing him like this, I decide to wait. To be patient with him because he's obviously dealing with his own demons, and for whatever reason, I don't want to hurt him worse.

"Do you remember the poetry readings we went to in college?" he asks, his expression morphing to one of wistful nostalgia.

Almost happy.

The poetry readings were our cheery memories, for the most part. The only reason he and I went alone was because they weren't Dave's thing. So, Aiden and I went while Dave was at his evening class one semester. We'd share a basket of cheese fries, and on the ride home, we'd talk about our favorite poems.

He never wrote any of his own, and I always appreciated that he indulged me by going. After he confessed his feelings for me, I realized the time alone was probably all he wanted.

"Yes," I whisper, the glass to my lips. Once I

swallow my sip, I say, "I still tear up when I think of the poem one of the girls shared. The one about her car wreck with a deer?"

"She was sadder that the deer died than the fact she broke her arm and doesn't have full functionality."

"That's the one." I pause. "It scrutinized our existence. How one unintentionally harms the other. How timing can be everything—create fortune or devastation. Tragically beautiful," I muse.

"Do you still write?"

"No." I inhale deeply and let it out slowly, keenly aware of my chest deflating as the breath leaves my body. "I haven't written anything in years. I actually found a box of old notebooks the other day filled with random notes and half-poems from college. They made me want to start writing again."

"You should. You always had a unique talent for it."

"Not sure magazines would agree, but thank you."

"Did you ever even submit them?"

"Some. Most were never finished, though."

"Were they not? Or were you scared?" he challenges.

He angles his body toward me and furrows his eyebrows, watching me, keeping me in my seat as I fight my urge to flee the bar so I don't have to answer.

He steals my breath with his questions, but I know underneath the few words, there's so much more.

He means more than my poems.

Us.

I squirm under his pointed scrutiny as the air shifts.

"Were you scared of putting yourself out there to be rejected? Of opening your heart only to have it smashed to pieces?" he continues, his voice rising with every word. When he says the last part, there's so much pain and regret in his eyes, and I fight my own tears. "Because I know the feeling, and I did it, anyway."

"What happened to us was..." I choke on the word *us*, then clear my throat to avoid causing a scene for the few patrons around us. "What happened to us wasn't entirely my fault, no matter how much you blame me. *You* left without a word and never came back. You left like I didn't mean anything to you."

He searches my expression as a lone tear falls down my cheek, and the flash of guilt is replaced with anger. "You left first." He slides off his barstool, giving me his back.

I take a few deep breaths, watching after him, feeling like the floor will swallow me whole if I step down to follow him.

But I do it, anyway.

I need this. We both do.

I march after him, my feet heavy but determined, and I shove the door open harder than is needed. I catch a glimpse of him as he rounds the corner to the alleyway, and I take off in that direction.

Once I catch up to him, he stands still, facing away from me. His shoulders are high and tense, and all I want to do is grab them and shake them.

"The night we were together... I *had* to leave the next morning." I approach him, my deep breaths matching my steps. "Not because I wanted to leave you, but because Dave found out his grandfather died. What was I supposed to do? We were broken up, but I'd been part of his family for years. I still cared about him—and his grandfather—and he was in shock. Grieving. His grandfather practically raised him. What the hell was I supposed to do, Aiden?" My voice is loud. Enraged. Desperate.

"Be with me." His voice is soft, and I barely hear him with his back still to me. He slowly turns, and his troubled gaze finds mine.

"I wanted to." I drop my hands to my sides as my chest heaves like I can't breathe in oxygen fast enough. "I wanted to be with you, but you didn't even give me the chance."

"I saw you at the funeral." His lips twist, his expression tortured. "You and Dave. I saw you together, and I couldn't stand by... I couldn't be on the outside anymore, not after I was finally with you." He rams his hands over his hair. "I couldn't watch you go back to him. I couldn't fucking take it."

"But I wasn't going to. I didn't have any intention of taking him back, Aiden."

"Don't lie to me." He drops his voice low.

"I'm not." I hold my arms out, ready to beg for him to listen.

"You kissed him!"

His outburst stops me in my tracks—my whole body freezes.

"I saw you." He points at me and takes measured steps toward me, his body rigid and enraged.

And underneath it all... hurt. He's so hurt.

"You kissed him that afternoon after the funeral. I went looking for you, and I wish I hadn't. I wish now that I hadn't had feelings for you at all."

"You don't mean that." I wrap my arms around my stomach like I can keep myself whole when all I want to do is crumble.

He throws his head up to the sky, a satirical laugh strangled in his throat as darkness washes over him. "Tell me, why did you and Dave split up?"

I narrow my gaze at him.

"You two were such a happy fucking couple, right?" he says, sarcasm dripping from every word like the tears I shed when he left. "So, what was the problem? Why the divorce? What happened to you now that's different than it was back then? Because the way I remember it, he was always a dick."

"Why were you even friends with him if you hated him so badly?"

"It wasn't exactly *him* I cared about." He stares at me pointedly, as if I should know by now that it was me he wanted to be close to.

I realized it when he confessed his feelings for me, but it was hard to keep believing his motivations after he ran away and made me question myself.

"How did you know we divorced?" I ask. *How long has he known? Why hasn't he asked about it until now?* I have questions to last a lifetime.

"I heard whispers from mutual friends, but I didn't believe them until I saw you. At the first meeting, I knew you left him because you're here. You wouldn't be if you were still married to him."

He's right. Dave didn't want this for me, or *us*. But Aiden... he always rooted for me and every desire I had.

I swallow the lump in my throat and rasp, "You."

He stands straighter.

"We broke up because he found out about you and—"

"Hey," a female voice sounds from beside us.

Aiden and I both turn our heads. Raven stands to our side, her arms crossed, her gaze pinned on Aiden and the little space between us. *How did we miss her approach?*

"For someone you *barely* knew, you're very close, history and all," she spits.

Oh God—she's been listening.

But before I can think of an explanation, her words ring in my head.

"That's what you said to her?" My mouth falls open in shock, feeling like he slapped me.

My heart stings.

All our memories together—the ones I've clung to over the years—are clearly a joke to him.

"It's not how it sounds."

"Then how is it exactly?" Raven puts her hands on her hips, her glare becoming murderous.

"He's a client." I turn my frown toward him, my eyes watering with unshed sadness.

"You *work* together?" she screeches and places her hand on her stomach like this piece of news sickens her.

"You didn't even tell her we have a working relationship?" I hiss, staring at him in disbelief.

"I knew you'd get worked up about it," he says to Raven.

"And why's that? If there's nothing between you and this woman, why would I get *worked up?*" She shakes her head like she doesn't want to know the answer. "You're a real asshole, aren't you?"

"I should go." I slump against the wall and brush

past Raven, not allowing either of them the satisfaction of seeing me break.

No more.

"Jersey, wait," Aiden calls after me, echoing in this alleyway and the walls of my heart, and Raven scoffs.

My heart sinks further.

The name he used to call me. Our friendship. Our night together—it's all ruined.

This is what I was afraid of. That I'd attempt to get closure, and it would blow up in my face.

But it turned out worse. So much worse.

He told his girlfriend he *barely knew* me, like I was a smudge on his life that he easily wiped away.

I hail a cab with little effort, and I'd like to celebrate. To turn around and smile at Aiden because the small victories used to give us life.

Picnics with cheap burgers.

Cheese fries at poetry readings.

Riding in the car with no destination in mind.

Now, it's the monumental disappointments that take it away and drive a wedge between us.

I give the driver the address to the train station, forcing myself not to look back. Not to see them making up.

Not to cry anymore.

I lean against the headrest as we hit traffic and close my eyes.

"What about this one?" I come out of the fitting room

wearing a navy and white striped dress that's short and flirty —perfect for summer. I walk down the hall to where Aiden sits cross-legged on the floor, leaning against the wall. "What do you think?"

He sits up straighter, raking his gaze over me. He's silent for a few seconds, making me shift from one foot to the other, nervous.

"The mannequin wore it better, didn't it?" I frown.

"No, that's not it at all." He stands, wiping his palms down his jeans. "You look great. Much better than the mannequin." His expression softens as a smile spreads. "You look like you're ready to go sailing."

"Good. I want to fit in with the yacht clubs of New York City someday, so I need to look the part now." I cover my laugh with one hand as we stare at each other.

"You'll fit right in."

I shrug, taking a deep breath, my smile faltering. "Dave's right. It's only a fantasy."

He moves toward me. "Sage, you've talked about this fantasy, as you call it, a lot since I met you. It's more than a fleeting thought." He puts his hands in his pocket like he's afraid to continue but does so, anyway. "And why shouldn't you want more? Why shouldn't you move to New York instead of back to your hometown? You can do whatever you want."

I bite my lip to keep myself from telling him how badly I want that more than moving back home. More than what a small town has to offer.

"It's good to dream. To want something seemingly impossible. It makes it that much more special and satisfying when you make it come true."

There's something in his eyes—a spark.

He gets it.

And I like it.

His phone dings, and he fishes it out of his pocket, his expression falling. "Dave's class let out early, and he needs a ride."

"Okay, let me change real fast, and we'll go."

"Toss me the dress, and I'll check out while you get ready."

My cheeks blush at his thoughtful gesture. "Thank you."

He gives me a tight-lipped smile, and I walk to the fitting room in a daze.

Why did my stomach flutter?

"We're here."

I open my eyes, and in the rearview mirror, I notice the driver watching me with concern, a crease between his thick brows. Thanking him, I swipe my card on his machine to pay and step onto the sidewalk in front of the train station.

I stare at my phone the entire way home, willing it to ring.

Willing Aiden's name to pop up.

But when I reach my apartment building, I still don't have any calls or texts from Aiden. No apologies. No explanation.

I shouldn't have expected any, but I hoped he

would call. That he would say it was all a misunder-standing.

I hoped he'd follow me here.

The whole way home—and ever since I saw him a few weeks ago—I hoped.

Because even after all these years, no matter how badly I don't want to let him affect me, he still makes my heart flutter.

The same heart he constantly crushes.

He didn't even tell his girlfriend about me.

I meant nothing to him back then, and it's the same now.

It's time I give up, right? Take the hint? Move on?

I have to.

CHAPTER TWELVE

AIDEN

I step inside my apartment with Raven on my heel. She slams the door behind her, and I steel myself for a fight.

I'm surprised when she doesn't immediately yell or throw everything she can find. The ride on the subway must've calmed her down. As I head to the refrigerator for a beer, Raven remains silent, and it might actually be worse than her hurling my toaster at me.

Bottle in hand, I lean my hip against the kitchen counter, waiting.

"I thought you were working late." She crosses her arms, and the hurt is more obvious than if she painted it across her forehead. She's more upset than furious.

My gut twists. "I *was* working, but Westin asked me to take the night off, so I could—"

"So you could hang out with your other girlfriend?"

Even though I know she's in pain, her calling Sage my girlfriend makes me see red. "She's not my girlfriend. She never was," I grind out, then take a sip of beer to wash down the angry distaste bubbling inside.

"You two sure were cozy in the alleyway."

"You have no idea what you're talking about, Raven."

"Probably because you won't tell me the truth about her. It's obvious you two don't just work together. You call her *Jersey*. I mean, you have a nick-name for her, for fuck's sake!"

She cringes when she says *Jersey* as if it repulses her.

And it makes me tense all over again.

We're at a standstill, watching each other as the silence stretches between us, and uncertainty surrounds us like a coffin.

I should apologize. Grovel. Get on my knees and beg her to stay.

But I don't move or say anything. My tongue feels like lead, tamping down the words.

"She's the one, isn't she?"

I meet her defeated gaze with my own confused one. "What do you mean?"

All disdain disappears from her voice and demeanor, leaving a sad and vulnerable woman in front of me. One I barely recognize, and it fucking kills me to know I'm doing this to her.

"She's what's been holding you back. Why I haven't moved in here with you. Why we aren't taking the next step. It's her you've been waiting for."

"You basically live here." I shake my head, my chest heavy and sullen.

"*Basically*. Not officially. My name isn't on the lease or the bills. I've been staying at my place more the last few weeks, ever since karaoke night at the bar with *Sage*," she bites out. "And you haven't even noticed."

"Raven, I've been busy with the company. You know I've had a lot—"

"Stop with the excuses, A. Be fucking straight with me like an adult."

I sip my beer, and it's hard to swallow. "I *am* an adult. It's you who keeps treating me like I'm not."

"Excuse me?" She scoffs.

"Come on, Raven. You want to take me shopping, you check up on me whenever I'm working late as if I've missed curfew—you baby me."

"You're mad because I'm nurturing? Because I care so much about you that I take time out of my schedule to make sure you eat?" She throws her hands up. "Unbelievable," she mutters more to herself than me.

"You know how much I appreciate it, but every now and then, it'd be nice to make my own decisions about the rug I use in *my* den." I pause, sighing with exasperation.

She drops her arms to her side.

I set my beer on the coffee table and pace.

This is it. The end. Even if I wasn't confused right now and wanted her to, Raven's not going to stick around after this. I've been unfair to her.

And even though what I've said about her is true, it's not the entire story. When I look at her, I sense she knows it too—I'm grasping at straws to avoid facing the real problem.

But I can't keep lying to her.

"This wasn't supposed to happen." I grip the back of my neck with both hands. "I thought it was behind me. I wasn't supposed to see her again."

"You can stop pretending you're not glad you did now." She shifts, staring at me like she doesn't know me anymore. As if I'm someone else entirely.

Part of me knows she's telling the truth, but I can't admit it—to her or to myself.

"That's it, then? You have nothing else to say?"

I can't look at her. If I do, I'll see the hurt I've caused her. The hurt I never intended.

No words can take that away, but I offer her one thing. "I'm sorry," I whisper, and I mean it.

"Don't." She shakes her head, backing toward the door. "I've wasted enough time here."

She leaves me standing in my loft with only the echo of the door slamming.

The coat rack she bought for the loft seems ten times bigger, towering over me.

The room feels small.

"She's what's been holding you back... It's her you've been waiting for."

My head is heavy as the truth of her statement weighs on me—I hate it. I hate that she's right. That I'm not over Sage.

I hate that I've loved her for far longer than two years in college.

And for the second time in my life, I've let Sage Matthews turn my world upside down.

Fuck.

———

"What're you doing here?" I blink.

Jersey's standing at my door, chest heaving, cheeks flushed, and I can't move. Not after what I said to her outside the bar earlier tonight.

"You said you like me." She pants like she ran here. "Did you mean what you said, or was it the beer talking?"

"I meant every word." I clench my jaw, and my gaze bores into hers so there's no room for misunderstanding or doubt. "But it doesn't matter, does it? Because you don't feel the same, so spare me."

"That's not fair. You didn't even give me a chance to think about this. I broke up with Dave two weeks ago, and you're his best friend. You're my friend. I don't want to hurt anyone."

"There's no avoiding that."

"I needed time," she whispers, her bottom lip trembling like she knows what she wants but is afraid to say it. "I thought I did, anyway, but now…"

"What? What do you need now?" I hold my breath as I wait for her answer, steeling myself for the worst, but hoping for the best.

"You. I need you."

She steps over the threshold, into my arms, and crushes her lips to mine. They're sweet and full and eager.

I can finally breathe.

With Sage in my arms, melting against me, everything feels right.

I exit the train station and find a taxi.

"Where to, boss?" the driver asks once I close the door behind me.

I rattle off her address and run my palms down my jeans, nausea rolling through me as I remember the best feeling Sage had ever given me—and the worst.

"Don't go to him," I plead, tugging her sleeve so she'll come back to bed. "Stay with me."

But she answers his call, moving to the next room, talking in hushed tones like she's trying to hide it from me.

In my gut, I know, though. The sun has risen, a new day, but the old feelings remain. It's hard to compete with her history with Dave.

A small part of me hangs on to hope, though. She came to my apartment last night. Spent the night in my bed. Made love to me.

It was perfect.

"I need to go." She returns, her gaze traveling from my bare chest to my eyes, and I'm crushed.

The small hope I was holding on to vanishes like a ghost in the night, questioning if it was ever here to begin with—if any of this was ever real.

She licks her lips. "Aiden, Dave's grandpa died. He's really upset and needs someone." She rushes around my room for her clothes, then leans over to kiss my cheek. "We'll talk soon, okay?"

Her lips say one thing, but her eyes say another.

And when I catch her kissing Dave two days later, I know I was right.

As the cab pulls to a stop in front of her building, I'm tempted to ask him to turn around. This is a mistake.

Sage and I are a natural disaster ready to take down everything around us—it already did that to Raven.

But I get out, anyway, because I know I won't be able to stay away from her. We'll always find each other, because someone out there in the universe likes to fuck with me.

I practically run to the elevator.

Down the hall.

My heart and rage ball in my throat as I knock.

Once Sage opens the door, her eyes wide and questioning, I step inside without an invitation and pace the small living room. "I broke up with Raven."

"Are you okay?"

I whirl around to her. "No," I seethe. "I'm *not* okay, and it's your fault."

She pushes off the door toward me, scoffing. "How is it *my* fault that you didn't tell your girlfriend the truth about me? Please, enlighten me."

I grind my teeth so hard I could crack a tooth. "Why would I tell her about the gut-wrenching pain you caused me? How I'm still not over it, even though I thought I was? That I can't stop thinking about why you said it was because of me that you and your husband divorced."

She stands back, crossing her arms.

"My God, Sage, why did you marry him in the first place?" My anger seeps out of the cracks in my voice as I unleash the questions I've been holding in. "I loved you. I would've given you everything."

"But you didn't." She starts to turn toward the kitchen, and I grab her arm to stop her. When she lifts her devastating brown eyes—eyes filled with ghosts that mirror my own—I suddenly want to hold her. To make her feel better, even though she's the cause of my pain.

"Why?" I whisper.

"I waited for you for weeks, which turned into months. I was alone and—" She sucks in a sharp breath like she wants to say something else. *She's hiding something.* Wiggling out of my grasp, she says, "You disappeared to fucking Europe, and I never saw you again. So maybe you should be explaining *why* to me, because from where I was sitting, watching your social media week after week, you didn't seem to care at all."

I cringe.

"You posted picture after picture with a new girl every week, so please, don't bullshit me. You weren't upset about me, and you definitely didn't love me, Aiden." She glares.

"I didn't—" I wince, my heart still racing. "I just needed to get away. After I saw you with Dave, I couldn't fucking see straight. I mean, you said it your-self that you and Dave had a history."

"And I wanted a future." She softens her expression a fraction as the lump in my throat grows. "A future with *you*."

"I didn't think I had that option, Jersey. I was stupid, but I loved you." I curse under my breath.

"If you loved me, you would've let me explain," she whispers. "I could've told you that I didn't kiss him back. That I told him it was over, even though that made me a bitch since his grandfather had died. But I wanted you, Aiden. I wanted to be with you."

The way she talks. The agony in her voice... This thing between us has haunted her as long as it has me.

But it doesn't make my anger dissipate.

My head spins with all the emotions coursing through me.

If what she's saying is true, that she loved me, then why? She didn't just go back to him—she fucking married him. It's why I've been so angry at her. *Why*—

"I was pregnant."

My heart stops—I freeze.

The sounds of the city, the hum of her refrigerator, her pants—everything is muffled.

What the...

CHAPTER THIRTEEN

I gulp, fearing what he'll say. What he'll think.

What I'll see when he stops spinning in place and faces me again.

This is it.

"I found out I was pregnant after your graduation. I was about to start my senior year of college," I continue, my voice shaky. "I didn't have a job. My meager scholarships weren't going to support a baby. My relationship with my mom had already become nonexistent, but I went to her for help, anyway. She freaked and refused. Said I got myself into that mess and had to deal with it myself. I was alone, Aiden. Scared. No plan. *Nothing.*"

He slowly turns, his throat bobbing as he swallows.

"Jersey..." He frowns, the lines in his forehead

prominent. His eyes dart from me to the floor to the window, as he seemingly tries to fill in the blanks.

I fidget with my hands in front of me as his lips twist.

Finally, he meets my gaze head-on. "Was it…"

"She was yours." My voice cracks.

He stumbles backward as I deliver the final blow. The one secret I've only ever uttered once before in a drunken haze to a close friend. The man I've been running from now knows.

"No, no, no," he whispers, his face pale.

I wipe a stray tear from my cheek, my body going numb.

His mouth hangs open as the other pieces of our past appear to fall into place for him like water fills every crevice. "That's why you married him."

I gulp, squeezing my eyes closed. "You disappeared, and Dave was there, confessing his love for me. Apologizing for being an ass. Wanting to marry me and provide support. A home for us."

Aiden curses under his breath, tugging at the ends of his hair.

"He found out about the baby and assumed it was his." I choke on a sob as I urge myself to get the words out, pushing through the weight of this moment as best I can, but it's difficult. The truth makes my tongue feel like it's grown three times in size, and my stomach churns as I relive those painful days. "He proposed before I could gather my wits enough to explain it wasn't. I tried, but I... I was too..."

My voice trails off, and my vision blurs as I'm taken back to those few months, when everything was so uncertain.

"I broke up with you for a reason." I shake my head, *walking away from him. "I can't be with someone who makes my decisions for me. Who laughs at my dreams, no matter how ridiculous they might sound. I want support. Someone who roots for me."*

"Sage, please."

I instinctively cringe at his use of my real name. I've gotten so used to Aiden's nickname for me that I miss it.

I miss him.

"I can be the man for you. I'll change. I'll be better, and we can dream together." Dave gently grips my shoulder and turns me to face him. "Sage, I'm so sorry. I've been such a fucking idiot, and I don't deserve you. But you're having our baby."

I pause.

Oh God—he thinks the baby is his.

He doesn't know I was with Aiden after Dave and I broke up. During his frantic pleas to win me back, he doesn't do the math and realize that this baby can't be his.

I have to tell him.

"The baby is not ours." I rub my temples, my voice strained, and steel myself to finally end our relationship. He'll never forgive me once he learns the truth. "It's mine and—"

"You can't take it away from me. It's mine too. Why not

let us be a family?" He squeezes my hands in his, desperation in his eyes. He loves this baby already, and it does something weird to my chest. "I'll provide for us. I already accepted a job—I start in two weeks. Salary and benefits for all three of us. You can move back home with me and finish your degree online or something. We can figure it out... together."

The more he talks, the more relief floods me.

The future he paints is what I want—stability. A loving home.

Can I really do this?

My mother has abandoned me. Naomi and I haven't been close for years. No one else can help me.

Dave places his hand on my stomach. I haven't started showing yet, but underneath, a baby is growing.

A baby to hold and love and cherish.

A baby that's part of Aiden and me that I'll forever have, even though he doesn't want us.

"I lost her." The tears stream down my face, and Aiden pales again. "I lost her after one hundred twenty-six days of holding her in my womb and close to my heart. For those few months, I had a special kind of peace filling me because I had a new life inside me. One you and I created, and the loss of her..." I hiccup. "It broke my heart... my whole *soul*... in ways I never imagined."

Aiden's chest heaves, and the silence around us thickens with grief, but anger still lingers. The room closes in on us as his breaths pick up, and his eyes grow dark.

"Why didn't you tell me?" His voice is low.

Accusatory.

He's grappling with this the only way he knows how—growing livid and placing blame. I know him well enough to expect as much, but it still stings that he's talking to me like I did something wrong when I'm hurting too.

Some days are as painful as the day I lost her, and he wasn't there to help me through it.

"You should've told me." He takes a measured step forward, his voice rising. "I could've been there for you. Done right by you, and—*fuck*." He dips his head, leaning his hands on his knees, then stands, his face red.

"I called you. I emailed. I went to your house," I say, understanding he's upset, but I refuse to let him take it out on me.

Because I'm angry at him too.

"I called you *many* times. What was I supposed to do? Leave a voicemail to let you know you're going to be a father?" I raise my voice to match his and grip his arm to stop him from pacing. "You never answered, and you never called me back. You didn't just go to Europe for a few weeks—you walked out of my fucking life when it was falling apart!"

My outburst visibly rattles him, but he composes himself, shrugging out of my hold.

"You can get mad at me all you want, Aiden, but you're to blame for this." I point between us, my voice trembling as my outrage surpasses his. "I shouldn't have married Dave out of desperation—it's a mistake I have to live with, but I accept it. I made that choice because I thought it was my best option at the time. Now, it's your turn to realize you're a fucking coward."

He stares back at me, and his expression is unreadable for the most part, except for the pain. Pain is always visible. There's no mask for it because it eats at you from the inside out until you burst.

And Aiden and me? We exploded in a mix of confessions and regret.

Of love and resentment.

Because even through my bitterness, there's a layer of love for him that I'm realizing I'll never rid my heart of.

My apartment is quieter than it usually is when Naomi works late like she is tonight. As we continue blinking at each other, the silence stretches between us in eerie waves until Aiden finally speaks up.

"You didn't even give me a chance to be the man for you. You picked him—you always did. But if I would've known about the baby, maybe..." His voice is laced with sadness. He clears his throat, then says, "I might've been a coward to leave, but you were in love with him. With your history. Your fucking high school prom and living in the past and—"

The sting of my palm against his cheek echoes between us.

My bottom lip quivers as I brush past him. When I reach the door, I take one last look at him.

As he rubs his cheek, his eyes are distant. Empty. Sullen.

The way I feel.

With no other words—with only crushing disappointment coursing through me—I throw open the door. "Get out."

He stands still for a moment, his posture deflated. Anguished.

And when he finally walks out, he takes more broken pieces of me with him.

As I drag my feet to my room, my body aching, there's a sinking feeling in the pit of my stomach that there's nothing left of me.

And it terrifies me.

All because Aiden Baxter cracked open my heart once again with one simple gaze—and I let him crawl inside.

But I'm done.

He finally knows the truth and chooses to blame me, but I'm done letting him disappoint me.

As I move to my bed and pull the covers over me, I stare at the ceiling.

The minutes tick by.

The shadows of the city outside my window float above me.

I know Aiden—he's in shock with this news. But even if he doesn't come around, if he doesn't come to terms with his role in our past, I make a vow to myself to stand tall.

Strong.

Like a tree... rooted... that even a hurricane can't whisk away...

Never again can I let myself crumble because of him.

CHAPTER FOURTEEN
AIDEN

For the next week, my head is a mess, as if I'm constantly hungover. She thinks I abandoned her in her time of need, when I didn't even know.

I didn't know about her and Dave until it was too fucking late to do anything about it, and all this time, I've resented her because of it. That I'd lost my chance.

But a baby? *My* baby?

A baby girl.

How do I wrap my mind around that?

It makes sense. What Dave said all those years ago. The memory has been on constant repeat.

"We're happy." Dave runs his hand over his head, and his wedding band shines under the sunlight. He's grinning like a fool in love, which he is, and I'm left feeling hollow. Every

word falling from his mouth is a stab to my chest. "Sage and me, we're really happy. We're going to be a family."

His voice becomes muffled as blood rushes to my ears.

The red in my vision.

I try to force a smile as I clap him on the shoulder. "Congratulations, man."

Last I heard, he'd moved back to his hometown, so I didn't expect to run into him here, our old college campus. We haven't talked since his grandfather's funeral, and from the sounds of it—from the fact that he hasn't kicked me in the balls—Sage never told him she and I slept together.

I brush past him, ready to finish packing up my condo.

I have a long drive ahead of me.

One that will take me far away from this place—from Dave and Sage.

She married him.

"Everything all right?" Dave stops me.

With my back to him, my emotions in my throat, I nod. "I need to get going. I'd like to get most of my drive out of the way before dark."

"Smart."

I'm not. If I was smart, I wouldn't have left. I wouldn't have gone to Europe in a fit of rage. Sage wouldn't have married Dave because I was going to win her over. I wouldn't have given her up.

But now I have to.

"Don't be a stranger, brother. We missed you the last few

months. You disappeared and—" He shuffles behind me, then says, "Oh wait, Sage is calling."

I turn to find him with the phone up to his ear, on the other end of which is Sage.

My Jersey.

My heart lurches at the sound of her name. At the fact she's so close, yet... I lost her.

I fucking lost her.

"Ready?" Westin says, clapping me on the back.

"Let's do this. Where's Jared?"

We both turn in every direction and find him by the snack table, wiping his hands on his jeans.

"Good thing he and I won't be in the video." I shake my head.

"He's an animal."

Jared makes his way over. "You guys talking about me?"

"I know you're not in the shot, but lose the beanie and wipe the crumbs off your pants, will you?" Westin points to his thigh.

"Oops." Jared grabs a napkin. "Hey, before we start, I just wanted to thank you guys again for letting me tag along. Jenson fucking Ross, man."

Jenson Ross enters from a side door of the independent studio, a tray of coffees in his hands. "Good morning, guys. My friend Ralph picked up some coffees, for which I was going to take credit for, but nah, he does too much around here." We chuckle with him and each accept a cup, thanking him in the process.

"Thanks again for having us too." Westin raises his cup, and Jared and I do the same.

Taylor waves from the corner.

When she arrived, I searched behind her for Sage.

I held my breath, preparing to see her, but she's not here, even though she's been by Taylor's side—*our* side—through it all. It would make sense if this was one of the smaller interviews we've done—even Taylor doesn't attend those—but this one is particularly important.

And Sage isn't here.

It pisses me off further. She can't even be in the same room as me now? She's the one who held out on me.

She's the one who was happy with someone else.

When I wanted to make her mine.

I didn't stand a chance, and I find out years later the truth of it all.

As the guys enter the room, Taylor, Jared, and I stand behind the glass. I cross my arms, trying to focus on what I know will be a turning point for us.

Westin's got this.

We can do this.

"We're happy. Sage and me, we're really happy."

I squeeze my eyes closed to the past before I ram my fist through a wall, then open them to my future.

CHAPTER FIFTEEN
SAGE

I can't sleep.

Every night, I toss and turn, and each time I close my eyes, I see him.

And her.

The baby girl I never met. The one I never got to cradle against my chest.

She haunts me, breaking me all over again.

Sighing, I lean over my bathroom counter and blend more concealer under my eyes to hide the dark circles there. I have to put on a brave face for work. For my future.

For me.

I haven't spoken to Aiden since he was here almost two weeks ago. Since he finally learned the truth about me and what happened all those years ago.

The secret I carried around like the weight of a

thousand pounds on my heart. The one that still plagues me.

Thankfully, Taylor didn't ask me to go with them to their interview with Jenson Ross. She needed me to stay in the office to work on our other accounts and a pitch for a new one we're after. I was more than happy to stay away.

But tonight... tonight I can't escape his hazel eyes with dark amber flecks in them like dust, quietly tainting his expression.

"What're you up to tonight?" Naomi asks as I stroll through the living room, adjusting the belt of my high-waisted dress pants. "You're wearing heels?"

I check my feet like I forgot what I was wearing. "I'm going out with Taylor and the guys from Jock Stock for a celebratory dinner."

"Oh?" She quirks her eyebrow.

"Yes, but it's a business dinner. No big deal."

"If you say so." Judging by her flat tone, she doesn't believe me, and I don't blame her—I'm not very convincing. That, and she knows about my miscarriage. About it being Aiden's baby. About the real reason I married Dave and why our wedding was so rushed.

Naomi found me crying on my bedroom floor a few nights ago, and I couldn't keep it from her anymore. We spent long hours going over every detail. All the things I remember. That I lied so much in my past, especially to Dave. I couldn't even tell him the truth about how far along in my pregnancy I was, so he wouldn't figure it out on his own.

I had no plan for the future. What I would tell Dave down the line—I knew I couldn't lie to him forever. But I was too terrified of everything, so I took it one day, one step, at a time.

Naomi and I talked about how I feel now. What Aiden said and did once I told him.

It was a relief to tell her. She didn't seem to know what to say other than to apologize and wish she'd been there for me, and she squeezed my hand and listened.

Sometimes, it's enough to unload our burdens on a friend.

"I'll probably be home late," I say as I grab my keys off the counter.

"I'll feed myself, don't you worry."

I walk to the door in a daze and barely miss her attempt at a joke.

"Hey, are you okay?" she asks as I turn the doorknob.

"Hmm?"

"You've been *off* since the other night. Like me when I work a twelve-hour shift."

"I'm fine." I give her the most reassuring smile I can muster. "Thanks, Naomi."

I yank the door open and head out, straightening

my posture as I walk to the elevators. My ankle rolls when I step off. *Damn heels.*

I wanted to dress up. To look nice for the guys' accomplishments.

Their interview with Jenson Ross went well—*really* well.

Westin was funny, relatable, and professional. He was knowledgeable and confident, like he lives and breathes sports and their product.

Which he does.

They all do at their company.

They work hard like I did when I opened my business. People say if you're doing something you love, that you'll never work a day in your life. I discovered firsthand that I don't agree. Because the business was mine, I worked even harder in order to make it successful.

Dave took a lot of my creative drive away over the course of our relationship, so my business was a much-needed outlet to stretch my proverbial imaginative fingers. He complained about all the hours I spent at work, but he hardly pushed it because he knew it's what made me happy. What made me want to stay in town, and he didn't want me getting any ideas of leaving. He wanted us to stay there, in the confines of our small town, because he liked it there. He felt secure and enjoyed knowing everyone.

He insisted it was the best place to raise a family, and at one point, I agreed. I loved living there.

It's where I grew up. Where I learned to ride a bike. Received a good education and met wonderful people.

But Dave's clutches around me made me hate it, long before we ever spoke of divorce and I left.

He wasn't always bad—rough around the edges, sure—but after he found out that the baby was Aiden's, he never got over it.

He drank heavily. Cursed and yelled at me. It's what led to the grocery store fiasco.

All his bad qualities were amplified after he learned the truth—that I'd slept with Aiden—but a baby? Dave lost it when he overheard me talking with my friend, confessing the whole story to her when I thought Dave was working late.

But he was home, eavesdropping from the hall.

It was the last straw.

I was only able to get him to sign the divorce papers through sheer luck that he was so angry with me when I stopped by; he simply signed to make me leave.

I find a seat on the train to cross the river and wrap my arms around my midsection as nausea settles in.

I made a mess of my life. No matter how much I resent Dave for his attitude and constant manipulation, I'm guilty too. I married him under false pretenses.

He assumed the baby was his, and even though I know I should've told him otherwise, I couldn't do it.

I was scared.

I knew if I told him it was Aiden's that Dave would've never forgiven me. He would've left me alone as everyone else had.

I did what I thought was best and accepted Dave's marriage proposal, but I should've told him the truth. Maybe he would've surprised me and forgiven me in time. Maybe things wouldn't have ended so badly between us.

But it would've ended, nonetheless, because he and I were never meant to be.

Being away from him the last few months has reassured me of that.

Thirty minutes later, I hold my head high, willing my nerves to calm down, and walk inside the restaurant.

Once I reach her stand, the hostess smiles. "Welcome. Do you have a reservation?"

"Yes. I'm with CJJ Promotions." I check the time on my phone. "I'm a little early."

"No problem. One of your party has already arrived." She comes around her stand. "Right this way."

It's a swanky New York restaurant—the ones I see

in movies and used to think how amazing it would be to eat at one.

Now, I am.

But it's hard to revel in this moment when I know the hostess is leading me toward Aiden.

I follow her, stuffing my hands in my pockets to smooth them out—and because I'm nervous.

My hands are shaking.

We're celebrating, and no matter how messed up things are between Aiden and me, I'm proud of him and his company. The creativity behind their ideas. *Them*. They deserve all the amazing things coming their way, and they definitely deserve a celebration tonight.

One I'll force a smile for.

"Your server will be right with you," the hostess says, then leaves us alone.

"You always did like to get everywhere early," I say, taking a seat.

"And when did you pick up the habit?"

"From you, actually," I admit. "I had to get everywhere twenty or thirty minutes early every time we hung out because I knew you'd be there and waiting. Guess the habit stuck."

"You're welcome." He smirks.

I roll my eyes.

For a brief moment, we feel like us again—the *us*

we once were. Easy. Fun. I catch glimpses of it every time we're together.

But as with every time before, it doesn't last long.

Silence falls between us, and I can feel the tension rolling off him like the sun's outer layer.

Fortunately, Taylor appears with Westin at her side, filling the silence. Jared isn't far behind them and arrives a few minutes later. Once we're settled, Aiden's frown is set in place like it's glued on, casting an awkward energy around us.

Or maybe it's only that way for me.

"Champagne all around, please," Westin says to the server, clapping his hands. "This is a celebration."

"Hear, hear," Jared chimes in.

I can't help but feel lighter with them here. These guys are fun to be around. The kind of friends you're drawn to because they make you feel like family too.

Once we all have drinks, Taylor raises hers, and the rest of us follow. "To hard work. A kick-ass team. And Jock Stock."

"To Jock Stock," Westin beams like it's his child instead of his company.

Nodding, we clink and sip our champagne. Aiden watches me with contempt while he drinks his in gulps.

I sputter, choking on mine like he probably wanted me to. "Excuse me," I croak.

"Here." Westin pushes my water glass toward me. "You all right?"

"Fine. It just went down the wrong pipe." I nod to the table, then sip my water.

I don't miss how Aiden sneers in Westin's direction, but Westin doesn't seem to notice.

What is his deal?

Westin never asked me out, as I suspected he wouldn't. I've often wondered the last couple weeks if it's because of Aiden. Even though I wouldn't have accepted, the thought that Aiden interfered pisses me off.

Our server returns for our orders, and the air around me feels stuffy. Like it's smoke instead of clean air.

We take turns ordering, then hand the server our menus before she disappears.

"Taylor, when's the big day?" Westin asks.

"In about three months now."

"Coming up soon." He raises his eyebrows.

"Yes, and there's still a lot of work to do. Thank God, Sage knows the right questions to ask the caterers, photographers, and everyone else. She's been a huge help."

"She does have the experience, after all," Aiden mumbles.

I furrow my eyebrows, blinking in his direction.

"Where's the ceremony?" Jared asks.

"We're having a small one on Long Island. It has a gorgeous view of the water." She pauses as they nod. "What about you guys? Ever been married?"

Aiden grunts, then downs the rest of his champagne while the rest of us aren't even halfway through ours. He signals the server for another as she walks by.

"Jared was close, but she burned his apartment down before he could pop the question," Westin teases.

"I was *not* close. I barely made it out of there alive." Jared scoffs.

"Do tell the story, please." Taylor leans forward as Jared rubs his temples.

The server comes by with Aiden's champagne and tops off our waters, reassuring us our appetizers are almost ready.

Aiden remains quiet as Jared says, "My sister came to visit, right? We're close in age—only a year apart—and she was in the shower when my then-girlfriend, Vanessa, stopped by. I forgot we'd made plans to cook lunch because my sister showed up unannounced. She does that." He checks our surroundings like Vanessa's lurking in the shadows. "And Vanessa flipped. Tossed the food she brought over to the ground, then grabbed a lighter and set my mattress on fire, calling me a liar and a cheat."

"No way." I cover my mouth.

"My sister and I managed to put out the fire while

Vanessa broke almost everything in my living room, then stormed out before I could even explain." Jared's eyes widen, dumbfounded, and I am too just by listening to it. I can't imagine living it.

"That's crazy." Taylor shakes her head. "Sounds like you dodged a bullet."

"Every now and then, you meet a girl. She's hot, funny, and seemingly sane... until she isn't," Westin jokes.

"Tell me about it." Aiden glares at me, and I mentally slap him for being an ass.

I shift in my seat as the server sets our appetizers in the middle of the table.

And Aiden asks for another champagne.

"Dude, chill," Westin tells him under his breath.

"We're celebrating, aren't we? All of our success," he spits like he's disappointed.

But it's probably only because of me. He's mad I'm the one he has to celebrate with, and my chest sinks.

I shouldn't have come.

"I have a story for you." Aiden rubs his hands together, and I hold my breath when he turns his dark gaze toward me. "Have you all heard about the time Sage got kicked out of a club? Sweet and innocent *Sage*. She realized she didn't like beer, but vodka... vodka she liked. She got wasted and—"

"Aiden," I hiss, narrowing my gaze at him as he

continues, anyway, his voice full of resentment and cruelty.

"—kept trying to dance with the bouncer. The bartender had to cut her off, and she got mad and wrote *asshole* on the bar with her lipstick. Well, she wrote *assho* because she forgot how to spell the whole word in her drunken—"

"Can I talk to you outside for a minute?" I grab his arm and nod toward the door, where we can avoid an audience, mainly my *boss*, although the damage is likely already done.

The server comes by with another drink and takes away his empty flute. Before I can pull him up, he takes a large gulp, then pushes his chair back. When he stands, his chair falls backward, making us all jump. Silently, he picks it back up and sets it upright.

"After you." He makes a show of holding his arm out, his voice sarcastic, and he doesn't seem to care that he's causing a scene.

"What is your problem?" I seethe once we're outside on the sidewalk. "Do you realize we're at a business dinner? This isn't a damn fraternity party."

"No, because if we were, you'd be making out with your fucking boyfriend. The one you married just so you wouldn't be alone."

"I wouldn't have had to be alone had you been an adult—"

"Ha," he yells. "And you were so grown up?"

"You're *still* a fucking child." I shake my head, brushing past him.

"And you're a liar."

I stop, hanging my head, my guilt weighing on me.

The sounds of cars passing, of the city carrying on, fill the heavy silence between us until he speaks again.

"You should've told me." I feel him right behind me. His heat. His pain. It rolls off him and onto me like we're connected. *One.*

But we're not.

We're nothing but a tragic memory.

"And you shouldn't have abandoned me, hooked up with countless women, because of what you thought you saw," I say without turning around.

I feel him lean down as he tucks my hair behind my ear. His breath is warm on my exposed neck. "You have no idea what happened that summer," he whispers, his voice distant, yet his fingertips graze my arms like he's in this moment with me.

And against my better judgment and restraint, my body responds to his touch of its own accord.

I'm drawn to him—every part of his anger, his intensity, *him*.

No matter how badly it hurts.

I slowly turn to face him, our lips close. "No, I don't know what happened, Aiden. All I know is that I was left to pick myself up and dry the tears I shed night after night. The overwhelming emptiness inside me because after I lost the baby"—my voice cracks —"I'd lost every part of you too."

He licks his lips, his fingers stopping on my wrists, curling around them like he wants to hold me, but instead, he brushes past me, nudging my shoulder with his along the way.

As he reaches the door, I wrap my arms around my waist and take a moment to catch my breath.

I'm reeling.

My nerves are shaken.

When my breaths finally come out evenly again, I return to our table inside. Our food has arrived, and Aiden and I eat in silence. I barely say anything as I mentally prepare to apologize to Taylor for tonight.

To apologize for Aiden's behavior. For letting my personal life interfere with a business dinner.

Mostly, right now, I only hope Aiden doesn't make it worse. Because, if he does, I might lose my job and have to start over once again.

But as we continue eating, as the servers come and go, what scares me almost more than losing my job right now, is how strong his pull is.

How badly I wanted Aiden to lean down and kiss me. When we were outside, his lips so close to mine, a large part of me wanted to give into him.

And that would be dangerous for so many reasons.

CHAPTER SIXTEEN

AIDEN

I let the roaring fire inside me fester.

And I drink champagne like it'll put out the flames, when it's really just stoking them.

She was pregnant with my baby and didn't tell me.

A baby.

My baby girl.

To make matters worse, Sage showed up here in heels that make her legs appear longer, lean and sexy, and all I can think about is wrapping them around me while I fuck the tension out of both our bodies.

Her red lipstick is seductive and taunting.

I almost kissed her outside.

For a moment, I thought about tugging her hair in my hand and biting her lip to punish her for the past, but mostly, I wanted her to pay for looking so damn perfect every time I see her as if she owns the world.

Like she owns my goddamn heart.

But I don't want her to.

I don't want to fucking *need* her like I do.

Once I reach the bottom of my third glass of champagne, and I'm still not drunk, I get even more pissed.

I drink two more glasses while they chatter around me. Their voices become faraway background noise as I disappear into the dark void inside me, spiraling into oblivion.

I thought she was happy with Dave.

When she was carrying our baby.

While I was miserable.

I take a generous sip of bubbly, my mind racing.

Jenson Ross was a big fucking success. Our following on every social media platform has increased by twenty percent already, and our engagement is up by twelve percent. People are excited about Jock Stock. About us.

About the future.

But with Sage's revelation, part of me is stuck in the past.

Before I know it, the uneaten food in front of me blurs and resembles a color wheel on my plate.

"Anything else you forgot to tell me?"

The room shifts in my vision.

"A secret life? Undercover FBI agent? I mean, did you ever even love me?"

A hard hammer hits my shin, like a doctor's checking my reflexes. It takes me a moment to feel the sting and realize Westin kicked me.

Which is when it hits me that I'm the one talking.

I'm saying these things out loud at the dinner table while my colleagues stare at me. I rapidly blink to try to clear my vision, but it's difficult. It feels like there's a blanket over my head.

"I think it's time to go." Westin grabs my arm to stand, and I go willingly.

I'm buzzed, but somewhere in the back of my mind, I know I've shoved my foot in my mouth.

But everything goes dark, except for Sage, the woman I've loved for years.

Her innocent eyes and soft curves.

Her fire.

I imagine her swollen stomach. A glow surrounding her.

A baby in her arms as she smiles at me.

CHAPTER SEVENTEEN

I bang on his door, cursing his name between knocks.

When he doesn't open, I drop my purse to the ground and use both fists, sure that his neighbors will wake and yell at me.

But I don't care. Right now, all I care about is strangling Aiden Baxter and kicking him in the balls so hard he'll think twice before humiliating me again.

After the guys left, I apologized repeatedly to Taylor. I don't think I took a single breath between pleas. She said she understands but that we need to talk on Monday.

The thought that it won't go well has me ready to vomit.

And punch Aiden in his crooked nose to break it all over again.

I continue banging, my hands growing numb, until he finally opens it.

There he stands, shirtless, his pajama pants hanging low on his hips, his wavy hair so wild and sexy that my breath almost hitches.

Almost.

He stands there like he doesn't have a care in the world when my whole life may have been ripped apart tonight.

Right when it was beginning.

"How dare you?" I hiss, brushing past him into his apartment. "This is my job. Whether or not you think I'm to blame for what happened eight years ago, I'm not going to lose it because of you. You were out of line!" I whirl around to him, sure that my cheeks are red.

Sure that my chest will explode any minute from how hard I'm panting.

"Sure, come in." Aiden closes the door.

"This isn't funny. This is not the time to be cute." My voice is squeaky. The madder I am, the more high-pitched it gets.

And right now, I'd make cats cry.

He stuffs his hands in his pockets, his gaze on the ground, his shoulders sagging. He seems... sad. Nothing like the Aiden at dinner.

"I'm sorry," he finally says, lifting his gaze to mine, and it steals my next breath.

The guilt in his eyes knocks me back like he shoved me.

Yet, they're still the same eyes I used to get lost in.

And it pisses me off further, because the Aiden I knew would've never done something like this.

I place my hands on my hips—he will not get away with this so easily. "Sorry for what exactly? Telling Taylor—my *boss*—about the night at the club in college? Embarrassing me? Or is it for acting like an ass since I moved here? Tell me, Aiden—"

"I'm sorry, okay?" He spreads his arms wide, naturally flexing his muscles, and raises his voice, bringing some of his anger back from earlier. "It hasn't exactly been easy seeing you again. To be around you again after all this time. Especially after what you told me. For fuck's sake, Jersey, I can't even process a baby."

I sharply inhale, my body stiffening.

"I've been... shocked. Angry. Ever since you told me, I've gone from one to the other, and tonight, I don't know. I snapped. I'm sorry, but..." His voice trails off, and his shoulders slump farther. "I can't help but think everything could've been different. With us. With the last few years." He shakes his head as if he knows his words are empty and futile.

"We don't have a time machine to take us to the past—we only have now." I step toward him. "We work together *now*. We need to find a way to do so without jeopardizing both of our careers."

"I don't know how to be your fucking client. How to sit across from you at meetings and keep my hands to myself. How to fight my urge to strangle you or kiss you." He swipes at the corners of his twitching lips like he's imagining crushing them on mine. "You drive me insane," he whispers.

I hardly register him stalking toward me.

I'm frozen, stunned by his admission.

That he feels anything for me aside from resentment.

Before I know it, he cups the back of my head and crushes his lips to mine.

It's surprising how well his lips mold to mine.

Heady.

My eyes automatically roll back as he sucks on my top lip, then moves to the bottom one, and I get lost in this kiss that I feel down to my toes. His tongue sweeps across mine in a punishing massage, sending heat to every lonely crevice of my body.

When he kisses me, the floor splits open, swallowing me whole, and catapults me to the past. To a past where I'm not a divorced, jaded woman starting her life over at nearly thirty years old.

At this moment, Aiden makes me feel like the twenty-year-old girl I used to be. One with hope for the future, optimistic that anything can happen. Hope that I'll be happy and finally find what I'm looking for.

Aiden kisses me with promise, even though I'm not sure it's valid.

How can he be real when he's in the past?

I shouldn't be enjoying his lips on mine. I shouldn't want him at all. Aiden is the one guy I shouldn't want. But here I am, letting his tongue push my mouth open. Letting him grip my hair so tightly—so sexy—as he pulls me against him by my waist.

Even though my job is at stake. Even though it ended badly the first time. Even though what happened between us threatens to rip through my heart—*again*.

It's hard to think straight right now, of all this will cost me, because he feels too good. This thing between us is too strong.

So, I kiss him back.

Sinking into him, I kiss Aiden Baxter because deep down, my heart—all the jagged pieces of it—never let him go. No matter how broken it is, his mere existence in my life has given me a shred of twisted joy. A second chance. Something to dream of, even if it's for one night only.

I melt into his kiss, his body, *him*.

I go willingly when he turns me toward the bed and sets me down. Hovering over me, he threads his fingers through my hair and wraps his free arm around my waist to scoot me higher until the cool glass of the window hits my back.

He nips at my bottom lip.

Fingers the belt around my pants.

Sends shivers down my spine.

His hand fists my shirt, pulling it out of my waistband, then reaches underneath until his fingertips graze the underwire of my bra, making me gasp into his mouth.

It seemingly fuels him to move more urgently.

He drags his eager lips across my jawline, down to my neck below my ear, and nips at me, then sucks on that spot.

My lungs seize.

He pulls my shirt over my head, then tugs on my pants as he captures my lips again, his tongue delving in to fight with mine in a deliciously painful way as we fight for control.

For power.

We pant, moving with urgent lust, both our arousals mixing in the air around us.

When he curls his thumbs around my panties, I'm very aware of his knuckles against my bare flesh, and everything that comes next feels like it's happening in slow motion. He pulls my panties down to my ankles, lifting one leg at a time to remove them the rest of the way.

He places a kiss on my calf.

A kiss on my knee.

Hooking my leg around his waist, he trails more

kisses up my inner thigh, then deeply inhales.

When he drags his tongue up the seam of me, my hips buck. The top of his head comes in and out of view as my chest rises and falls.

I pant.

I squirm.

I give in to each sensation, and the desire pools between my legs the longer he teases me.

The cool surface of the window on my back jolts me, and when Aiden's tongue finds the right spot, the tension builds.

Behind me, a whole world exists. One that's a blur—invisible—as Aiden continues working me to the edge of ecstasy.

He switches from licking to sucking on that sensitive spot, making my eyes fly open. "Yes... yes, Aiden, right... there." I gasp.

He sinks his finger into me, hooking it inside me, and I move with him.

His mouth. His finger.

I thrust my hips upward in a frenzy until I reach my climax. He holds my hip down with his free hand, letting me ride the waves of my pleasure.

When my breaths are even, he stands, pulling his pants down, freeing his length. I instinctively lick my lips, and his eyes widen.

They grow darker.

Hungrier.

I want to scream. To beg. To tug him closer.

A feral sound escapes from deep in his throat as he kisses me again.

It's raw.

Passionate.

Electrifying.

"I'm on the pill," I breathe against his lips and lower myself, lying all the way down, and he positions himself at my entrance.

Without a wasted moment, he thrusts into me. Wrapping my leg around him, he angles himself deeper inside me, and I cling to his shoulders, adjusting to the size of him. He pushes against the glass above my head with his free hand, using it to brace himself as he pumps in and out of me.

I let my head fall back, bumping against the window with a delicious pain that I welcome.

The bed squeaks with every thrust.

With one hand, I reach up the ridges of his abs, to his pecs, wanting to feel him. Wanting to feel his heart thundering there.

For this moment.

For me.

After all these years, we're together again.

There's an aching desire deep inside me, heating my core, building the tension again the longer he moves.

His thrusts are purposeful. They speak volumes of the war raging inside him.

His kisses are feverish.

Leaning over me, he lets a strangled grunt loose and pulls out, and I instantly feel the loss of him.

He pumps himself into his hand, then releases onto my stomach.

Our lips part in awe as we watch the white streaks trail down between my legs.

He captures my mouth with his once more, then slides off the bed, making his way to the bathroom.

All while I admire the full view of his backside.

He's stronger than the guy I knew in college.

More muscled.

A man.

He was a boy when we met. Thinking back, I'm starting to realize just how young and innocent we were. How we both made mistakes. Things we regret.

He returns with a washcloth, a dazed look in his eyes like he's high.

He kisses my cheek, then my lips, as he wipes between my legs, pausing to massage the spot he worked raw. It's sensitive, and the more he massages me, the more lost I am in all he's doing—all he's making me feel.

"I'm not done with you," he whispers, and the hairs on the back of my neck stand.

As he starts to back away, my emotions are caught

in my throat. I grab his cheeks in both hands and kiss him, wanting to hold on to the beauty of this moment.

Because we're not a one-night stand, not with our history, and I don't know what Monday will bring.

Where we go from here.

What this means for us.

But I know I want to extend this moment forever.

He sweeps his tongue against mine, sending heat down to my toes. "Jersey, we can figure this out," he whispers between kisses. "Please, I want to. I need you."

I think I nod.

I definitely moan.

Because being here with him, him kissing me with conviction as my hands run over the ridges of his back, I forget anything outside of *us*.

CHAPTER EIGHTEEN
AIDEN

"I really am sorry about earlier tonight and for how I reacted when you told me about the baby." I squeeze her tighter against my side, letting her body heat wash over me, comforting me. "I'll talk to Taylor and apologize to her too. I'll do everything I can to make this right."

"Thank you." She sighs, her breath warm on my bare chest. "I'm sorry too. For not telling you about our baby," she whispers, her sadness evident.

I tilt her face up to mine, so I can get a good look into her eyes. "I wish we would've gotten the chance to meet her."

She gives me a watery smile, one that makes my stomach sink.

How crushed she must've been.

For days, I've been alternating between rage and devastation, full of *what ifs*.

What if she'd told me back then?

What if she hadn't miscarried?

What if... *I hadn't left in the first place?*

My stupid mistakes eat at me.

"I wish I was there to help you through it," I add, my voice cracking by the end of the sentence, and I hold her tighter as we lie still with only our quiet breaths between us.

Her low voice sounds moments later.

"Do you ever wonder what we would've been like with a baby?" Her lips tremble against my chest. After another short pause, she peers up at me, resting her chin on my pec. "Would we have been a happy family?"

"Definitely," I say without hesitation. There's no doubt in my mind that Sage would've been an amazing mother, and she would've helped me be a good father.

Because she makes me want to be and do better.

I cup her cheek and bring her to me for a kiss. I kiss her eyelids, then her lone tear sliding down her cheek, and I melt into the bed with her in my arms.

"Tell me about her. About our baby. Did she kick? Were you nauseous?"

I imagine her with a round stomach, carrying the love we created, and an ache so strong overcomes me that I might break.

Break even more, anyway.

"You don't have to answer if you're not comfortable or—"

"I want to," she says, and as she shakes her head, her wisps of hair tickle my chest. "I was swollen from head to toe. Not cute." She giggles.

"I bet you were," I say into her hair as I idly run my fingers up and down her bare back.

"I felt her kick a few times." I feel the wetness of her tears on my skin, and my hand stops along her forearm as I listen to her smooth voice.

A song of the past, sad and gut-wrenching.

"I remember the first time she kicked so vividly. It was a soft thump, like the small flutter of a baby bird's wings, against my stomach. That's when it really hit me that it was happening—I was having a baby." She sniffles. "It was beautiful."

I remain silent, imagining her cradling her stomach, holding our baby girl close.

I never thought about kids. Back then, all I thought about was saving the world with the law degree I'd get. A family felt like it was eons into the future, so far off my radar that I didn't even comprehend the concept until friends started having kids after college.

Now, hearing Sage—my Jersey—talk about ours, I can't help but think about how different our lives would be with a baby girl to raise. We'd be together, a family, but we'd be in love too.

We'd be happy.

"When I lost her, I didn't think I'd ever recover."

"I'm so fucking sorry, Jersey." I wrap both my arms around her and let her cry.

I hold Sage while she lets out her anguish—while she lets go.

Her tears are hot on my bare chest, squeezing around my heart underneath, and they run down to my stomach.

She's crying for our baby. Our lost years. Our lives that have been forever changed.

One heavy tear after another slides down my own cheek, and I cry with her too.

CHAPTER NINETEEN

SAGE

He holds me in a hug so powerful and comforting, I just cry harder.

I snuggle into Aiden's side, soaking in his comfort, and I get lost in it and the memories.

All those years ago, I yearned for him to hold me like this when I found out I was pregnant. I ached for him to come back to me and tell me it would be all right. That we'd figure it out together.

And when I lost her, I begged God to send him back to me so he could kiss away my tears and put the pieces of my shattered heart back together.

With Aiden here to hold me now, I unleash my pent-up sobs.

He kisses my cheeks, soaking up my sadness, letting me share it with the one person I always wanted to.

I felt guilty when I cried with Dave, but with Aiden now, I can finally grieve openly, causing a strange sense of relief to wash over me.

"I'm so fucking sorry," he repeats against my cheek, then places a kiss there.

A kiss to my nose.

To my forehead.

Another apology like he's asking God to forgive him.

Soft sobs choke me as I let go of some of the pain I've been clinging to all these years. The pain that kept me from being happy.

And I cling to Aiden Baxter like I need him to show me the rest of the way to the light.

To peace.

I eventually tire myself from crying and fall asleep in his arms. It's a deep slumber where I dream of the sun shining.

The birds chirping.

Aiden's deep voice...

"What kind of toss was that?" He runs, almost tripping over our picnic, and the sounds of his laughter carry between us.

"Oops!" I call out, giggling. "You know I'm still practicing."

"You need a lot more practice."

I stick my tongue out at him as he finally reaches the Frisbee and throws it back to me. "See? That's a perfect throw.

All in the wrist and middle finger."

"I'll give you a middle finger," I grumble.

"I heard that."

"Wasn't being quiet." I roll my eyes, then get into position to throw it back to him.

But instead of going straight toward him like I thought, the Frisbee veers to the right like a lost kite.

"It's impossible." I cover my face with my hands.

He jogs to the Frisbee, then toward me. "You're not doing it the way I showed you."

"Maybe you're a bad teacher. Why did they let you on their intramural team, anyway?" I tease.

He scoffs sarcastically. "Because they want to win, and with me on their team, they will."

"Bring the arrogance down a notch, will you?"

He grabs my hand, his touch unexpected.

I sharply inhale, dropping my gaze to his fingers curled around my wrist, where he flips it so my palm faces up.

His soft touch sucks the humor from my next joke like a rug being pulled out from under me.

I look up at him, and his eyes find mine.

There's a pause.

Surprise crosses his features, and it mirrors my own.

His voice drops low when he says, "You throw it like this." He flicks his wrist, all while his gaze remains on mine.

I don't see where the Frisbee goes.

Instead, I gulp and know I'm in trouble.

CHAPTER TWENTY

AIDEN

"There's a woman doing yoga in her underwear." Sage stands by the window, pointing across the alleyway, then takes a sip of her hot coffee. The steam is visible with the incoming light, giving her a special glow.

Mesmerizing—that's what she is.

I wrap my arms around her waist from behind, nuzzling her neck, breathing her sweet aroma in. "That's Tina and her regular morning routine."

"And she doesn't care that the whole world can see her?" She scrunches her nose, and I kiss her cheek, unable to stop myself.

"She brings me cookies every Sunday, so I say, she can do what she wants." I smirk.

"What?"

I shrug. "I ran into her when I first moved in. She noticed my college sweatshirt and mentioned her brother went to the same school, coincidentally. We talk every Sunday now."

She hums, taking a sip of her drink. "Maybe in return, as a real friend, you could buy her some curtains."

"Especially for when she has male company over."

She covers her mouth. "*No*. Tell me she doesn't have sexy time where everyone can see..."

"I'm afraid she does. And I'm afraid we all see."

"Perverts." She giggles, leaning into me.

I place hot kisses down her neck, making her sigh, which makes me hard. Pressing against her backside, I let her feel her effect on me.

How much I want her.

How much she's been part of me for years. Even though I fought it, she's always been my Jersey.

"Breakfast?" I croak.

"I don't think I'm hungry for eggs," she whispers, setting her coffee on the windowsill, then pulls the curtains shut.

"Good thing that's not what I was offering."

She yelps when I scoop her in my arms and toss her onto the bed. As she scoots up to the edge, I catch sight of the window above her head.

The one with my hand still printed on the glass.

The thought of having her again, spread wide for me, makes me pull my clothes off like I'm on fire—I can't get them off fast enough.

By the time I'm done, Sage is also bare.

Her bottom lip tugged between her teeth.

Her eyes lust-filled and teasing with a lazy tilt in the corners from sleep.

I put one knee onto the bed and climb toward her, the anticipation rising with every inch I close between us. When I reach her, I kiss her, gently at first, happily getting to know her perfect lips all over again.

She moans when I cup her between her legs —she's wet.

Needy.

And it makes me want to pound my chest with caveman pride.

I kiss her as I slide two fingers into her, making her arch her back, and her breasts push against my chest, her hard nipples teasing me.

I relish the sensual sounds she makes. Like they're escaping her swollen lips of their own accord. Strangled and hot.

It's sexy, the way she gives herself to me, letting herself feel everything.

She tries to speak, but her words end on a sharp inhale as I continue working her while trailing kisses down her neck.

She clenches around my fingers, and when I dip my head to capture her nipple between my teeth and bite down, she falls off the edge, trembling beneath me.

I can feel every shake as her climax consumes her.

I'm hard, stiff, and ready for her.

My restraint snaps, and with one swift thrust, I slide into her wet heat like I belong there. I pump in and out of her as she wraps her hands around my neck, holding me close.

I get lost in the special comfort only she has ever provided, but I forgot what it was like to be with someone who has this power over me like Sage does.

As I continue moving inside her—as I continue reveling in the feel of her—I'm reborn.

Having her in my life makes me feel like the last few years without her have been one giant fog, and my vision has finally cleared now.

"So close," she pants, moving her hips in sync with mine at a rapid pace, like we're trying to tear the whole building down. "Don't stop, Aiden. Don't," she whispers, and her eyes roll into the back of her head.

Her cheeks are tinted pink.

Her hair a wild mess of honey blond, bright against my black pillowcases like auroras in the sky.

I thrust into her once more, then pull out, pumping my release onto her stomach and continue coming until there's nothing left.

Until I'm sated.

I move her hair from her shining eyes, my heart cracking. Like a solar storm, Sage Mathews re-entered my life like the natural order of things.

Like destiny.

Even though the last time we were together ended in a colossal explosion of broken hearts, being here with her now, two small specks in a New York City loft after years of our souls wandering, the pain of the past seems easy to forget.

To forgive.

Right now, it's easy to imagine we can finally move forward—*together*.

Sage pulls the covers higher under her cheek, making me smile.

I clutch my phone tighter in my hand, pressing it to my ear, trying to focus on what Westin's saying when my mind is a blur of all things Sage.

"Are you listening?" Westin asks.

Her natural blush.

The curve of her shoulders and slender arms.

Her lips so swollen from our kissing that the bow of her top lip is barely visible.

"Hello?"

I shake my head. "Yes, man, I'm here. I'll be at the office in less than an hour. I'm dressed and every-thing," I assure him as Sage gives me a peek of her bare nipple, her lips curling in a mischievous smile. I invol-untarily groan.

"What the hell are you doing?"

"Nothing. See you soon." I hang up and tsk at Sage. "That was dirty, Jersey, and you will most definitely pay for that."

"Do your worst," she challenges.

"You're going to kill me, aren't you?"

"That's the plan. Re-enter your life just to sex you to death."

"I knew it." I capture her lips in mine, cupping the back of her head with my hand. I press my forehead to hers, my voice strained as I say, "I wish I didn't have to go, but I have a ton of work to do."

"Go," she whispers. "I'll lock up."

"Meet me for a late dinner." I brush soft kisses across her knuckles. "Please?"

"You said please?" She raises her eyebrows. "Who even are you?"

I roll my eyes, standing from the bed. I take one last look at her, sitting upright with the covers bunched around her waist.

Feminine perfection.

"Dinner," I rasp. "I'll call you with details."

"I'll be ready." She smiles so bright, I know it'll stay with me through the rest of the day as I try to focus on Jock Stock.

On our company that two guys dreamed up five years ago.

A dream that's looking more and more like the beginning of something real. Of something big.

And having Sage through it all has turned out to be the blessing of good luck I didn't know I needed.

I take the subway toward our building.

Grab a coffee on my way in.

Sidestep people on their phones, taking pictures, and hailing cabs.

It's the same routine, but different in so many ways.

When I reach our office, I stroll in a new man, and the guys notice too.

Westin takes one look at me and asks, "What's different about you?"

"What do you mean?" I shrug, my expression coy. "It's Saturday. The weekend. Hashtag weekend vibes, or whatever the trendy millennials like to say."

Westin rolls his eyes, and Jared walks toward his office, a steaming cup of coffee in his hand. He glances at me, stops, then backtracks. "What's going on here?" he asks, waving his free hand in front of my face. "I thought you'd be hungover and moody like a middle-aged man going through *man*-opause."

Westin and I both stare at him, but he just shrugs, then sips his coffee. "Ow!" He grimaces. "Burned my tongue."

"Serves you right." I smirk.

"What did I do? You're the one who ruined dinner."

I wince.

"So? What happened last night?" Westin asks, and his frown makes me feel like scum.

My shoulders slump. "I'm sorry. I drank too much and let it get the best of me. I'm going to call Taylor on Monday too and apologize for being a dick."

"That's a start." Westin relaxes a fraction. "And Sage?"

A slow smile spreads across my face as I sit in my desk chair and lean back. "Sage is... she and I talked."

"And?"

I finally admitted I was wrong.

That I was angry and holding too much resentment toward the woman who didn't deserve it.

At last, I'm putting it behind me. I thought I'd done it once before, but it wasn't real then.

This is different. True. I'm finally feeling peaceful.

"We worked things out."

"You dog!" Jared slaps his leg.

I drop my smile, my demeanor sobering. "We really did talk too. Worked through some of our baggage. Shit from the past."

"Which part? Seemed like you had a lot to deal with." Westin's concern is obvious in the crease of his forehead.

I nod slowly, my expression falling, deciding to finally tell them what she told me two weeks ago. The main reason I've been on edge for days and a dick last night.

"She was pregnant."

Westin and Jared both stand taller, peering at each other in question.

"She only told me a couple weeks ago that she was pregnant with my baby in college, but she had a miscarriage." Shaking my head, I rub my aching chest as I tell my friends the truth about us. "It's why I was such an asshole last night. It's no excuse, but I was mad at her for not telling me before. I was... devastated that she lost our baby. I didn't handle any of it well."

"Dude..." Jared starts, his coffee long forgotten.

"I'm sorry, man..." Westin's voice trails off as he frowns even harder than before.

They're at a loss for words, like I've been.

"Are you okay?" Westin squeezes my shoulder like he's my dad instead of my friend and business partner. He's only two years older than me, but he tends to act like he's sixty and wise from a long life lived. "If you need to talk, you know you can come to us."

"Thanks." I give them both a tight-lipped smile. "But I'll be fine. Better than fine. Sage and I... we're going to be okay." I rock in my seat, and my good mood from when I first walked in comes back full force as I think about her.

Her laugh brightening my loft.

Her soft touch.

Her tight body wrapped around me.

I didn't realize how much I missed her until she showed up in my life like a thief in the night.

"Oh, God. Don't tell me you're going to be all dopey now." Jared groans. "Love is not a good look on you."

Westin chuckles as I sit upright. "It's not love, asshole. I mean, Raven and I broke up two weeks ago. We were distant for far longer, but still." I run my hand through my loose hair and sigh, the guilt over Raven still weighing on me.

She packed her things from my place while I was at work. That's how much she didn't want to see me, but we did the right thing by splitting up. We weren't right for each other, and being with Sage last night only reassured me of it.

"Sage and I just reconnected. Taking things slow, starting with dinner tonight."

"Then we better get to work, so we can get out of here at a normal hour and enjoy a Saturday night for once, like regular people." Westin backs away.

"Yeah, leave me alone," I joke as I hook my laptop up, and they leave me to work.

I'm sure Westin and I will have a more in-depth conversation about what went down, as it's not in his nature to be satisfied by simple answers. No, he needs the details. To know that I'm truly okay and that there isn't anything left unresolved.

He's a problem-solver, which makes him a good friend and leader.

But until then, I'm content and surprisingly at ease, although a few more thoughts do surface as I log in to my computer to check my reports and data.

Raven was right.

I had been subconsciously biding my time, waiting for the right person to reappear and fill a void I didn't realize existed. That it was Sage I've been waiting for.

Half an hour later, Jared pops his head back into my office. "Ready?"

"Let's do it." I grab my laptop and follow him into the conference room.

Lila's already waiting, her steaming cup of tea on the table in front of her. Ethan from quality assurance joins us a moment later too. He's been coming to our meetings since our launch is coming up so quickly, and that way, we're all on the same page. A process that will likely change once our team grows, as will the need for Saturday morning meetings, but for now, this is working well.

It's business as usual, for the most part, but I'm lighter and happier.

And it's because of tonight.

Because of my date with Sage Matthews.

CHAPTER TWENTY-ONE

SAGE

"Where's he taking you?" Naomi asks, sitting on my bed. She cups her hot tea with both hands and blows on it, causing ripples through the dark liquid.

"I'm not sure. He's surprising me with something special that New York City has to offer," I repeat what Aiden told me, then sigh, in a dreamy daze. "Isn't that romantic?"

She swallows her sip of tea. "Yes, which is why you need the perfect outfit. What're you wearing?"

"He said casual, so I'm thinking one of these two shirts with jeans." I hold up a flowy top with a high neckline in one hand and a floral shirt in the other. "What do you think?"

She studies the two options and finally points to the flowy top. "That one. And you can borrow my suede jacket."

"The gray one? Perfect." I hang the floral top back in the closet, a grin on my face.

Part of me is still worried about my discussion with Taylor on Monday. Aiden said he'd speak with her too, and my hope is that she can look past Friday night and trust that Aiden and I can be civil and professional for the remaining few months of our contract.

Until then, I can exist in the moment. Tonight... tonight, it's simply Aiden and me.

"Are you finally going to tell me what happened between you two last night, or what? You've been smiling like an ass all day." She rolls her eyes, but her lips twitch in the corners.

"We talked." I toss the clothes over a chair in the corner and sit on the bed with her. "We *really* talked. We got things out in the open and cleared the air. It was cathartic, being able to share my grief with him. We grieved without the tension between us, you know?"

"That's huge." She sets her tea down and gives me her full attention.

"He was a dick at dinner, so I went to his place to yell at him afterward—and I did. But we ended up talking and... um"—my face heats—"having sex too." I cover my mouth, feeling giddy.

I feel like I'm young again—carefree and happy.

When Aiden held me while I cried, I could feel the

bitterness dissolve with each tear. Each exhale. Each of his kisses.

I needed last night to finally let go of the burden that's weighed me down like an anchor, tying me to the past.

"Look at you. You're glowing." She pats my hand.

My smile grows wider. "I'm just... really excited for tonight."

She squeezes my hand. "Do you need help with your hair or makeup? You can't tell by looking at me, but I'm pretty good at both."

I scoff. "You're the sexiest nurse I know."

"I'm the *only* nurse you know," she teases, then stands, pulling me with her. "Now, let's get moving."

We move to her bathroom, and I spill the details of my confessions with Aiden while Naomi does my makeup and curls my hair. An hour later, I'm dolled up and ready for my date.

"It's perfect. Thanks for helping me." I watch Naomi from the mirror.

"Anytime." She puts the makeup brushes in her bag and zips it up as I stand from the chair we pulled in here from the kitchen.

I start to hoist it up to put it back in its place, but she gently touches my shoulder, stopping me.

"Listen, I'm really happy for you, Sage. That you and Aiden talked, and I hope you don't take this the wrong way, but given what happened with Dave, I'd never forgive myself if I didn't speak up this time."

"What do you mean?"

"I don't know Aiden, but from what you've said, he caused you a lot of pain. It was difficult watching you struggle through so much... heartache the other night when you told me about how Aiden abandoned you. Since he's back in your life now, there's light in your eyes again, but I... I want you to be careful, is all. Promise me you will."

"I will." I gulp, searching her gaze.

This is the most she's said in one breath in a while, and it seems her words of caution are hard to get out. But she said them, anyway. Like a sister might.

Before I leave her room, I turn to her. "I haven't said it enough, but thank you for everything. For not giving up on me. For taking me in when I needed family and a friend. I know I can count on you to have my back, and it means a lot."

She smiles a rare smile and follows me into the kitchen. She grabs her keys from the counter, then tugs on her top—black scrubs tonight for her grave-yard shift. "I'll see you tomorrow."

I sit on the couch, twiddling my thumbs, when my phone vibrates with an incoming message.

Aiden: *On my way to pick you up.*

When he called about our date earlier, I offered to meet him, since it's likely more tedious for him to come to my apartment, then go all the way back across the river.

But he insisted he pick me up.

And I have to admit—it made me feel special.

He left to hook up with girl after girl while you cried for him.

I blink into the empty room, my nagging thoughts in the back of my mind.

"I want you to be careful."

Half an hour later, there's a knock on my door. I run my palms down my jeans and tuck the front of my top into the waistband. Touching the side of my head, I check the bobby pin in my hair that's keeping it back in what Naomi called the "classy bitch" style.

Inhaling, I open the door, and my exhale comes out with a resounding whoosh as I take in Aiden. He stands there, one hand against the frame and a single red rose in the other.

His wavy hair is pulled back in a low bun, and his plaid shirt is buttoned over a black T-shirt. It's an outfit he normally wears, but tonight, he's even sexier.

And when his lips stretch in a smile that reaches his eyes, my stomach flutters like a butterfly garden.

Gulping, I tug the suede jacket around me. "Hey," I breathe.

He steps into my apartment, offering the rose to me. "For you."

"Thank you." I accept it and smell it like I'd inhale the fresh scent of a meadow, then grab a tall glass from the cabinet. After I fill it with water, I set the rose inside. It's much taller than the glass, but it'll have to do for now. "Are we ready?"

"I only need one more thing." He cups my cheek in his large hand and captures my lips in a heady kiss that leaves my head spinning when he pulls back. "All set." He winks, grabbing my hand, then leads us out the door.

Once it's locked behind us, we head down the hall, down the elevator, and onto the sidewalk.

We walk in the direction of the train, our fingers intertwined, and the night sky vast above us.

"Where are we going?" I skip to keep up with his pace.

"You'll see." He watches me out of the corner of his eye, amused.

"Can I guess?"

"You could, but this is New York. You'll be guessing for the next ten years before you think of everything there is to do here." He chuckles, and the deep sound tugs on my heart.

"Fine." I pretend to pout.

I let the crisp spring air distract me, instead. It's

April, and the nights are still chilly here. They remind me of late winter nights in North Carolina.

The soft breeze.

The quiet calm around us, even though we're in a much bigger city. Not many people are out in these parts right now.

Together, the anticipation of this date builds. *Where is he taking me?*

When we reach the station, Aiden doesn't let go of my hand while we wait a few minutes for the next train. He holds it as we board along with the rest of the crowd and find two empty seats. As we ride into the city, the chatter of the other passengers falls over us as I lean my head on his shoulder, letting his spicy cologne and the rattling sounds of the train soothe me.

"You ready to see what I have planned?"

I nod against him, at a loss for words, realizing I'd be content to simply ride to Manhattan and back with him.

His warm confidence and intensity are addictive—they always have been.

In his presence, I'm confident too. He brings out a side of me I love. Wild. Content.

"Do you keep in touch with your friend Carter from college?" I ask.

"Jacobs?" He chuckles, referring to Carter's last name. "We still talk from time to time. He's a loan officer now and married with two kids."

"Really?" I sit up and face him. Carter was always a jokester—Jared reminds me a lot of him, come to think of it. It's hard to imagine Carter as a dad with a career. "How grownup of him."

We spend the rest of the train ride catching up—we have years' worth of life to fill each other in on. Since I first ran into him, we've focused so much on the things we left unsaid over eight years ago.

With all that behind us, we're able to talk about other, much happier things now. The conversation flows, and I silently give thanks to have my best friend back.

The more we talk, no matter how inane the topic is, there's something else here too. A spark we didn't have before.

I didn't know of his feelings when we were friends in college. I didn't have the same feelings for him as I do now, so it seems new. Familiar yet exciting.

I lean closer and closer into him, stealing a peck or two, as we let our easy chatter fill the ride.

"We're here." He leads the way off the train and through the crowded station.

Once we emerge onto the sidewalk, I ask, "Where to now?"

"This way."

He takes off, and I again quicken my pace to keep up with his long strides. Once we're separated from the crowd outside the station, he hails a taxi, and a few minutes later, we come to a stop in front of a rustic bar with a small patio out front. The rails enclose two long wooden tables with benches, and the soft lighting from the lanterns gives them and the few people there a romantic glow.

"This is it." Aiden stretches his hand out and leads me inside.

On the way in, I notice the chalkboard by the door says:

Poetry Night.

Oh my God.

We step inside, feeling as if we're entering a different world, one full of creativity and promise.

Of all the places he could have taken me, he brings me to one with such special value for us both. It's nostalgic, in a way, yet it's a place where we can make new memories.

"... In the night, you're all I see like the stars in the sky. While the world sleeps, I talk to you, my ghost of love..." the man recites as the audience sips their drinks and nods along.

Aiden tugs on my hand to find a table, and my feet move of their own accord as I'm in a daze, breathing it all in.

Once we're seated, a server sets down two napkins and drink menus.

"This place is... *wow*," I gush in a low voice, leaning toward Aiden, admiring the room.

Suspended wooden trellises are overhead, and the glass windows have matching wrought iron designs down the middle. Several plants are scattered throughout the intimate space, and it's all cozy yet classy—the perfect setting for a poetry night.

His eyes shine as he agrees. "I thought you'd like it."

We turn our attention to the stage, from where the man's words float around us. "Won't you come back to me? Won't you join the rest of the world with me? My ghost of love, let me take you on a walk. Let me show you the city when the sun comes up..."

I watch him with appreciation of his hauntingly beautiful words.

"For how can I live this reality with only the ghost of love?" He lifts his gaze to the crowd and drops his hand, clutching the paper to his side, and the cheers are loud and supportive. "Thank you all very much." He nods and waves as he makes his way to his table, where they clap him on the back.

"That was beautiful." I smile at Aiden across from me.

The server returns for our drink orders, and we sit back as the next reader steps onto the stage. "This one's for you, Sarah." The young woman points to the sky, making me gulp.

I instinctively reach for Aiden's hand, and he rubs his thumb over my knuckles, offering me comfort and strength, as we listen to her poem. To her truth. To the part of her that she only shares in her art.

I recognize it in her expression because it's the same for me.

"The light you *were* is the light you *are*. Shining on the ones you left behind. Gone too young, you were a special goby fish in the sea of life..."

The server sets our drinks down, and I have to tear my eyes away from the woman, whose voice still rings out across the room. She speaks with dedication and emotion. Captivating and devastating.

"I wish I was that brave," I whisper, meeting Aiden's gaze.

"You are."

"I'm not." I let out a small laugh. "Hiding my poems in notebooks in a box under my bed isn't brave."

He flips my hand over in his, then uses his thumb to rub circles on my palm like he's tracing the lines, memorizing them. "You should read here."

I blink in his direction like he suggested I take my top off in front of all these people.

"I'm serious." His eyes are dark and very sober when he peers at me—I almost volunteer to get up there right now. "You have a gift, and you should share it. Make people feel what you're feeling now, listening to the painful truths of life."

I open my mouth to object, but he stops me.

"I'm not suggesting you get up there now, unless you want to." One side of his lip curls. "But tell me you'll think about it. And when you're ready, we'll come back."

"Okay," I whisper, threading my fingers through his, our palms connected.

"Now"—he picks up the food menu—"should we order cheese fries, or what?"

"We have to. It's not a poetry night without them."

He laughs, and I could melt into my seat. It's senti-mental—his laugh, poetry echoing in the room, cheese fries.

It's like we're in college again going to poetry open mic nights, but it's different.

There's no Dave.

We're in the present, where Aiden and I freely spend intimate moments together.

There's no guilt between us.

We are in the *now*, and that fact wraps around me like a comforting hug.

It's liberating.

The rest of the night, we listen to poems of all kinds—sad and satirical, haikus and free verse—and we chat quietly in between readers.

We sip our drinks.

The spark where our hands meet grows.

And when we reach his apartment a few hours later, the chemistry explodes between us.

We're barely inside his door when his hands are on me, stripping me of my clothes.

I kick my shoes off as he pulls his shirt over his head. When he does, some of his hair falls out of his bun and into his face.

He's unraveled.

I lick my lips and continue assessing him, my gaze traveling over his sculpted arms.

His strong abs.

His low-hanging jeans.

My breath hitches when he pulls me into his arms and lifts me up. I wrap my legs around him as he walks us to the bed. Setting me down, he hovers over me, pinning me there with the delicious weight of his body.

"God, I've missed you, Jersey," he growls against my cheek, then raises my hands above my head and kisses me. Parting my lips, he tangles his tongue with mine while my hands remain pinned above my head.

I'm at his mercy, and still, I feel free.

Alive.

Sexy.

Being with Aiden again feels good. Like I'm in the right place for the first time in years. And I get lost in this feeling.

When he chucks his jeans to the side and fills me to the hilt, I'm complete.

I arch my back off the bed as he stays deep inside me.

"You're mine, you know?" His gruff voice against my lips sends shivers down my spine. "You've always been mine, even when you weren't."

I gasp, my eyes flying open, as he moves inside me, stretching me more with every thrust. He moves with fluid motions like a poem, flowing beautifully from one line to the next.

Full of passion.

He trails his fingers down my arms, then briefly cups my cheek as he kisses me. He continues moving his hand down to my chest and massages my breast.

His steady pace is heady.

Sensual.

As he makes love to me, my heart swells.

"Yes... yes..." I pant against his cheek as the tension inside me builds.

He quickens his pace, his hips meeting mine with purpose.

Skin against skin.

Heart against heart.

Heat snakes down my spine to my toes before I explode in a blur of bright lights and pleasure.

He grunts as I cling to him, my fingers tangled in his hair, keeping him close.

He thrusts one more time, then comes undone. His hair and eyes wild, nostrils flaring, shoulder muscles defined and round and sexy. He pulses inside me, and warmth settles into the pit of my stomach.

I close my eyes when he softly kisses my lips, lingering there like a secret.

"Don't move," he whispers. When he stands to go to the bathroom, I stretch my arms to my sides, sighing. I'm sated.

Spent.

Whole.

Tonight was... perfect.

We were *us*, but so much more.

CHAPTER TWENTY-TWO

AIDEN

I'm crazy about Sage.

Her dancing in the kitchen when she cooks.

Her humming in the shower.

Her soapy breasts full and enticing.

During the two weeks since our date, Sage and I have spent every spare moment together, whether it's a short lunch or spending the night at my place since I live alone.

Our schedules don't align to meet up every day, but we call and text often.

The guys groan every time I smile at my phone, and if I were them, I'd call myself an annoying pussy too.

It's so hard to care, though, when Sage sends me pictures of her lacy black one-piece that comes up high above her hips. During the nights we can't spend together, the pictures help.

They also give me the extra motivation I need to get through my workload. Whether it's because of our history or not, my feelings for her are strong, and I'm desperate to spend time with Sage.

This is different than what I had with Raven—it becomes more and more obvious to me every day. With Raven, I always felt obligated to hurry and finish work, so I could meet her for dinner, drinks, or her art show.

But Jersey... she gives me a new sense of purpose and is making me realize I have more to look forward to once I leave this office.

Smiling to myself, I focus on my computer. With the football draft, the team and I have been preoccupied building profiles for the new players and updating current ones too.

The weekend is a short two days away, and Sage and I made plans to spend Saturday afternoon together. I promised her we'd take the ferry from her apartment to downtown Manhattan, where we'd wander around the Financial District and find somewhere for dinner and drinks.

Her eyes shined when she mentioned the ferry as if she'd be getting on a Mediterranean cruise instead of an old boat on its last leg.

"I swear, if you keep smiling into space like that,

I'm going to vomit on your stupid plaid shirts. All of them. I'll break into your apartment and vomit all over every plaid shirt you own." Jared looks at me pointedly, his eyes narrowed as he rolls up an empty chip bag and tosses it in the trash.

I throw my hands up. "Okay, okay." But I can't help the laugh that escapes me.

"Prick."

"Fuck you." I flip him off. "I'm happy."

"And we like seeing you this way," Westin says, appearing at my side and leaning on my desk. "I can only assume our next meeting with CJJ will go swimmingly, unlike the previous disasters?"

"When was I ever a disaster, man?"

He quirks his eyebrow, and I can practically hear Jared's eye roll.

"Okay, you're right. Once again, I'm sorry."

Nikki stands from her desk in the corner, her eyes wide. "Guys, you might want to come see this."

Westin, Jared, and I exchange confused glances.

Once we make our way over, we stand behind her and stare at her computer screen. She starts a video on *YouTube* of Tank McAllister, a professional football player. He sits across from the host of a show for an interview about his recent draft.

"So, Tank, you've heard of an app called Jock Stock? What're your thoughts?" the host asks, folding his hands in his lap.

I start to high five the guys, but Nikki stops our mini celebration, pointing to the screen. "Wait."

"I have heard of them, and they're a total scam." Tank waves his hands.

"Care to elaborate?"

"An amateur created the algorithm. He's a sports enthusiast, not a coder, and users are expected to put their faith in that? They're supposed to spend their hard-earned cash on a finicky app? They're better off tossing their money in the Hudson River."

My face falls.

"Strong words, Tank," the interviewer says.

"Listen, Ken, I'm all for innovation, creativity, and the like, but there are too many sports, variables, and factors to consider when you're talking about an algorithm to determine a player's stock value based on performance. A task that large is for someone like Bill Gates, not two kids with bachelor's degrees in unrelated fields. I mean, one of the owners has a political science degree. He takes a few computer science courses online and thinks he's a sports expert? I took a few history courses in college too, but I don't call myself a museum curator."

The host chuckles, shaking his head as the screen changes to an ad.

Blood rushes to my ears.

I open and close my fists.

"How many views?" Westin clenches his jaw, pinching his nose.

Nikki hesitates. "Five thousand and counting. It was posted only an hour ago."

"*Christ.*" Westin paces, and the anger bubbles inside me.

How did Tank know anything about my background?

This is exactly why I've kept my mouth shut when asked about how I got started. We've taken extra precautions to keep that information from being used against us, yet it's coming back to bite me—the whole team—in the ass, as I was afraid it would.

"Tank McAllister also posted his thoughts on Twitter, and it's being re-tweeted like crazy." Nikki's eyes are wide as she continues scanning her screen.

"*Jesus.*" I want to curse and scream, but I bite my tongue since Nikki's here. I try to turn, my head ready to explode, but Westin grabs my arm.

"I already have a couple missed calls from Taylor." He holds his phone up. "We'll fix this."

"How? This is a nightmare. The whole—" I curse under my breath, lowering my voice as I pull Westin to the side. "The whole fucking country knows McAllister. A handful know us, by comparison. This is a complete nightmare."

He grips my shoulders and repeats. "We'll fix this, man. It's a small bump in the road. We've encountered them plenty of times before and overcame them. We'll do the same now."

"We weren't so close to the launch then. We didn't have investors riding on us then. We—"

"Aiden, I need you to keep it together." He squeezes my shoulder before he lets go, then pulls his phone out of his pocket. "Look, it's Taylor again. She's already on this."

I nod, grinding my teeth.

He retreats to his office, his phone to his ear, and I'm sure smoke is coming out of mine.

I walk by Jared's office, and he immediately clicks out of his browser, chewing on the inside of his cheek. His eyes are wide like he's been caught watching porn on his company computer.

"What?" I growl, stopping next to his desk.

"It's, uh…"

"Yeah?" I need to jog. To set a personal record for barbell squats. Any kind of physical exertion will do to rid myself of my nerves.

"The comments on the interview are brutal, man." Jared grips the back of his neck, his face red.

"Fantastic." I smack the doorframe with my palm, welcoming the sting of it, and head outside.

I pace the sidewalk, tilting my head toward the sky.

Shit.

Fuck.

Fucking hell.

I'm letting everyone down.

I'm an imposter, and now the world knows it too.

Fucking shit.

I pull my phone out and dial the one person I want to talk to.

"Hey."

Her simple greeting makes my shoulders relax, just like that. "Hey, Jersey."

"I saw the interview..."

I exhale. "It's bad, isn't it?"

"Yes," she says without hesitation.

"Ouch. You're supposed to make me feel better."

"Let me try again." She giggles. "Yes, it's bad, but not irreparable. Taylor and I are on this. I cleared her schedule, so we can come up with and implement a game plan. No one will remember McAllister's asshole comments by the time the launch rolls around."

I sigh with relief.

"Otherwise, I'll just kick the douchebag's ass for messing with you."

I throw my head back and laugh.

She scoffs. There's shuffling on her end like she's balling up a wrapper, then says, "Or maybe I'll kick *your* ass for not thinking I'm tough."

"You're tough, you're tough." I grin. "I just like it when you're riled up, especially on my behalf."

"I kind of like you, so..."

"Kind of? Ouch, again."

"I would say I like you a lot, but I've forgotten what you even look like. It has been three whole days, you know."

I groan. "Trust me, I know. And I'm doing everything I can to make sure we are uninterrupted on Saturday." I drop my voice low. "Only you, me, and so much sex you'll need help walking to the subway."

"Is that a promise?"

"You know it."

"Then what're you waiting for? Get back to work."

"God, I—" I bite my tongue, swallowing the rest of my words to the depths of my fucked-up heart. I pause, my body frozen.

"What's that? You cut out."

After another moment of silence, I clear my throat. "I need to get back to work, Jersey. I'll call you later."

"Yes, I need to make sure Piper isn't spitting in my coffee. I'm going to need it to get through the damage control that's about to commence. Talk to you later."

I walk to the spot where Sage and I talked after our first meeting together. The one where I hugged her for the first time in eight years.

So much has changed in such a short amount of time.

One might say we're dating. We're definitely fucking.

Making love.

I work my jaw back and forth—*love.*

I almost told her I loved her.

It felt comfortable talking with her on the phone about our day. Even though a major fucking shit storm floats above us.

I wanted to tell her I love her. It felt natural, even, yet... in the middle of these crazy few weeks, right before we're about to launch?

So quickly after we started dating? We haven't even discussed what we're doing.

Do I love her?

No matter the answer, I'm glad I didn't say it, especially over the phone. Plus, we're not ready for any declarations of love.

Not yet.

CHAPTER TWENTY-THREE

SAGE

"How did this happen?" Westin paces the conference room at CJJ the day after Tank McAllister's interview went live. "I mean, they singled Aiden out like they had a vendetta against him. How did they even know about his background? We've been so meticulous about keeping it under wraps, and even when we do discuss it publicly, we have a carefully constructed narrative to control the situation. Now, this?"

Aiden's square jaw hardens. He hasn't said much since he and Westin arrived for our meeting.

Taylor shakes her head. "I wish I knew. We keep our files locked. Our computers are password protected. The only ones here who have access to client information, including Aiden's background, are Sage and me."

Aiden's eyes flicker up to mine, and even though

there's obvious anger there from the dilemma, there's a softness there too the longer we stare at each other.

I fight my urge to reach across the table and squeeze his hand. To comfort him.

I hate this for him.

It physically pains me to know someone out there attacked him and his credibility after all he's worked for and accomplished.

In a way, I know what it's like.

With Dave, after we split, he spread nasty rumors all around town. That we were divorcing because I'd been unfaithful. That I was mentally unstable.

Most didn't believe him. They were loyal to me, but his lies certainly didn't help my business and its reputation.

To be wrongfully attacked like that is disheartening, to say the least.

"Sage and I have been working on scheduling a meeting with McAllister. We've been drafting social media posts and mailers, and I'm making calls to move some of your interviews up. The sooner we get you out there, talking to people and reassuring them, the better."

Westin slumps into a seat as Aiden turns to us.

"What about Jared?" Aiden suggests. "He has a computer science degree. We can push him into the spotlight, and I'll fade to the background. I work best in private, anyway."

"Whoa, whoa." Westin angles his body toward Aiden, resting his hand on the armrest of his chair. "You're the brains behind all this. I'm not going to let them drag you through the mud. We'll find another—"

"Listen, if it's best for the company right now, it's what we should do." Aiden sighs.

"It might be a good idea to shift focus to Jock Stock's strong suits," Taylor offers, cringing as she says it.

I start to speak up but sit back quietly instead as they continue. It's moments like these when I wish I had more authority in matters. More control. And not only because it's Aiden, but because I'm confident in my ideas.

Taylor's been a great mentor to bring me up to speed on how this world in New York City works, but my job duties don't involve taking the lead. I practically have to bite my tongue to keep myself in line.

"I'm not suggesting we cut Aiden out entirely, but for now, at least until we can meet with McAllister and his people, it would be helpful to emphasize the other members of your team and restore faith in the company. Besides, you are a team at Jock Stock. Working together so well is what makes you unstoppable." She eyes them both. "This is what I'm thinking, but at the end of the day, it's your call."

"We'll do it." Aiden doesn't hesitate.

"But only for the first few interviews." Westin leans

forward, then looks over his shoulder at Aiden. "I'm not going to pretend Aiden isn't my business partner and lead engineer, but I'll try to steer the conversation toward Jared and his qualifications. For a short while. We'll see how it goes."

"And I'll keep trying McAllister's agent. We'll keep you posted."

We go over a couple minor items for the remainder of this emergency meeting. At one point, it feels like we're running their political campaign and updating them on their poll numbers—which I imagine is similar, in many ways.

At the end, I stand alongside Taylor and shake their hands, trying not to linger on Aiden's.

He doesn't try to sneak a meeting this time. He's too upset. It's obvious in the defeated way he slumps his shoulders as he follows Westin outside.

If we ever do get a face-to-face with McAllister, I will seriously consider kicking his ass—he'd deserve it.

When I exit the conference room and head toward my desk, Piper's there.

"Can I help you find something?" I ask, trying to keep the irritation out of my voice.

She holds up a pack of bright pink Post-It Notes, which coincidentally match her top. "I ran out." She shuts my top drawer with her hip.

I cross my arms. "Take those, but you don't have to sneak them out of my desk. I don't mind—"

"You were busy, so I helped myself." She winks, then nods toward the conference room. "You all sure looked tense in there. Hope everything's okay."

"It will be." I square my shoulders.

She hums as she struts away, leaving me confused.

I study my desk for anything that might be out of place, but everything seems to be exactly as I left it. I click my computer open and log in—nothing out of the ordinary there.

Besides, even if she wanted to go through my computer, she wouldn't be able to since it's password protected.

Why would she snoop through my things, anyway?

My investigation is cut short when Taylor comes back from the restroom. "I'm heading out to meet with Joe and our wedding band. I'll be as fast as possible since we have a lot of work to do."

"Of course. What can I do while you're gone?"

"Make some talking points to highlight Jared's role in Jock Stock. Anything relevant, and we can go over them when I come back." Taylor disappears into her office and returns a few seconds later, black purse in hand. "You're doing great, Sage. Keep it up."

I nod and watch her back as she walks away, very aware of how lucky I am.

From what she's told me, I already have more tasks than she did when she was Catherine's assistant, which should make me glad. After all, I've only been here for a little over two months. No one is promoted after such a short time.

I knew when I moved to the city that I would have to start somewhere and work my way up.

I only need to be patient and keep working hard, starting with Aiden and the guys.

———

"For you." I hand Taylor the smoothie I got for her when she texted that she was on her way back.

"Oh my God, thank you." Her shoulders sag as we both enter her office.

"How was the meeting with the band?"

"Longer than expected." She throws her purse into her chair and places her hands on her hips, sighing. "It went well, but they had to listen to Joe and me argue for fifteen minutes about the last dance song. Which was *great*." She rolls her eyes sarcastically.

"That's so sweet," I gush.

"That we argued?"

I wave my hands. "No, no. That you're doing the last dance song. The idea is very romantic."

"You didn't do one at yours?"

"Dave wasn't exactly all about the romance." Her face falls, and I wave my hands again, inwardly scolding myself for putting my foot in my mouth. "He was. At first, anyway. Flowers, date nights, wooing. But we grew apart. We never seemed to be on the same page. Then I... um...” I clear my throat. “Anyway, you know the rest.”

“Wow, I’m sorry, but it sounds like it was the right move to separate.” She rounds her desk and squeezes my hand. “Plus, I’d be lost without you.”

“You and me both.” I smile. “On another note, I have more ideas for the Jock Stock issue.”

“For Hurricane McAllister?”

“Is that what we’re calling it?” I raise my eyebrows as she sips her smoothie.

“Yes, and you have to call it that too,” Taylor jokes, then sobers. “How are the guys doing?”

It’s only been a day since Tank McAllister publicly bashed Jock Stock, but it feels like it’s been a week. In the single day, Taylor and I have worked nonstop to put together press releases and social media blasts to counteract the blow to Jock Stock’s reputation and legitimacy.

The most obvious response is for us to talk with Tank himself and state our case, but we’ve had trouble getting through to his agent. I don’t doubt Taylor’s resilience for a second, though.

“They’re getting heat from investors. The potential board members they’ve been vetting are also shaken, but the guys have faith in us. Last night, Aiden—” I stop myself, and her eyebrows shoot up. “I mean... last night, Aiden messaged me...” I clear my throat to shake the high-pitched squeak from it. "They're as fine as can be. It hasn't slowed them down. They've had their work cut out for them with the recent football draft. Every now and then, he tries to explain exactly what he does, but it usually goes over my head." I laugh as the phone rings behind me.

I rush to answer it—our new client confirming a meeting.

After we end the call, I remain frozen, my back stiff.

I almost outed myself to my boss. I haven't told her Aiden and I have been sleeping together. That I talked to him last night, in his bed, while we were naked.

That I see him naked often.

She had many theories and suspicions after the disastrous dinner a few weeks ago, but Aiden kept his word and apologized for his behavior, which Taylor accepted. She also said she understood how sometimes personal lives interfere with business, and she's glad it was only her and not an interview broadcast for many people.

Which is what she warned us both against on separate occasions, but we reassured her we wouldn't have another incident. And we haven't.

We've remained cordial and professional during every interaction since then.

I'm happy to say she and I have moved on from it.

But now, there's the new issue of seeing Aiden outside work.

I know I should tell her that he and I have moved on too, to a more *agreeable* situation, but I don't know what Aiden and I are doing or where we're going—*if* we're going anywhere.

We've been enjoying the present. We don't talk about the past much anymore, but we don't talk about the future, either.

Telling Taylor about us will only mean we have to make the hard decisions about us and risk our business relationship and careers.

So, for now, I'll keep quiet.

By the time the sun starts setting, my eyelids are heavy, and my feet even more so. I rub under one eye and yawn as Piper walks by.

"Oh no, don't tell me you're already tired, honey." She lifts one thick eyebrow. "You're not going to last long in that case, fancy degree and experience or not."

"Good thing I have plenty of energy left in me." I nod to my coffee on the corner of my desk.

"Try to drink this one instead of wearing it." She snickers, then continues to her office.

I peer down at the brown stain on my blouse from when she *accidentally* ran into me earlier and adjust my cardigan to cover it up.

I flip her off behind her back because that's how mature she makes me feel.

"God, she's the kind of person I want to trip when she's walking. It'd be so easy to casually stick my foot out. Like this"—Taylor raises her red heel an inch off the floor—"that's all it would take."

I cover my laugh with my hand. "She's the worst."

"You know what's awesome, though?" She waggles her eyebrows. "My bachelorette party is in three weeks. We're having it way before the wedding, so we don't have to worry about anyone being hung over the day of."

"Planning a wild weekend, then?"

"Catherine is planning something fun, for sure, but she will only tell me it's in Vegas. Guess we'll see about the rest." Her eyes dance with excitement.

"Actually, Naomi mentioned a friend of hers is a dancer for Naked Heat." My cheeks redden. "It's a, uh... male revue show."

"Sounds *interesting*." She grins.

"I'll ask her for more information."

She checks her watch, backing into her office. "You should head home. It's getting late."

"Are you sure you don't need anything?"

She waves me off. "No. Go. Enjoy your night."

"Thanks. See you tomorrow."

By the time I finish up, log out of my computer, and gather my things, the sun has completely set. I head toward the subway, stretching my neck from side to side, winding down from the stress of the week.

I also keep my purse clutched to my side and glance around me, aware of the people scurrying about. I'm still getting acclimated to the city. To walking alone. To getting on the subway and taking the train at night. I've heard so many horror stories of New York, and they were almost enough to keep me from coming here.

But so far, I haven't felt unsafe.

My life here has started to feel natural and satisfying. Like I've finally settled into my new routine in the city. Thanks to Aiden, Naomi, and Taylor, I've found a real home here.

As I board the subway and find an empty seat, my phone vibrates with an incoming message.

Then another.

And another.

And a fourth.

"What the hell?" I mutter, then apologize to the woman holding her baby next to me.

As I read my messages, my stomach sinks.

Dave: You're in New York????

Dave: Of course, you went running to fucking Aiden. After everything I've done for you.

Dave: I knew you and him always had a thing on the side. You fucking cheater.

Dave: I can't believe this is the thanks I get. I wish I'd never taken you back. I would've been happier without your fucking drama.

What the... How did he find out?

My short breaths are labored.

How did he know Aiden lives here?

Has Dave been keeping tabs on him since he found out my secret?

I bite my lip, trying to keep the string of curse words to myself, to avoid unleashing them on the mother next to me and the rest of the passengers.

Instead of answering Dave, I call Aiden.

"Hey," he answers, and I relax into my seat.

"How's it going? Tired yet?"

"Only every day for the last five years." He chuckles, and I wish I could reach out to him.

To kiss him.

To feel him against me.

"It's all worth it."

"That's what we keep telling ourselves. Except for Jared. He's still pissy he hasn't found an apartment close by yet. None of the ones he likes are available for months, so he's been camping out in the office like a squatter."

"I heard that," Jared's voice is muffled in the background.

"Why do you insist on sleeping here? Are you

afraid Vanessa will find you at your place?" Aiden teases.

"She probably would. She's a fucking witch, I'm telling you."

I laugh along with them. "Sounds like you guys are having too much fun."

"Have to pass the time somehow. Until I see you again."

"You make me want to puke," Jared's voice sounds again.

After a pause, there's a thud, then more silence.

"Sorry about that. Had to kick some sense into him."

"Don't kill your number two," I joke.

"I think about it at times."

"I'm almost at my stop. Just wanted to hear your voice."

"You okay?" His humor is replaced with a concern that warms my chest.

"More than okay. See you tomorrow?"

"Or sooner. Not sure how I'll last until tomorrow afternoon."

"How about I send you more"—I drop my voice to a whisper—"pictures?"

He groans. "Yes, *please*."

After we say our goodbyes, I hang up and head toward the train station, thinking of nothing but Aiden.

No Dave.

So what if he figured out I'm in New York? It's not like he could really find me here. I never even told my mom my address.

I have nothing to worry about, except what I'll wear on my date with Aiden tomorrow.

The thought of seeing him is enough to settle my nerves, and that's all I need right now.

"After you."

"Thank you, sir." Jersey curtseys like she's boarding the Titanic instead of the ferry.

I like this playful side of her, reminding me that even though we're adults now with careers, we can still joke and have fun. Which I definitely need, given how brutal this last week was.

Once we're on board, I try to sit, but she pulls on my arm to keep walking. "What're you doing? We can't sit."

"Why not?"

She throws a mischievous grin over her shoulder as she leads me outside. We emerge onto the deck, where three other people stand, admiring the view of Manhattan.

"It's beautiful," Sage says, her voice filled with awe. "Sometimes I can't believe I'm living here," she whispers, wrapping her arms around my waist, pulling me tighter.

I kiss her temple, breathing her in, the breeze cool on my face. "I know what you mean," I say without turning away from her.

The boat pulls away from the dock, making her bump into me. She peers up at me through her long lashes. "I've been writing again."

"Yeah?"

"Bits and pieces of poems that come to me when I'm on the subway or cooking." She tucks her hair behind her ear, keeping her gaze on mine. "I've been revising my old stuff too. It's not much, but it feels good to get words onto a page again, even if it is only three at a time."

I dip my head low and kiss her lips, lingering there as the wind wraps around us like a cocoon, keeping us close—right where we're supposed to be.

Leaning her forehead to mine, she whispers, "What was that for?"

"You," I answer honestly. "You're amazing, and I'm happy for you. I know how rewarding it can be to do things you love. For yourself."

She watches me with watery eyes.

"What?"

"It's…" She clears her throat, her lips twitching. "You make me feel as if anything's possible. I like that you want me to go for it."

Her statement throws me off. "Why wouldn't I want you to do the things that make you happy?"

"You'd be surprised." She steps out of my hold and studies the view around us as the sun sets across the skyline. "Some people only want to see you fail in order to feel better about themselves."

I grip the rail in front of me, cursing under my breath. The small waves crash against the ferry like my heart hammers in my chest. "Is that what happened with Dave?" I ask. It makes me cringe, but I want to know because no matter how much I hate it, he's part of her past.

I'm scared of her answer, but knowing it means I can understand her better—who she is *now*.

"You know how he always laughed about my New York dream?"

I clench my jaw. "Yes, and I fucking hated it, Jersey. I couldn't take the way your face fell each time."

The bastard and I were friends. We had a few classes together and watched football every week. It was always a good time, but it didn't take long to figure out the kind of person he truly was.

He never deserved Sage.

"Well, it never got better. When I opened my own

business and was successful, to him, it meant I thought I was better than him. At first, he was happy and encouraging, then quiet. It got worse from there. The jealousy, the insecurities. It got to him so badly that I started keeping my work to myself to ease the tension." She shakes her head. "I'm sorry. This is a date. I shouldn't be talking about Dave."

"I want to know you. All of you. And that includes Dave, although I wish what you had to say didn't make me want to punch him in the jaw."

"You did once."

I turn my back against the rail and cross my arms. "I did what? Punch him?"

"Well, you elbowed him in the chin during intramural basketball. You claimed it was a mistake, but after we slept together, I started wondering if it was on purpose." Her eyes shine, amused, as she waits for an answer.

I exhale, hanging my head. "It was definitely on purpose."

"Is it bad that I'm smiling? What does that say about me?"

"That you're pretty ruthless." I pull her into my arms and clasp my fingers behind her. "That you're confident and so fucking sexy I've thought about you nonstop for days. Weeks. Years, even when I didn't know it."

She smooths the collar of my jacket down. "No more talk of the past, okay?" A shadow casts over her expression before she smiles up at me.

Thinking she doesn't want me worrying about Dave, I let it go. I kiss her lips, then mumble against them, "Sounds like a plan." I kiss her again, groaning under my breath, then look at the skyline, squinting in the direction of my place. "I can practically see my loft from here. We could run to it, get naked, and still have enough time for dinner and drinks."

She smacks my chest as the boat slows. "We're being spontaneous about dinner and drinks, remember?"

"What's more spontaneous than skipping dinner to get naked?"

She stands on her tiptoes as the boat comes to a stop and says, "Take me to dinner first because I'm starving. Then, we'll grab a bottle of wine on our way to your place, and I'll make it worth your while." She kisses me, and when she pulls back, her eyes sparkle.

I thread my fingers through hers and follow her off the boat, nearly sprinting to find the first place that sells food.

We haven't seen each other much this week, and she's too optimistic about my resolve.

When it comes to Sage, though, I'm merely a twenty-one-year-old with too much excitement.

"You're wearing the lacy black one-piece?" My mouth hangs open as Sage shuts the bathroom door behind her.

It rises above her hipbone on each side.

The lace dips in a V down below her chest.

She's a fucking goddess.

"I told you I'd make it worth your while." She sashays toward me, to where I sit in only my boxers, my back against the window. "I've been properly dined. Had my wine. Now, I'm ready for something I couldn't find on the menu."

I sit up straighter as she gets to the edge of the bed and crawls toward me, her lips teasing.

Her eyes shining.

Her cleavage so sexy.

I'm rock hard, and my hands itch to touch her.

But I like this little game she's playing too much.

She runs her palms down my chest, to my abs, to the waistband of my boxers, and I fight the urge to toss her beneath me.

But the thought of having her on top stops me.

She tugs at my boxers, and I lift myself off the bed to help her. When I'm free, she takes me in her mouth without hesitation, only intention.

Intention to drive me mad.

"Fuck..." I groan, drawing out the word as she works me slowly.

Deliberately.

She wraps her fingers around the length of me, her black fingernails matching her lingerie.

She's confident and hot, and I won't last long, not with her head bobbing up and down, her warm and wet mouth sucking me into oblivion.

My chest heaves.

Her mouth clamps tighter around me, her teeth grazing my head, taking me deeper until I hit the back of her throat.

I might pass out from the sensations.

The heat.

Tugging on a fistful of her hair, I thrust my hips upward—*close*.

So damn close.

"That's it," I mutter, my voice raspy, strained, overwhelmed with what this woman does to me.

My release comes fast and hard, shooting down her throat, but she doesn't move.

She fucking swallows. *My God*...

I groan, leaning my head back with a thud, spent.

When I open my eyes again, she uses her fingers to wipe her mouth. "Forgive me yet for making you wait?" She quirks her eyebrow.

"Oh, you are more than forgiven. I am definitely in *your* debt," I pant, pulling her against me.

"I accept cookies, coffee, or sexy time." She laughs against my chest, and it's a sound that echoes in my head.

Suddenly, the whispers of the past are loud and clear, hitting me square in the stomach.

She used to mesmerize me with that sound like a siren's call, and it does the same to me now.

My heart thunders like a damn rainstorm.

"You posted picture after picture with one girl after another."

I grip her as the weight of what I did to her—how I made her doubt me and my feelings for her—causes a crushing pain to my chest.

My guilt is heavy on my conscience.

This woman... she deserved better.

And she needs to know the truth of what happened.

Caught in my emotions, I turn to my side to face her. "About what happened back then... there's something I need to tell you. When I left, I was so stupid. Angry. Hurt. I wasn't thinking, but those girls in the pictures... I didn't—" I pause when she tenses against me. Clearing my throat, I'm ready to continue, but she stops me, placing her hand on my chest and splaying her delicate fingers across my pec.

Her gaze is glued there—distant. "Let's stay here, in the present. Okay?" She peeks up at me as she swipes her tongue across her bottom lip. "Let's stay here," she whispers, then kisses the corner of my mouth before fully planting her lips on mine.

My vision blurs the longer we kiss. The longer we tangle our legs together in the sheets.

The nagging voice in my head is muffled by her sighs and moans the longer she's in my arms.

I blink at my phone to make sure I'm not hallucinating, then swipe to answer. "Mom?"

There's a short pause, then, "Hi, Sage."

I wait for her to go on, but when she doesn't, I ask, "How are you? Haven't spoken in a while."

She pauses again, and I wonder if she hung up. I'm about to pull the phone back to check when I hear, "I've been very busy, as I'm sure you have as well." I hear what I assume is her back door sliding open. "I'm remodeling the kitchen, and I haven't been able to decide on the right colors."

I nod, unsurprised. She's redone every room in her house several times over the years—there aren't any new colors left at this point.

"How are you doing? Ginger keeps me in the loop with the occasional phone call, whenever I can answer.

I didn't even know you moved in with Naomi until last week."

I take a deep breath, steadying my voice. "I told you that before I left. Where did you think I've been living this whole time?"

She sighs as if I annoy her with the truth. "You've moved around a lot. It's hard to keep up with you and your choices of the week. Honestly, Sage, you can't expect me to know every detail."

And she never does.

Suddenly, I wish she wouldn't have called. I could go without her constant judgment that I'm doing everything wrong. If anything, I'm creating a better life for myself by being here and doing well, both personally and professionally.

Of all people, I'd think she would understand that.

"Glad you called, Mother," I say sarcastically, looking toward the sky.

"Watch your tone. I raised you better than that."

"Right," I mumble.

There's a muffled commotion in the background. "I need to go, Sage. They're working in the kitchen and knocked a vase over."

She doesn't wait for me to respond before she hangs up, but I'm not surprised.

I am in shock, though, that she called to begin with. After all, she didn't have anything nice to say. She didn't even wait to hear how I'm doing. What I'm up to. Who I'm seeing.

She almost seemed indifferent—more than usual, anyway. *What the hell is up with her?*

There's no use in trying to ask that question. I haven't understood her my entire life. It won't change now.

I stare out at the parking lot. I was about to enter the grocery store when my mother called. Blinking, I try to remember what I was here to get.

Food.

Food to cook dinner.

Dinner with Aiden tomorrow night.

"Right," I mutter to myself and stand from the bench. I don't remember sitting down, but it's not unusual, given how flustered I get every time my mother's involved.

As I walk through the aisles of noodles, my mind flashes to Aiden and his family. From what he's said, he hasn't seen them in a while, but they're still close and keep up with each other.

A twinge of jealousy stabs at me as the crushing realization that I might never be close to my mom settles in.

———

"Are you almost here?" I switch my phone from one shoulder to the other as I sway my hips and stir the Alfredo sauce together.

The smell of garlic and herbs fills the room like musical notes, and I dance along to the rhythm.

Naomi has the graveyard shift again tonight, so Aiden and I are cooking and eating here for a change. Although, I miss his apartment. The kitchen is much bigger there.

"The train is stopping now, so I'll be there shortly," Aiden reassures me.

"Food's almost ready, and I don't want to have to start without you," I tease.

"I'm running."

Humming, I hang up, and a few minutes later, there's a knock. "He must've been closer than he thought," I say to myself as I open the door. "You didn't have—"

The rest of my sentence gets caught in my throat, along with my stomach.

"Dave..." I take in his wrinkled shirt. The dark circles under his eyes. His frown. "How did you... What're you doing here?" I sputter as he brushes past me, leaving me in the doorway, stunned.

Turning around the small space, he places one hand on his narrow hip above the waistband of his dark jeans, a small blue notebook in his other hand. His dark hair is buzzed on the sides, and he seems leaner than before.

Otherwise, he's the same.

As he takes in my apartment, he wears the identical disapproving frown he's worn most of my adult life.

Same glare he's been giving me for over a year.

And the same distaste is in my mouth as I've had for a while when it comes to him.

How did he find me? My mom called yesterday for the first time in months, and now Dave? What the Hell?

I cross my arms and ask again, "What are you doing here?"

"I cannot believe you gave up our life together for this shithole." He laughs like the villain in every movie. Sadistic. Mocking. His disappointed gaze lands on me, and right when I'm sure he's going to spew another insult, I catch white sauce bubbling over the pot in my periphery.

"Shit," I mumble, rushing to turn the stove off. A hissing sound from where the sauce meets the hot stove fills the silence, and my hands shake as I clean it up.

"Who are you cooking for?" Dave asks, his tone accusatory.

And he's right behind me.

"Where is that fucker?" he sneers, stepping up to

meet my back, his breath hot against my neck.

"How did you know he lives in New York?" Cringing, I stare at a spot of chipped tile on the wall in front of me as I wait for his answer.

"We still have a mutual friend. Heard a while back that he moved."

"How did you find me?"

"Would you believe it if I said your mom?" He laughs, but nothing about this is funny. *My mother?*

"What're you talking about?"

"Turns out, she does like me. She finally sees *you* were the problem all along and not me."

I tense when he sweeps my hair over my shoulder.

No.

My mother wouldn't...

Would she?

"Don't touch me," I warn, moving over, trying to put distance between us.

But this kitchen is too small, and he traps me in the corner of the counter.

"Are you fucking him?" He raises his voice, slamming his palm on the counter next to me, and I hear the echo in my head.

I narrow my gaze at him, refusing to cower. I've put up with his bullshit for long enough. "Don't yell at me, Dave. Don't come to my home to yell at me like a jealous fucking teenager whining over his lost girlfriend."

"Of course, I'm jealous." His lips twist, and his eyes are full of pain. "I miss you, and he doesn't deserve you."

As I stare into his eyes, I almost feel bad for him right now. The truth is, I do feel bad. For years, I've been crippled by my guilt because I lied to him, but his attitude has always been a problem, even before my lie.

And it's only gotten worse.

"Back away," Aiden's voice rings out.

I peer over Dave's shoulder at him. He steels himself in the doorway, a white box in his hands. He narrows his gaze—he looks lethal.

His glare is murderous.

"You motherfucker." Dave leaps after him.

I try to grab ahold of his arm, but it's no use. Aiden drops the box on the floor, ignoring the cookies that spill out, and meets him halfway.

"Stop!" I yell before they get into a brawl in my kitchen. I stand between them, refusing Aiden's attempt to push me behind him. "Don't." I make Aiden look at me and soften my voice. "Please don't."

His expression morphs as he steps back, then turns his attention to Dave again.

"I cannot believe you," Dave seethes. "You were my best friend. *My best friend*, asshole, and then you quit on me. After my grandpa died, you disappeared for years, and then I find out you fucked my wife when you were supposed to have my back!"

"Watch how you talk about her." Aiden's voice is low.

"Oh, now you want to act like a gentleman? Are you fucking kidding me?" Dave's sarcastic laughs echo between us.

"Guys, calm down—"

"I watched you hook up with whore after whore, and you think you're better than me now? Don't kid yourself. Sage is too good for you, you coward."

"She *is* too good for me—we can agree on that. At least I know and admit it. But as true as that may be, she's better off with me than she ever was with you." Aiden takes a threatening step toward him. "She never even wanted you. She *settled*."

Dave lunges, and again, I jump between them before either one of them can throw a punch.

Dave looks at me, his jaw ticking, shaking his head. *Broken.*

"After everything, I can't believe you ran to him. I held you when you miscarried. I wiped your fucking tears." He never takes his attention off me as his face reddens, and he raises his voice. "*I* picked up the pieces while you sat on our bedroom floor, crippled by depression, as you wrote these." He shoves the blue notebook at my chest, and I curl my hands around it.

I don't realize I'm crying until the sound of a sob fills the room—*mine*.

Clutching the notebook to my chest, I feel the

tears stream down my face.

I don't have to look inside to know the devastating sadness that the pages of this notebook hold. The poems I wrote when I came back from the doctor's office that afternoon. The ones that haunt me like the words are floating around me, strangling me.

When I wrote them, I was in a grieving trance. I hardly remember the words themselves—fragments of phrases, bits and pieces of angry and defeated imagery, the sad rhythm—but the feelings? The despair, the ache, my heart breaking over and over again—I remember those all too well.

When I look at Aiden, he stumbles backward like I punched him.

"No..." Aiden rams his hands through his hair.

"I'm the one who helped her back up. Who held her hand and helped her put her life back together. Where the hell were you, Aiden? Huh?" Dave continues, stepping toward him, and I cry harder as the emotions grab hold of my chest and squeeze. Dave snaps his fingers. "That's right. You were having yourself a European sex-cation."

I cover my mouth, unable to look at either one of them.

Dave whirls around to me. "Instead of thanking me, I have to chase you down to New York, to find you with *him*. Whoring yourself to the son of a bitch who didn't give two shits—"

I gasp as Aiden's fist strikes Dave's cheek, making him stumble into the back of the couch.

Dave bounces off the back of it, making it scrape against the floor.

The scraping mixes with my voice when I try to stop them. "Don't..." I cough, trying to find my voice through the weight on my heart.

My stomach rolls.

"Stop it..." I whisper as they shove each other, and Aiden pins Dave against the wall by the door. I shake my head and pull on them both. "Stop it!"

"That's not what happened. I didn't fucking abandon her..." Aiden says, putting his arm against Dave's throat in an arm bar. "I loved her. I wanted to be with her. I came back for her!"

"You what?" I suck in a sharp breath, a new round of tears spilling.

My head hurts.

My heart aches.

"You're a coward. You never loved her, but I did. I *still* do," Dave chokes out.

I sit on the couch, the notebook still clutched to my chest like a Bible. I don't know how long I sit here or what makes them finally stop trying to hurt each other, but suddenly, they're both in front of me.

"Baby, you're pale." Dave tries to feel my forehead, but Aiden steps in.

"Talk to me, Jersey. What's wrong?"

"I... I need..." My gaze darts between them and finally settles on Aiden. "I think you should both go."

"I'm not leaving you," Aiden says at the same time Dave says, "Yes, he does need to go."

I squeeze my eyes closed—I can't look at Aiden right now.

He came back for me?

He never told me he tried to find me. To win me back. To tell me he loved me.

For years, I believed he didn't have strong enough feelings for me. That he left because he didn't love me.

That he hooked up with all those women in Europe because I wasn't worth the fight.

He left me alone.

"Please go." I grind my teeth as I push them off me and stand, dropping the notebook behind me on the couch.

"Jersey, let me explain." Aiden holds my shoulders, but I shrug him off.

"I'm not leaving until he leaves." Dave crosses his arms.

"Why am I not surprised you're the childish one?" I steel myself when Dave walks toward me. He takes my hand while Aiden growls.

"I want to talk. I came all this way—after everything we've been through—can we talk for a few minutes? Please?" Dave frowns.

He said *please* for probably the second time in his

life.

The man I married.

We exchanged vows—vows that we meant to each other at one point, even if they don't hold any weight now.

I won't go crawling back to him.

I won't use him as a crutch again.

I can't forget all the hurtful things he's called me, today and in the past, and I won't. His name-calling and attitude are only a couple of the reasons we're not together anymore, after all, so they're nothing new. I'm not surprised, either, that he came here to shame me.

Which is why we need to talk. We need to put our history to rest, once and for all.

"Okay." I slowly nod, and in my periphery, Aiden steels himself. "We'll talk, but that's it. No more harassing me—I mean it, Dave."

"Harassing you? You're my wife," Dave says at the same time Aiden says, "I'm not leaving. Not this time. I'm not walking out of here without you."

"I'm not your fucking wife," I grind out, then turn to Aiden and whisper, "Go."

"Are you kidding me?" Aiden walks toward me, his hands out, pleading.

"She said leave, asshole." Dave steps between us.

"I didn't sleep with those girls." Aiden brushes past him, his eyes full of pain.

"What?" I stiffen.

"The girls in the pictures—I didn't sleep with any of them. All I could think about was you."

More he kept from me.

When I was already vulnerable back then, Aiden made me feel worse, and now he's telling me it was a lie? That none of what his pictures suggested was real?

Dave scoffs, turning to me. "You can't seriously believe him, can you? He's only saying this to stop you from kicking his ass to the curb."

"This is between me and her." Aiden holds his hand up to stop him.

Everything hurts.

"Please go, Aiden."

"Jersey—"

I squeeze my eyes closed. "Don't... don't call me that."

Aiden drops his hands, his gaze searing into me, branding himself on my heart—but all I feel is the sting of it. "You'll always be my Jersey, no matter what. This isn't over."

My chest aches.

Every fragile piece of my heart finally snaps. It was held together only by the thought of my second chance with him, but Aiden never said he tried to find me. He never told me he fought for me. Never explained about the pictures that haunted me each night.

What was his angle with the pictures, then? To

make me jealous?

My stomach churns—*I'm going to be sick*.

The longer I look at him, the more crushed I am. Because when I look at him... all I can think about is the disgust and devastating disappointment I felt when I saw one smiling picture after another with a different woman every week.

While I carried—*and lost*—our baby.

Once the door shuts behind him, I almost forget Dave until he smirks.

He pushes his hip off the kitchen counter, his sullen expression from before now replaced with amusement. Like he's won.

As if it's ever been a competition between him and Aiden.

The truth is, I did settle. I settled because I was young and forced to make a decision I wasn't emotionally equipped to make.

And it all could've been avoided if Aiden hadn't run.

If he'd chased me... instead of running in the other direction.

"Why don't we go out for dinner?" He eyes the ruined pasta, his lips curling. "Don't think we'll be able to eat here. We can go out to a nice meal and talk."

"You just called me a whore, Dave, so no, I won't be going anywhere with you. We can talk here." I square my shoulders, steeling myself.

"You *are* fucking him." The pain in his eyes almost makes me feel worse—he's always been good at that. At making me feel like it's always my fault.

But I haven't done anything wrong, not now.

He shakes his head. "That was the one thing..." He swipes at the corners of his mouth and pauses. "The whole way up here—the last few months—I've been prepared to forgive you. I told myself not to care about what happened in the past, because it didn't matter. It didn't matter because it was over between you and him, but now, you've been *fucking him*."

"You and I are divorced, Dave. You have no right to be pissed or act like I've wronged you."

"I don't know how to forgive you for this," he continues as though he doesn't hear me.

"It's over, Dave. If it's closure you want, I'll gladly give it to you, but other than that, it's over—"

"What the fuck does that mean? We were married. You can't throw that away."

"We're *divorced*, Dave," I repeat more loudly, hoping he truly hears me this time. "You can't keep contacting me like nothing's changed since we first started dating in high school. Everything's changed, mainly who we are."

He shakes his head.

"Dave." I place my hand on his forearm, but he jerks it away.

And the anger bubbles inside me.

"You spread nasty shit about me to all my clients. You yelled at me in the middle of a grocery store. Did you forget all that? You made me feel *this* small." I hold my thumb and forefinger an inch apart. "You humiliated me in front of half the town. That's not how you treat the people you claim to care about."

"I said I was sorry for everything, and I came all this way to apologize for that and so many things. You'd think you could appreciate that. I mean, what the hell else do you want?"

"I want you to stop being a dick," I spit.

"*I'm* the dick? That's rich. Compared to Aiden, I'm a fucking saint." He puts his hands on his hips.

"It was never a comparison." My shoulders fall, hoping the truth lifts the cloak that's blinded him all these years. "I fell for Aiden in college, and I'm sorry I wasn't stronger. That I didn't tell you the truth before we got married. I was selfish—"

"Damn right."

"I deserve that." I sigh, steadying my voice, and put my hands up, praying for him and for strength. "But don't pretend like you're not also to blame. We both made mistakes."

He scoffs.

"I can't tell you how much I appreciate what you did for me back then. You were my rock, my hope. You made me see the light. And I'm sorry for not telling you the truth sooner... But it's in the past." I lick my lips. "I don't owe you my future. So stop holding it over my head like a damn debt that'll never be repaid." I lower my voice. "Don't text me anymore. Don't call. Don't guilt me into thinking our divorce was all my fault. Just *don't*."

"Sage, I've loved you since we were sixteen. I don't know... forget it." He turns on his heel and stomps toward the door.

I gulp, hurt from the way things exploded between us, and all we're left with now are shattered hearts.

With shaking hands, I pick up the notebook Dave brought with him. I must've forgotten it at our old house when I hurriedly packed my things.

"You know..." He pauses, his hand on the doorknob, then looks over his shoulder at me. "What makes you think Aiden is the one for you?"

Emotion clogs my throat.

"How can you trust him? Because the girl I know... the one who wrote those"—he nods to my notebook—"she'd never be naïve enough to think Aiden won't abandon her again."

Another tear falls as his words settle around me like debris. "You don't know him."

"I know him well enough to know that I'm not the one who should be kicked out of your life." He shakes his head, roughly exhaling in defeat as he leaves my apartment.

And I know it's the last I'll hear from him.

Sadness seeps into my heart as if I already miss him, but as I sit on my couch, taking deep breaths, I realize it's the comfort he provided that I'll miss.

The truth is, no matter how awful he was, I could always count on him to be there for me. I knew that he'd stick by me. That he wouldn't run off to Europe when things got difficult.

In my heart, I know that I'll miss the security. The certainty of knowing he'll be there when I'm alone. When the darkness gets to me.

I peer down at the notebook in my shaking hands. Bile rises up my throat, and before I know it, I sprint to the bathroom. My head in the toilet, I heave.

I try to catch my breath, but my stomach cramps as I continue throwing up.

Once I think I'm finished, I sit back on my heels and reach for a towel out of the cabinet to wipe my mouth.

Inhaling, I brace myself as I stand on wobbly feet. I splash water from the sink on my face, drinking some of it in the process.

I make my way back into the living room, where my notebook is face down on the floor. Picking it up, I read the poem on the page.

This is the first time I'm reading any since I wrote them. I sink onto the couch, my stomach growing more and more queasy as I turn page after page, and the fear inside me grows too.

The shadows of the trees dance in the moonlight.
The air hums.
Still I lie as they taunt me.
As nothing but empty groans sound from my stomach,
with the faint whispers of a heartbeat
only in my memories.

Through blurry vision, I keep reading, poem after poem, line after line, until my tears spill onto the pages and smudge the ink.

Inhaling, I curl onto the couch with the book in my hands, my body aching, suffocating from what Aiden said.

Was it all a cruel game to him? To get back at me for what he thought he saw when Dave kissed me?

Eight years ago, Aiden disappeared, and I lost part of myself.

That's what happened when I lost my baby—I lost part of my own heart and soul.

And Aiden... the man I thought could take away the heartache.

He left, and I've spent years wondering how he could do that so easily.

"How can you trust him?"

Fear and confusion grip me as my chest heaves, and my sobs fill the apartment.

I don't know the answer to that anymore.

CHAPTER TWENTY-SIX

AIDEN

I throw the covers off and pace my loft. It's the middle of the night, and I have only my thoughts and the whispers of her cries to keep me company.

I sense her sobs in my soul.

If I stay quiet enough, I might hear them like a ghost haunts the living. I should've gone back. I shouldn't have let her kick me out—we should've talked.

I should've told her everything from the start.

I should've groveled and pleaded and begged her to accept my apology that I didn't explain sooner. And fucking Dave... how were we friends once? What kind of person treats someone as good as Sage like he has? One look at him, and my skin crawled.

He's a fool.

And me? I'm an even bigger fool.

I spent years and the first few weeks of her back in my life, resenting her for marrying Dave. I spent so much time thinking I was wronged and hurt by her when it was me.

I drove her to him without realizing it.

And those fucking pictures... I posted them because I knew she'd see them. And for what? My childish games to get revenge on the one girl I really cared about. That's why it hurt that much more to see her kiss Dave.

To see her in another man's arms when I thought she was finally going to choose me.

But looking back, I was immature. A coward.

I hang my head, defeated and angry, so fucking angry at myself.

I trudge back to my bed, but my emotions keep me up the rest of the night.

I toss and turn.

Get up and drink a beer.

Stare at the ceiling.

I curse—a lot—until the sun rises, bright and shining, like it's taunting me.

My sour mood only grows worse as I drag myself to work. Did I brush my teeth? Did I even put clean clothes on? I stare down at my pants, trying to figure out where they came from—the bathroom floor or the dryer?

When I step inside our office, Jared's the first

person I come across. "What happened to you? You look worse than a gorilla's ass."

"The fuck, man?" I growl, tucking my hair behind my ears.

"Forget your haircut? Again?" Jared raises his eyebrows, then stuffs a large chip in his mouth.

"Chips?" I challenge, shifting the strap of my bag over my shoulder. "It's not even eight yet."

I continue toward my office when my phone rings, the comforting name on the screen one I often see but not this early in the morning. "Avril? Is everything okay?"

"Of course, no need to start burning down cities yet." She giggles on the other end.

"You know I would, though, right?" My shoulders relax a fraction.

"You're my first call if I need that." It makes me smile for the first time in the last twelve hours. My little sister has that effect on me. "We're on our way to our final debate competition for the year."

Suddenly, it makes sense why she's calling first thing today. "And you need a pep talk?"

"Can you?" Her voice is small and innocent. Even though she's a freshman in college, she sounds so much younger.

I lose more of the edge in my voice as I say, "Whoever you're up against, you'll beat them. You're smart. Scrappy. And special. Don't forget the three

Ss." She echoes me on the last line. "You're ready, Avril."

"Thanks, big brother."

Westin knocks on my door and pops his head in.

"Listen, I need to run, but good luck today. Let me know how it goes." I nod as she agrees and hangs up.

My hint of a smile turns into a full-on grimace as I rejoin my reality. Staring at Westin, I wait for him to speak. And the longer he stays silent, the more pissed I get.

"What?" I finally ask.

"Jared was right—you're pissy. That was his word, not mine, but it seems accurate."

I swivel in my chair to face my computer. "I'm pissy because you're in my office first thing in the morning and don't have anything to say."

"If this is about the McAllister thing, I thought we talked about this. The investors are happy again. The potential board members are as well. It could've been a lot worse, but we're fine."

"It better be." I scoff, staring at a scratch on the wall. "After all, I've given five years of my life to this company. *Five years*." I turn my attention to Westin. "I'm damn good at what I do, and I'm sick of people only caring about my credentials. My background. Pieces of fucking paper instead of who I am."

"Okay, guess this is about more than that."

I let out a defeated laugh, thinking about Dave and

Sage talking yesterday. Thinking of them alone together. Thinking about all they had to say while I had to walk away.

She looked like she was choking on the past.

"*Go.*"

Her voice... it was so dejected.

Because of me.

"I have the past—every tiny piece of it—coming to bite me in the ass around every fucking corner. So yeah, I'm pissy."

Westin continues standing tall and doesn't seem fazed. I don't have to worry with him—he knows I don't mean to take it out on him.

But when he remains quiet, it makes me want to take it out on him a little. Maybe a good jab in the nose for being so fucking reasonable and calm all the time like he's Buddha. For once, I'd like to see him unraveled.

"Do you know why we work so well together? Why we're friends?" he finally asks.

"Enlighten me," I grind out.

"Because we're different. Two different temperaments. Different pasts. Unique perspectives. We complement each other." He shrugs.

I wait for him to say more, but my patience wears thin. "And?"

"And I'm good at calming you down. Which is what I'm trying to do."

"You're making it worse."

"I'm making you focus on something else, aren't I?"

"Yes, how much I want to wipe the damn smirk off your face with a swift kick in the shin."

"Better than wanting to crawl into bed with a bottle of whiskey, though, right?"

I roll my eyes and rock in my chair.

"I'm sorry about the interviews. About diverting questions when anyone asked about you."

I sigh, interlocking my fingers above my head. "It's not your fault. I agreed to this. It was my fucking idea."

"But you're a major part of the team, man. We'll talk to Taylor about a new plan now that some of the heat is off our backs. She even got in touch with McAllister's agent, mainly because he was annoyed that she called so frequently and at all hours of the night, but they're in the process of setting up a meeting."

"Good." Part of the weight lifts from my chest. "Maybe I can kick him in the shin when we do meet. Teach him—"

He holds his hands up, chuckling. "Let's leave the kicks to the MMA fighters, okay?"

I sigh. "When are we meeting with Taylor again?"

"Next week."

That's when I'll see Sage.

But I hope to God she calls me, ready to talk,

before then, because I don't know how long I'll last without hearing her voice.

Her laugh.

She's become the center of my world again, and I can't lose her this time—I won't.

I avert my attention to the ground as I get lost in the events of yesterday.

Of her sullen expression and dark eyes.

My ears ring from lack of sleep and water.

From guilt and anger.

"What happened, Aiden?" Westin whispers.

When I lift my gaze, he's studying me, frowning and pitying me. "I need to get back to work."

"Don't—" He sighs when his ringing phone interrupts us. "This isn't over," he says before he answers, taking the call to his own office.

I furiously type on my computer, slamming my fingers on the keys as I study updates on athletes. If any have been injured, delaying them from playing. I pull up stats to stay up to date on athletes' performances.

I don't know how long I type.

I thought working would keep my mind busy, but every second I stop, I think of Sage and how we'll get through this.

We have to get through this... right?

CHAPTER TWENTY-SEVEN

SAGE

"How could you?" I hiss into my phone, pacing my bedroom.

"You had relations with another man. When you were supposed to be committed to your husband." My mother's cold voice makes me cringe.

I was finally able to get ahold of her after trying for days, but after two seconds of this call, I wish she wouldn't have answered.

"Dave wasn't my husband when I was with Aiden. You don't even have the facts. You have Dave's poor-wounded-puppy version. I admit, I was in the wrong for not being honest with Dave from the start, but I wouldn't have felt like I had to lie if I had anyone else to rely on. If I would've had *you*, Mother."

"Don't blame this on me, Sage. Be an adult and admit your mistakes."

"I just did. Your turn."

The anger rolls off me in waves. How dare she? How dare my mother ignore me most of my life, then come back to ruin it because she thinks she has a right to? Because she knows anything about what happened to me?

She's made it a point to miss everything in my adult life, yet she wants to pretend she's doing me a favor now.

How fucking dare she?

"What have I to apologize for? You're the one acting akin to a heathen, committing adultery. That's not how I raised you."

I exhale, stopping next to my bed, my stomach churning. "You're right. It's not how you raised me." I pause as my body deflates with a realization that I should've accepted long ago. "You didn't raise me at all. It's not enough to call yourself a mother—you have to actually act like one and pay attention when your kid needs you."

"Sage, I was a single mother with a lucrative business, so I taught you to fend for yourself. Are you really mad that I taught you independence?"

"No." I clench my fist at my side. "No, I'm only mad that you truly believe you did me a favor with your absence."

I end the call, frozen in my spot, staring out my window.

My own mother is on Dave's side. She believes I did him wrong. Even though I am to blame for some of what happened with Dave, she had no right to tell him where I live.

To betray me and my trust when she didn't deserve to have it in the first place.

I clutch my stomach, nausea rolling, and I rush to the bathroom.

Between work, this thing with Aiden, my mother—it's too much. *Too overwhelming.*

When I stand, I step back, dizzy. I lean on the counter for support and study my pale reflection.

"Get a grip," I mutter, then turn the water on until it's warm before washing my hands and face.

Once I exit my room, I find Naomi on the couch with a pint of ice cream. "Was that your mom on the phone? What did she have to say for herself?"

I sigh. "She blamed me, as always. For once, I finally thought she'd see that she's gone too far, but that's what I get for hoping."

"I can't fucking believe she stooped so low, though. To go out of her way to actually hurt you."

"In her own twisted way, she thought she was helping by making me face Dave and take responsibility for my actions."

She furrows her brows at me, swallowing her bite of dessert. "You don't really believe that, do you?"

I sigh again, slumping against the doorframe to my

room, my hand on my stomach. "No, but it's better than admitting she's just selfish with a skewed perception of reality."

"I think it's time to accept it, unfortunately." She holds her ice cream high as she crosses her legs on the couch. "Don't get me wrong, I'll always love Aunt Cheryl, but I don't have to like her."

I smile, glad that Naomi's on my side, at least.

She points to her ice cream with her spoon. "You want some?"

I stand upright, shaking my head, as if she offered me bugs instead.

"Really?" She scoops a spoonful of the creamy dessert. "You never say no to ice cream."

I freeze, pausing with my hand still on my stomach.

No...

She glances at me, setting her spoon in the container. "What?"

Can it be?

"Sage? Are you okay?"

"The only time I didn't want ice cream was when..."

Oh my God.

"When what?" Naomi leans forward and sets the ice cream on the coffee table in front of her. "You're scaring me. What's going on?" She rushes toward me. Placing the back of her hand on my forehead, she searches my gaze. "Talk to me, girl. What're you feeling?"

I try to swallow to wet my dry throat. "Um... I need to get to a drugstore."

———

"Slow down." Naomi shuffles behind me as I run to the 24-Hour CVS.

It's late, but I can't wait.

"I'm sorry, Naomi, but I have to find out for sure." I come to a screeching halt in front of the well-lit storefront and red letters across the door.

"Hey." Naomi pulls me by my arm away from the door and dips her head to meet me at eye level. "Listen, no matter what happens, I'm here for you, okay? You're not alone this time."

I slink into her and wrap my arms around her neck. "Thank you," I whisper over her tight curls.

Squeezing her one last time, we both exhale, then go into the store together. When we come to a stop in front of the tests, I stare at them.

I instinctively touch my stomach as memories of my swollen belly invade. Of singing to my baby. Of feeling her kick.

Of dreaming of holding her.

My chest squeezes.

I didn't have Aiden then, and I don't know where

he and I stand now. The way we left things... we have yet to clear the air. To figure out how to move forward with us—if it's possible.

But a baby?

As I stare at the tests, this is all too familiar.

"Sage?" Naomi rubs my back in soothing circles.

"I'm fine. I was just remembering..." My voice trails off as my throat constricts.

"Listen, we don't have to do this right now. You can come with me to the hospital tomorrow for a checkup, and—"

I place my hand on her arm. "I want to do this. I have to know."

She nods, then picks up a few boxes, turning them over in her hands. I pick one up as well, but she speaks before I've even read the first word. "This one." She sets the others back on the shelves.

I walk to the counter on wobbly knees as if I've forgotten how to walk. My mind is racing.

The thought of being pregnant again has my heart thundering in tune with the beeping of the register as the cashier checks us out.

I didn't know if another pregnancy would be in my future. Dave and I agreed to wait after my miscarriage, and before we knew it, the months turned into years. He always said he wasn't ready, and I didn't argue.

I didn't feel ready, either. It never felt right.

Naomi and I remain quiet the rest of the way back to our apartment.

Once inside, the bag rustles in my hand where I grip it tightly, and I stop outside my bedroom. Hugging Naomi one more time, I whisper, "Thank you. I'll let you know what the results are—"

She pulls back, gripping my arms. "Are you insane? I'm waiting in your room with you."

I sigh with relief, and together, we go into my room, where she sits on the end of the bed.

"I'll be right here when you come out."

I close the bathroom door behind me, and with trembling hands, I set the box on the counter. "I can do this," I tell my reflection, then take a few deep breaths and open the box.

Once I'm finished, I open the door and sit next to Naomi on the bed, the test in my hands. We stare ahead, remaining still.

The city beyond our apartment seems to stop its bustle.

The seconds feel like hours.

After a few more beats of silence, Naomi looks up from her watch and says, "It's time."

My shoulders tense as I look at the thin stick in my hands like it's an explosive, and I'm supposed to defuse it.

"Okay," I whisper, but it's mostly to myself. "Okay, here we go."

We both sharply inhale as I turn the test over.

Two lines stare back at me.

And instantly, I imagine two tiny eyes peeking up at me as I hold him or her to my chest.

Naomi holds her palms together over her mouth.

"Positive," I say, my voice shaky. "It's positive."

"Oh my God," she whispers, and a slow smile spreads on her lips.

"I'm pregnant."

"You are." She nods, then full-on grins.

"Aiden and I are having a baby," I say more firmly, and a sob escapes me as she tugs me to her in a tight embrace.

"Tomorrow, we need to schedule an appointment. I know a great OBGYN, and I'll help you every step of the way with anything you need."

We're having a baby.

My body grows limp in her arms.

She rocks us from side to side, and I'm relieved that I'm not alone this time.

I have family, who's also a friend, with me, unlike all those years ago when Naomi was already in New York City. We weren't as close as we are now, either, and I bask in this rare outpouring of affection from her.

She's happy for me, and I too shed tears of joy on her shoulder as her grip on me tightens.

But what remains the same from my previous pregnancy is that the baby is Aiden's, and he's not here.

Fear creeps down my spine, momentarily dampening the good news.

Naomi must sense it after I stiffen. "What's wrong?" she asks, pulling back.

"I have to tell him. Aiden, he needs to know." My bottom lip quivers.

Her grin turns into a frown as understanding visibly dawns. She knows what happened. What Aiden confessed a few days ago and how badly it hurt me—how much it still pains me.

"What will he say?" I whisper more to myself than to her.

"There's only one way to find out, honey." She squeezes my hand with both of hers.

"What if..." I lift my scared and haunted gaze to hers, recalling my loneliness during this moment of déjà vu. "What if he runs again? Leaves me alone again? A baby... I mean, this is huge. What if history repeats itself?"

"Sage, I meant what I said. No matter what, you are not alone. I will be here for you." She looks down at the test still in my hand. "But you need to tell him. He needs the chance to be the man he wasn't back then."

"Do you believe he can be?"

I'm taken aback when she smiles. "I think people

can surprise you. A lot of people change for the worse, but many of us change for the better—take it from me."

I tilt my head toward her.

"I'll save that story for another time, but all I'm trying to say is… don't be afraid he'll leave. He didn't know you were pregnant last time. This will be different—I know it."

I bite my lip.

"Right now, we need to talk baby names."

"Baby names? You realize I just found out, right?" I can't help but laugh.

She lies back on the bed, bringing me to lie next to her. "It's never too early to plan."

As we chat, I'm wrapped up in the familiarity of it all. Of lying with Naomi like this when we were kids as she told me funny stories or tried to cheer me up when I was upset after my mom didn't attend my school play or when she threw my report cards away.

Naomi always had the right thing to say to make me feel loved and just… *better*.

She giggles as she lists the names she insists I absolutely cannot use. "Those are too overdone and unoriginal. You need a cute-ass name for your angel."

Never would I have imagined Naomi being giddy. Who knew all it took was a baby to get her smiling like a lunatic?

My emotions are caught in my throat as I peer at her. "I've missed this. Us."

She gives me a small smile. "I've missed you too, girl."

We stay like this for another hour, laughing and talking, and it works wonders to distract me from my fears.

All that matters is that I'm having a baby.

A miracle.

I deeply inhale as we make our way to CJJ—to see Jersey.

All I've thought about is her.

She hasn't answered or returned my calls or texts.

Is she that pissed at me?

The elevator dings, and the doors open on their floor.

Sage is in a flowy skirt that reaches her knees. Red flats. A black short-sleeved shirt that clings to the perfect curves of her full breasts.

There's a new glow about her. It's only been a week, but it feels much longer.

It's been too long since I last held her.

When her gaze meets mine, her eyes widen, and indecision crosses her features.

"Hey, guys."

I tear my attention from Sage and force a smile when Taylor greets us, then leads us to their conference room.

Westin and I sit, and Jared grabs a cookie from the end of the table before he sits on the other side of Westin. Jared doesn't normally come with us, but we thought it was time to include him. Westin and I may have started the company, but Jared's played a major role in making it what it's become.

We go over the guest list for our launch party so far and a few more interviews that are scheduled.

"Last but not least, Tank McAllister." For the first time since his Tweet went berserk, Taylor doesn't cringe when she says his name.

Instinctively, I lean in.

"We have a meeting tomorrow to discuss his public apology." Taylor smirks.

"What do you mean?" Westin asks.

"Certain information has come to light." She holds her hands up when we—including Sage—start to ask for more details. "I won't share until I confirm, but we may have a lead as to where he got his *misguided* information. I'm going to meet with him and his agent tomorrow, just the three of us, and hash it out. I'll give you guys a call the minute we're finished."

Westin, Jared, and I glance at each other, exhaling with relief.

"Where does that leave us with Aiden?" Westin

points to me, and for the hundredth time since I met him, I'm glad I took that IT sales job because I met him.

Westin always has my back.

"I'm confident I can get McAllister and his people on our—and Aiden's—side. I'll let you know tomorrow for sure, but either way, I think it's time Aiden comes out of hiding. We now need to shift to the results. Hurricane McAllister was only a setback, and we need to get people focusing instead on the results, which you guys are killing." Taylor smiles, and it relieves me even more.

I didn't realize how pissed I was about the whole thing until yesterday, when I hid Jared's chips under my desk to get back at him for all the attention he's getting.

As if pouring five years of my life into this company has meant nothing.

But I quickly realized it's not Jared or anyone else's fault. It's the way of the world. Image, background, and experience matter, but so do results, as Taylor says. Which we're getting, and the team and I continue doing so every day.

"Oh, one last thing. It's pretty huge and will definitely give us a boost, to say the least." She pauses for what I assume is dramatic effect. "*Forbes* is doing an online article on Jock Stock in their spotlight of up-and-coming companies with a bright future." She drops her pen like she would a microphone, and we jump out of our seats.

"Holy shit," we say in unison.

"*Forbes*? Seriously?" Westin's eyes bug out of his head like the time our first investor told us how much money he wanted to give us.

"Dead serious." Taylor holds her arms out. "Turns out, one of the writers and I have a mutual friend, so I asked for an introduction. I pitched him Jock Stock, and he loved it."

"Oh my God." Jared paces, rubbing his palms down his pants.

This is it.

Westin and I never imagined all our late nights and headaches would lead us here. For *Forbes* to even know who we are, let alone want to write about us—me, a guy from the middle-of-nowhere, Virginia, and Westin, a loud kid with too much determination for his own good.

And Jared, of course, the junk food addict with a brain the size of Earth.

Jersey celebrates with us, and I wish I could crawl over the table to kiss her.

We were together at our last meeting.

She and I exchanged coy glances—we were a team inside and outside of the conference room as she helped me navigate the crazy world we're now in.

"I think that's a good place for us to stop today.

We'll meet back up in a few weeks to finalize the guest list for the launch party and itinerary. Like I said, I'll also update you on McAllister. As for you guys"—she points to Westin, Jared, and me—"keep being awesome."

We thank her and Sage again for all they're doing.

Before we separate, I lean down to Sage and whisper, "We should talk. I don't like the way we left things. Meet me at Hemingway House tonight?"

"I can't. I have to work. We have—"

"Please give me a chance." I inhale her sweet scent and pick my heavy feet up. I keep walking and don't stop until I'm on the sidewalk, waiting for an open cab.

Only a few hours until I can speak my piece.

My Jersey and me.

I pull my phone out on the way back to the office and text her to meet me at eight tonight, and when I get to work, I know I'll count down the minutes until then.

CHAPTER TWENTY-NINE

SAGE

I walk into Hemingway House fifteen minutes before eight, and as suspected, Aiden's already here, sitting at the bar in all his plaid glory.

My nerves are jittery like I drank three pots of coffee, but when Aiden turns his pleading gaze toward me, I stop.

Being in his presence has always calmed me, and even though I'm still mad at him, it doesn't change the way the lazy tilt of his lips warms me from the inside out.

It was so difficult sitting across from him at the meeting today. I felt like we were separated by several miles instead of only a few feet.

As I approach, he stands and hugs me. I inhale deeply, ignoring how much I love his cologne. How much his presence soothes me.

How much I wish I could tell him I'm having our baby, so he could hold me.

But I can't tell him yet.

I can't tell him while I'm still mad at him because then, I know I'll fast-track this thing between us and get back with him only because of the baby.

And I refuse to enter another relationship under false pretenses. The next time I get married will be out of pure and honest love.

Aiden and I have a while to go to get there.

"What can I get you to drink?" Joey asks, leaning on the bar toward us.

"A red wi—" I clear my throat. *Damn, no drinking.* "A water, please."

"Nothing to drink?" Aiden asks.

I shake my head. "Water is great."

He shrugs, then finishes his beer and tilts it toward Joey. "I'll take another."

There are plenty of people around, but none of their chatter reaches my ears. All I can think about is where Aiden and I will go from here.

He scratches his chin, the silence thick with tension, then angles his body toward me. "I thought you'd be happy."

"Happy?" I blink at him.

He drops his hands in his lap, making him hunch forward, giving him a strange vulnerability. "That I came back for you. That I didn't sleep with those girls. That I loved you then, and I love you now."

I let out a shaky exhale, fighting the way my heart lurches toward him and his love like a plant toward the sun.

Part of me is happy, but it's not enough.

"You don't get it." I furrow my brows. "Had you told me this years ago. Had you been there for me years ago... Yes, I would've been happy, but you made me believe otherwise. It took Dave coming here for you to finally tell me the truth, that you played childish games with me when I really needed you, and you expect me to be happy?"

"I tried to tell you before."

"Well, you didn't try hard enough." I breathe in and out, glancing around me as I lower my voice. "For years, I believed the worst in myself because of you. If you wouldn't have tried to fuck with my head by posting misleading pictures, I wouldn't have married Dave. I wouldn't have felt so guilty for what I did to him. I wouldn't be so angry with you right now when I know I need—"

A stray tear falls down my cheek like the dew from my cold glass of water. Swiping it away, I swallow down the rest of my tears.

"Jersey... I had no idea."

After a short pause, I nod. "We need space."

He grabs my hand and squeezes, reminding me

what it was like for him to touch me. To own my heart and soul.

And he still does.

Because I love Aiden, but our love isn't simple.

It's not as easy as confessing a few words—it's the actions. It's overcoming the ghosts of our decisions and learning to trust each other again after all the mistakes we've made.

We need time to do that.

He leans forward, cupping my cheek, weakening my defenses as warmth from his palm travels down to my chest.

"Don't," I whisper, squeezing my eyes closed, shaking out of his hold. "We're broken, Aiden. You and I... we're broken. And it's not going to fix itself overnight."

"I was stupid back then, but that's not who I am now." He grabs my hands again and peers down at them, rubbing my knuckles with his thumb. "I'm so fucking sorry."

The comfort, the special kind I've only ever received from him, reaches deep into my soul and forces the sob from my throat as I retract my hand.

I pull it from him and stand.

I don't say a word for fear I won't be able to leave. But I have to, for now, anyway. It's the right thing to do.

"I'm not letting you go, Jersey."

I stop with my back to him.

"I'm going to fight like hell to win you over. Be ready."

It's a promise.

One I need him to keep.

CHAPTER THIRTY

SAGE

"Sage?"

I squeeze my eyes closed.

"Sage?" the voice repeats, then a hand gently nudges my shoulder, shaking me awake.

"Naomi?" I squint, trying to bring her into focus. "What day is it?"

"Wow." She sits on the couch next to me. "You must've really been out."

I keep my eyes closed, thinking back to last weekend.

Vegas.

Taylor's bachelorette party.

They had shots. So many lemon drop shots, while I sat back, making excuses as to why I wasn't drinking. Once Taylor started to guilt-trip me that it was her bachelorette party, and I should join their fun, I had to use logic against them. That we were in a strange city, and one of us had to stay sober to keep the others in line.

Which wasn't a bad idea, actually.

I finally got the chance to meet Catherine and thank her for being the encouraging mentor she was to Taylor. It's because of her that Taylor's the mentor she is to me now. I thought I knew a lot about this industry, and I do, but with Taylor's guidance, I've learned to apply many of my skills on a new scale. Plus, I've made many connections that will be invaluable as I build my career.

Frankly, I've been able to level up, as Aiden might say—he loves his video games.

I sit up, rubbing the sleep from my eyes. When I open them again, a sharp pain slices through my forehead. "Damn it." I squeeze my eyes closed again.

"What's wrong?" She touches my head with the back of her hand. "Are you nauseated? Cramping? Do you—"

"No, nothing like that." I open and close my eyes, cautious of setting off another jolt of pain. "It's been a hell of a week. I had to go straight to work after we got back from Vegas, and it's been one thing after another each day. Even if I wasn't almost seven weeks pregnant, I'd be exhausted." I glance around me, noticing my purse on the floor. It's on its side, and the contents have spilled out. "Guess it all caught up to me, and I passed out before I made it to my room."

Naomi continues studying my eyes and feels my lymph nodes.

"I'll catch up on sleep this weekend. I'm fine."

"Please, take it easy." She sighs, sitting back, and rests her elbow on the back of the couch. "Talk to me."

"There's nothing to say," I whisper.

"What's going on with Aiden? Have you spoken to him since you told him you needed space?"

"No." My face falls, and my crushing loneliness threatens to devour me.

I miss him. His intensity. His eyes. Even how infuriating he can be.

"He's called and texted, but I don't know... I asked for space, and he hasn't gone a single day without trying to reach me."

"What did you expect? Seems like he's just a guy in love."

I scoff, then go to stand, but Naomi pulls me back.

"Let me tell you a story."

I raise my eyebrows. "A story about *you*?"

"Don't be so shocked. I talk about myself plenty."

"That couldn't be more false." I nudge her.

"Well, get comfortable." She peers down at her slender fingers, fidgeting with her chipped nails. "When I was in college, my best friend's name was

Charlie. She's the one I've mentioned before, but I never told you what happened."

"Okay..."

"We were twenty-one-year-old art students. We went to Coney Island on spontaneous trips. Every now and then, we'd get high. We partied. Laughed—we laughed *a lot*. She was a hit everywhere we went." She rubs her palms down her scrubs. "We didn't think about death. We weren't supposed to, not then."

Chills run down to my toes.

I gulp, and through my fear, I manage to ask, "What happened to her?"

"We were supposed to meet one night to study for our exam, but I was running late, so she went to pick up snacks and coffee..." She pauses, tears in her eyes as she lifts her gaze to meet mine. "I should've been there. It should've been me," she whispers.

"No, Naomi, no." I scoot closer to her.

"She was... my best friend. Charlie was shot and killed that night."

"Oh my God." I wrap my arms around her, shocked. "Naomi, I had no idea."

"I got there as the ambulance shut its doors. The blue and red lights. The caution tape. It was a night-mare. No one would say anything other than a young woman was shot and killed. And I knew even before I got to the hospital that it was Charlie. I *knew*." She licks her lips as she pulls back, then swipes under her eye at a tear. "Her brother Ty... he's the exotic dancer for Naked Heat I told you about."

"Oh..." Understanding dawns as I recall the male revue show we attended for Taylor's bachelorette party after Naomi suggested it, but she never mentioned how she knew any of the guys. "Ty... he was the one with the tattoos?"

"A bunch of tattoos. My weakness." She gives me a small smile, but then her expression darkens. "He and I got close afterward. We formed a connection. A bond. No one else understood, but we did. We *got* each other, and I became addicted to it. To him. To the point where I thought I was in love with him." She laughs, shaking her head. "Over a year ago, I even told him we should be together. We could have a future. I made an idiot of myself."

"What do you mean?"

"He found someone else, and I embarrassed myself."

"I'm sure you didn't."

"But I did." She exhales. "I tried to tear him away from her. I was the villain in their story, but... I was hurting."

"I'm sorry, Naomi." My heart is heavy for her. She's been struggling all this time.

"Don't be." She waves me off, a strange peace settling around her as she continues. "It's for the best. He did me a favor, anyway. Even though I was hurt, I eventually realized it wasn't him I was in love with. I loved the idea of having someone understand. Sharing a unique connection with someone. But the truth is, our past, when we were together, it wasn't real. We were caught up in the addiction of feeling *seen*."

"That's all most of us want."

She exhales a shaky breath, shifting on the couch. "Our past is exactly that—history. When I told Ty how I felt, I got closure. *Real* closure. And although I couldn't admit it at the time, it was truly a relief. I felt like I could finally move forward. Try to find someone real."

"And you will."

"Maybe." Our eyes lock. "You and Aiden, though? I know I cautioned you a few weeks ago, but that was before I realized how well you two fit. No matter what happened in college, you have something real, *now*. You're different people."

I exhale, my lungs feeling like they're shriveling.

"You're mad and scared and so many other things, and I get it. I don't blame you, but ask yourself if it's enough to keep you apart. If it's enough to keep you from trying to be a family. Be honest with yourself about your feelings, and if you need extra help"—she stands, holding her hands out for me to stand too—"write."

"Write," I repeat as if I'm trying a new food, rolling it on my tongue, seeing how it tastes.

And I like it.

"No matter what we're feeling, art is how some of us express ourselves and take a deeper look into our psyche. Every emotion sweeps onto the page with every brush or pencil stroke. Every word. Every image. It's a tapestry of our lives in that moment."

"I couldn't agree more." I fight the lump in my throat.

She nods to my room. "Then write."

When I reach my door, my mind still troubled from her past yet more optimistic for our future, I stop with my hand on the knob. "Do you ever paint anymore?"

She hugs her midsection. She's unusually meek, almost fragile, and my heart breaks all over again. "Sometimes, especially when I want to be close to Charlie." She shrugs, offering me a sad smile. "But now, I mostly throw myself into my career. Nursing is how I deal with my loss, the guilt of what happened, and who I turned into after that. But helping people gives me the purpose I so desperately need."

I nod, understanding where she's coming from. "Thanks... for sharing that. I know what it's like to suffer alone, and I'm sorry you do too. You've been there for me, and I hope you know you don't have to be alone anymore, either. We have each other, right? Family?"

"Friends." Naomi smiles. "We're more than family

who's usually obligated to love each other. We're friends who choose to do so."

I grin, thankful that the mess in my life brought me back to her after years of distance.

"Now, get out of here. I've talked more in the last hour than I have all week, and I'm exhausted from all this wisdom I'm spewing."

Laughing, I hold my hands up, inching into my room. "And I have to pee because... pregnancy bladder."

She chuckles, making me smile harder.

Naomi's wise words swirl in my head as I retrieve my notebook from my nightstand. My urge to write is strong. I need to let the words and emotions out of the cage they've been rattling for years.

Like I wouldn't think twice to take my next breath, I don't think about the perfect way to begin. I don't spend hours contemplating the flow, the rhythm, the line breaks to create riveting enjambment.

I simply write.

As the night sky deepens, the minutes tick, the neighbors surely put dinner on the table, I continue writing until my hand cramps—and then write some more.

Our love shattered
like glass in slow motion.
Only echoes of kisses in the distance like

cries of help.
You left,
and the memories collected like dust
I never wiped away.

The words that come out take me back to eight years ago. To my old bedroom where I sat hunched over my notebook. Where my hand hurt to write anymore because I was trying so hard to work out my frustrations on the paper.

I'm transported to my time in college. Years have passed, but I never really healed.

When I laid eyes on Aiden at our first meeting, my old wounds he created split wide open, and he poured salt inside with his confession of the mess we created.

It's why it hurt so badly to learn the truth about his trip and those girls—that it was all a ruse.

You left like a plane during takeoff.
I would've stood at the gate, waving
goodbye
had I known it was me
you were leaving behind.
Had you known I wasn't the only one
you deserted, would you
have flapped your wings and disappeared
into the night? Or would you have stayed and run
through the gate into my arms?

I blink, rereading the question in the last poem, considering the answer.

"That's not who I am now."

People do change—Aiden and I have. We've grown, evolved, and the experiences of our past shaped us.

In every broken piece of me, I know the truth.

"I loved you then, and I love you now."

I believe him. I believe he loves me, and one day, he'll love this baby too.

CHAPTER THIRTY-ONE

AIDEN

"You're in love."

My throat closes as if I ate a strawberry—my only allergy.

"You're in love with Sage, and she obviously loves you back, yet you're still moping."

I turn in my chair to face Westin.

He grimaces like it hurts to see me in this state. Granted, I could've combed my hair and tried harder to match my shoes to today's choice of plaid, but his obvious disgust makes me feel even worse.

"What happened to you two, man? You were doing so well before her husband surprised her with a visit. Does she think they have a chance again? Are you jealous? What is it?"

I smirk. "No, there's no chance of them getting back together. Not after spending time with me. She and I... we're meant to be together, and I know she knows it, but she's asking for space instead." I ram my hands through my hair and tug on the ends. "And I don't fucking blame her."

I tell Westin the rest of the story, of what happened the last few weeks.

I was an ass.

I didn't realize the damage I'd done to her by running away before she could explain.

When we first saw each other again, at our first meeting, I was angry with her for not choosing me. I resented her because I thought she didn't feel the same for me. I thought she ruined me for love.

But I hurt her too.

I took so much from her.

We both made mistakes, and now I'm left with nothing but guilt and self-loathing.

"Have you tried to talk to her?" Westin asks.

"Of course, I have. I've called and texted. Left way too many voicemails than is appropriate after she asked for space, but I can't help it. I'm losing my shit."

"You have a..." He points to my head, and I smooth my wavy hair down.

"Thanks." I stand, rolling my eyes, and wipe the Pop-Tart crumbs from my pants. "I have to take a piss."

He nods, stepping out of my way.

When I return from the restroom, Jared and Westin are huddled around my desk.

"What're you doing?"

"We're plotting how to get your girl back." Jared rubs his hands together.

"There's nothing you can do—I don't even know what to fucking do."

"You're not in this alone." Westin grips my shoulder. "You have us."

"Now, sit down so we can strategize." Jared snaps his fingers, inching away. "Or should we use the SMART Board in the conference room?"

I grab both of them by the collars of their shirts and drag them back. "What makes you think she even wants me back? She would've answered even a single call if she did."

"She loves you, man." Westin smacks my hand away. "You just need to show her you do too."

"I've already told her, and it didn't work." I sigh, dropping my hands to my sides, defeated. I'm spent from all the sleep I've lost alternating between berating myself and wishing I could turn back time.

"That's why I said you need to *show* her. It's not enough to say the words, not after your messy history. You need a grand gesture. One so big romantic comedy fans will swoon right into a coma. Which means you need help—you need us." Westin points between him and Jared.

"What he said." Jared shrugs.

I work my jaw back and forth, staring at their collars and the wrinkles from where I gripped them.

Westin, the son of bitch, always has the right thing to say. The wisest of us three. His head is on straight. His focus is laser-tight and narrow. It's why Jared and I would follow him to the end of the earth—like brothers.

Family.

How do I get Sage's attention?

How do I win her over, for good this time?

Because I want her. *I love her*.

My gaze bounces between my two best friends as my mind sorts through different options until it lands on an idea. My eyes widen when it hits me. "I know what to do. We only need to figure out how to get her to meet me there."

"We'll do anything we can to help." Jared claps his hands.

"What he said." Westin grins.

And together, we use the SMART Board to draw up a plan to win the girl.

CHAPTER THIRTY-TWO

SAGE

I pull the account files on my desk and skim through them, brainstorming ideas for press releases and social media, but the one I focus on the most is Jock Stock.

Their launch is coming up fast, and I need to put together a few mailers and confirm details with the venue for the party. We're expecting more guests now than originally planned, which is great, but it also means more food, drinks, and seating.

This week, I've been more like an event planner than a publicist's assistant with planning the details for the party and helping Taylor with her wedding, but I've enjoyed it.

It's been a welcomed distraction for the time being.

By the time I check everything off my to-do list for

the day, the sun has already started setting. Yawning, I walk to Taylor's office.

"I meant to ask, how was the meeting with the venue earlier?" I lean on Taylor's doorframe.

She sighs in her chair behind her desk. "It went well, and I think we're pretty much set for the big day."

"I can't believe there are only two weeks left," I gush.

"It doesn't seem real, but time has flown."

"I think we lost a month during our Vegas trip."

"Yeah, right. You came to work that Monday morning looking like you'd spent three days at a spa." She scoffs. "How could you refuse shots of lemon sweetness from hot, tatted bartenders?"

I smile, pointing at her. "I thought you were going to fight me for that one guy's attention at the first club, so I steered clear afterward."

"That was the shots talking." She throws her head back and laughs. "He was *fine*, but no one compares to Joe, of course."

"Not even the sexy strippers," I muse.

She pauses, as if she's mentally comparing the exotic male dancers from Naked Heat to Joe. "Nah, I'd still take Joe over anyone." She grins.

I'm about to turn when she stops me.

"How are you and Aiden?"

"What do you mean?" I freeze.

"Have you two made up yet?" She tilts her head, rocking back in her seat.

"I don't... I don't know what you mean." I cross my arms over my chest, then wince, extra aware of how sensitive my breasts are becoming.

"Come on, Sage." She smiles, and it's genuine. Her posture is relaxed—no sign of anger—which puts me at ease. "I've known about you two for a while. It's pretty obvious given the way you look at each other."

"And how's that?" I ask, purposely stalling.

"The way Joe and I look at each other—like you're in love."

I exhale, shifting from one foot to the other, and give up the charade. "I'm sorry I didn't tell you sooner."

She waves her hand. "I'd be mad, but your work performance has been too fantastic. I mean, I would not have been able to take on more clients and do so well without you. You know your stuff."

My chest blooms. "Thank you."

"Now, about Aiden..." She eyes me.

"It's very... complicated."

"But do you love him?"

"Yes."

"Then, don't give up."

Nodding, I'm grateful for her advice and also relieved she doesn't give me a hard time for being with Aiden in the first place.

She's an understanding person, an admirable publicist, and a respectable and excellent boss.

I still can't believe my good fortune for working here.

"In fact, why don't you head out for the night?" she suggests.

"But we have work to do for Jock Stock and the new clothing line account."

"I'll finish up the more urgent matters, and you and I can get to the rest tomorrow."

"Okay, if you're sure..."

"I am."

Once I gather my things, I make my way to the elevator. When I get on, I tap my foot, my nerves jumbled. I don't have anywhere to go.

No drinks with Naomi.

No date with Aiden.

I miss him like crazy. Like a leaf separated from its branch, I miss Aiden Baxter, no matter how exasperating and stubborn he can be.

He's also warm and sexy and makes me feel loved.

Sighing, I exit the elevator and walk out the door until I'm outside. I abruptly stop when my gaze falls on Jared.

He's standing on the sidewalk, rocking back and forth on his heels. "My lady." He holds his arm out to show me to the taxi waiting behind him.

I furrow my eyebrows, standing firmly in place. "What's going on?"

"Your chariot awaits." He shrugs.

The driver leans out the window. "Are you getting in, or what?"

Reluctantly, I get into the cab, and Jared follows, giving him an address.

"Where are we going?" I ask.

"You'll see."

I sigh. "Look, Jared, I'm sure Aiden put you up to this, but he's not respecting the space I asked him for. He is *so*—"

"I know." When he looks at me, his eyes are sad and sympathetic. "But this is different. Please hear him out."

I cross my arms.

Jared places his hand on my shoulder. "Please. He's really sorry, and he wants to talk to you."

"Why didn't he come himself, then? Why did he send you?"

"Because you wouldn't have gone with him, obviously."

"Good point."

"You know Aiden better than Westin and I do. He's complicated. Prickly."

"A broody dick ninety percent of the time."

"That too." He cracks a smile. "But he has a big heart. And he really cares about you. He's been a mess since your fight, and I can't take seeing him this way. I know you miss him too."

I study him. His lightly stubbled jaw. His clear eyes staring back at me. There's no sign of his teasing nature. "Why are you being so... normal?"

He chuckles as we take a turn and pull to a stop. "Sometimes, life isn't all fun and games. Every now and then, love makes us serious."

"What do you know about love?"

Jared finishes paying and opens the door. "Not much, but when I look at you and Aiden? It makes me want to find out."

I remain in my seat, peering out the windshield at the horizon and back to Jared.

He holds his hand out and quirks his eyebrow. "Coming?"

The driver exhales, clearly annoyed, and I jump out of the car before he throws me out.

When he drives away, I turn to Jared, who taps at his phone. After a short pause, he asks, "Ready?"

I sharply inhale, then nod.

"Good answer." He laughs, holding his hand out for me to lead the way, which is when I look up.

The outdoor patio with cute red umbrellas.

The wrought iron rails and wooden tables.

The place Aiden brought me for poetry night.

I step toward the door like I'm walking a tightrope and pass the familiar chalkboard, announcing it's open-mic poetry night again. Speechless, I open the door and cross the threshold. It looks the same, except for the red rose petals sprinkled across each table.

And Aiden walks to the center of the stage, holding a single rose in one hand and a piece of paper in the other.

I gasp.

The room silences.

Aiden's voice echoes around us, sending a shiver down my spine.

"How's everyone doing tonight?" He wrinkles the piece of paper in his hand, and his voice shakes as people murmur a resounding answer. "I've, uh, never done this before, but I want to impress a girl."

My heart cracks when he locks eyes with me and gives me a sheepish smile. The one he gave me all those nights ago in college when he told me how he really felt about me.

How much he liked me.

How much he still loves me.

"She once told me I had poetry in me, and I disagreed." He works his jaw back and forth, glancing down at his paper and up at me again. "She told me all I had to do was speak from the heart, and that's what I'm doing."

The room erupts with an *aww* and a few claps as my stomach flutters.

My lips tremble with a watery grin as he begins.

"We were young. Too young to live. To love. To know.
But we loved each other—that much we were sure of.
It was a soul-shattering love,
one that awakens the heart, like the sun
rattles a new day.
Because of you, I saw the world anew.
The little things became extraordinary
because you made me believe,
like a man reborn,
a new heart with which to love.
A heart that forever beats for you, no matter
the number of sunrises, the storms, or the distance.
Because our love awakened the best parts of me—you."

He clears his throat, flicking his gaze toward the crowd until he finds me, then folds the paper in his hand. "I love you, Jersey."

I clutch my chest, letting the stream of tears fall.

"You said we're broken, and although that might be true, we're not over. Don't you see?" He smiles, his gaze hopeful and unwavering. "Our broken pieces fit. *We* fit. We're strong, and together, we're unbreakable."

He waits expectantly as the room stills. The crowd follows his gaze to where I stand. Some hold their breath, and others smile.

Together, they wait.

My tears continue falling one by one.

Nodding, I rush to the front where Aiden climbs down from the small stage, and I jump into his arms.

The cheers are instant and deafening as I plant my lips on his in a kiss that's too heated for an audience.

But I don't care.

Because I'm in Aiden's arms, and he kisses me with no regrets.

No guilt.

Only love. I have all his love—all of *him*.

I pull back, giggling, and in my periphery, the people in the crowd have stood up, clapping.

Leaning my head on his strong chest, I laugh, and he joins me.

We wave like this is the end of our play, and we even bow, which causes a new round of laughs from us.

Westin and Jared stand in the back clapping as well. I squint to make sure I'm seeing the woman standing next to them correctly—Naomi.

I grin wider when she shrugs, her lips curling at the corners.

I snuggle deeper into Aiden's side and accept the rose from him as he leads us out onto the sidewalk.

In the crisp early summer air, I bring his lips to mine, kissing him with more emotion than I could manage with words.

"I'm sorry," he mutters against my lips, and I swallow them like I would water. "So fucking sorry."

"I'm sorry too." I place my hand on his chest, sharply inhaling.

He leans his forehead to mine, holding my hand over his pec, squeezing it.

"I love you too," I whisper.

He crushes his lips to mine, brushing across my mouth with intention. Want. Fervor. He then parts my lips with his tongue, firmly exploring my mouth.

My breaths become labored as he steals each one like he stole my heart all those years ago.

On this chipped sidewalk in the middle of New York City, underneath the evening sky, showered with twinkling lights from the surrounding buildings, Aiden kisses me like he's a dying man.

By the time he pulls back, we're panting.

"Your place?" I ask, winded from his kiss—and him.

Without a word, he grabs my hand and waves for the first taxi we see.

As the buildings blur, his leg bounces faster and faster.

I bite my lip.

The cab buzzes with excitement—with newfound hope.

And my chest swells.

When I look at Aiden, I feel the planet shift. It rights itself. I'm in New York, where I always dreamed I'd be. I'm doing well at my job. I've rekindled my relationship with my cousin, and she's becoming my best friend.

Then there's Aiden. In a few weeks, his company will really take off. He's successful and happy.

We're together, right where we're supposed to be.

"Thanks," he says to the driver when we stop in front of his building.

As he leads me out, I grip his hand, feeling the heated tension rolling off him as we reach the elevator. Once inside, we're alone.

And he snaps.

I gasp when he pushes me against the wall, assaulting my lips in a kiss so passionate, I feel it in my bones.

His lust.

His love.

The intensity of this man is something I crave, and I'll never tire of it.

The elevator dings, and the doors open on his floor. He lets go of my hair and grabs my hand instead. I skip to keep up with him, and once we're inside his loft, we don't waste any time.

We keep the lights off, and his apartment is quiet, except for the soft echo where he drops his keys to the floor.

He flings his shirt off in one swift motion.

I pull my dress up over my head and am left in only a lacy red bra and black panties.

He licks his lips.

I squeeze my trembling thighs together.

Heat creeps down my back like a low whisper across my skin.

He kisses me, placing his hands on my waist to hoist me up, and I wrap my legs around him as he carries me to his bed.

When he sets me down, he doesn't pull back. Instead, he hovers over me, fumbling with his belt.

"Let me." I grab his pants, pulling him toward me as he peppers kisses on my temple, in my hair, right below my ear.

I moan, and he growls in response as he unclasps my bra. "Hurry," he rasps. "I need you."

I pull his pants down, and his length springs free, making my mouth water.

My body hums as the anticipation grows.

He lays me back, covering my body with his, and places warm kisses along my throat, running his hands up my sides until he cups my breasts.

Dipping his head, he swirls his tongue around my sensitive nipple, making me arch my back against the bed, into his touch.

Squirming, I reach for him, clawing at his shoulders —his teasing is frustrating yet delicious, making the ache in my core grow.

I angle myself so that his tip is at my entrance, and my whole body trembles.

He looks up at me, his hazel eyes brighter in the dark. "I love you."

The determination in his voice matches his expression. There's a strong crease in his brow as he says the words I've waited all my life to hear, from the one person who means them the most.

I gulp as the emotions surround us like a backdrop of this night. "I love you too," I whisper.

He inches himself inside me, and I memorize the feel of him stretching me.

The feel of something new waiting for us at the start of a new day, the start of something real for us.

He rolls his hips, and I writhe beneath him as we get re-acquainted after the last few weeks apart. And I lock everything he gives me in my heart.

He stays close as he picks up his pace, his cheek against mine, his breaths coming out in pants like my own.

We move in sync as the cool sheets rustle beneath us. As the bed molds to our shape. As the city blinks beyond the window behind us like it's cheering us on.

I wrap my arms around his back as we make love. Sensual, tender love that makes my eyes water with happiness.

Aiden has always held my heart, all the broken pieces of it.

But with him by my side, living as one, we truly are unbreakable.

CHAPTER THIRTY-THREE

AIDEN

"Your poem was..."

I trail my fingertips from her shoulder down to her elbow and back. "I hope the end of your sentence is good. You should've seen how hard I worked on it, especially when Jared kept trying to help."

Laughing, she grips my arm like she needs the support. "I can hardly imagine."

"All I'll say is that he can rhyme a lot of words with *ass*."

Her eyes sparkle, dancing with amusement, and after a moment, she sobers. "I always knew you were a poet."

"Only when it comes to you." I tuck her silky hair behind her ear.

"It was beautiful," she whispers.

I move across the pillow to kiss her forehead, then wrap my arm around her shoulders and hold her close. Her body fits into mine like it's always meant to be there.

After a few beats of silence, she untangles herself from me and stands. Pacing by the bed, she fidgets with her hands in front of her.

I sit up and cross my arms around my knees. The longer she remains quiet, the higher my heart rate spikes. "Jersey?"

"Aiden, I need to tell you something."

"What's wrong?"

She shakes her head, smiling. "Nothing's wrong. I've wanted to tell you this for a couple weeks, but I wanted us to be sure about our feelings for each other first. And, well, I can't wait another moment to tell you."

I slide to the edge of the bed, waiting.

"I'm pregnant."

My stomach lurches. "What?"

"I'm pregnant, Aiden."

I blink.

Shocked doesn't even begin to cover what I'm feeling.

"I'm on the pill, but things happen..." She takes hesitant steps toward me, her lips trembling. "I know this isn't what we planned, and maybe the timing isn't great, but this is our second chance. Our second chance to be a family."

I remain frozen, my mind racing with a million thoughts.

My Jersey's swollen stomach. Cradling a baby in my arms.

A tiny hand wrapping around my finger.

"Please say something." She wrings her hands in front of her.

"A baby... we're having a baby." I exhale and jolt forward to scoop her up. "Fucking hell, we're having a baby!"

Her giggles echo around us as I spin her in my arms, my head buried between her breasts.

"I'm going to be a dad," I whisper, setting her back on her feet. I rub my hand down my face, my eyes welling. "We're going to be parents."

"My checkup went well, but there are still many uncertainties, especially given what happened the last time." She gulps. "But you're happy?"

I cup both her cheeks and kiss her. "Of course, I'm happy. I'm ecstatic, and I can't wait to scream it to the world. *A baby*."

She kisses me, squeezing her arms around me. "Yes, but we shouldn't say anything, not yet. I'm still early in my first trimester, and I'd prefer to wait until I'm almost to my third before we tell people."

"Whatever you want." I pull her to me, wrapping my arms around her, breathing her in.

My world.

I'm holding my entire world right here in my arms, and I'll never let go.

CHAPTER THIRTY-FOUR

SAGE

The next morning, I wake up in Aiden's arms, a new sense of peace settled in my chest.

I hum as I stretch my arms above my head, and Aiden's scruffy jaw tickles my cheek as he kisses me there, then places a hot kiss below my ear. His fingertips travel down my arm, my side, until they grip my bare hip.

He captures my lips with his, delving his tongue inside my mouth to gently explore.

The way he wants me—it drives me wild.

"Good morning," he whispers, a smile tugging at his lips.

"Mmm..." I snuggle into him, kissing him as my hands roam his back. "What's for breakfast? We need food. Energy. Coffee—decaf for me, of course."

"Definitely coffee." His gruff voice makes goosebumps erupt down my arms. "That's what I was thinking."

He palms my ass—he is definitely *not* thinking about coffee.

"How about we grab breakfast from the bakery around the corner, and then we come back here for..." I clear my throat. "A shower." My expression is coy when I pull back, and I lift my eyebrow suggestively.

He jumps out of bed like I shocked him and tosses me my bra and shirt.

I laugh as I halfway dress, and he races around the room like this is a restaurant and the health inspector is stopping by.

"You sure are hungry for pastries," I tease.

"Yeah, that's what I'm hungry for." He rolls his eyes, then comes back to bed. Leaning over, his nostrils flare before he nibbles on my bottom lip. "Get your sexy ass out of bed. We need to eat, and then I can have my way with you."

"Yes, sir."

He groans, squeezing his eyes closed. "Don't do that, or we won't make it to breakfast."

"So, you like it when I call you *sir?*" I throw my feet over the edge of the bed and walk to him. Tugging on his shirt, I whisper, "I'll keep that in mind."

He crushes his lips to mine, fisting my hair in his large hand.

Pulling back, he groans again and slaps my ass. "Put some pants on. You're killing me, woman."

Once we're fully dressed, we walk down to the bakery, and his hand grips mine the entire way.

I practically skip, and not just because I'm excited about tasty pastries and hot coffee.

It's because of Aiden.

Because of last night. It was so romantic. What many girls dream of—the guy they love being vulnerable and real with their feelings. Aiden isn't one for the spotlight. When he stood in front of a group of strangers and recited poetry, it made me melt.

It was a grand gesture if there ever was one.

"Are you having any special cravings or anything?" Aiden asks.

"The opposite—I haven't wanted ice cream. Makes me sick even looking at it."

He stops and faces me. "Excuse me? Ice cream? That's blasphemy."

"Right? That's what I said to the baby, but he or she did not care about my needs. Crazy, huh?" I laugh.

"He or she *is* the boss, so we'll go with that."

"But until then, I'm the boss, and I want butter... flaky... everything."

"Yes, ma'am," he mumbles against my lips, then squeezes my hand as we continue walking.

Once inside the bakery, the smell of sweet treats and coffee fills the air, along with the exciting buzz from people starting their day. When we get in line, Aiden kisses the back of my hand and whispers in my ear, "Want to get this to-go? Breakfast in bed?"

"Good idea."

We move up in line, and he never lets go of my hand.

I never want him to.

CHAPTER THIRTY-FIVE
AIDEN

I swallow the last bite of my breakfast sandwich and pick up the remaining item in the box of breakfast foods. "You have to try this cronut."

"I've never had one."

My jaw drops. "You're living in New York now."

"Well, Jersey City, but so?"

I roll my eyes. "I know, Jersey, but it's too close to the city to never have tried a cronut." I hover the pastry by her thin lips. "It's not Dominique Ansel's, but it's one of the best I've had. Crunchy, yet creamy and thick. Heavenly."

"Who's Dominique Ansel?"

I sigh and almost drop the pastry. "You need to be a better New Yorker."

She lifts my hand to her lips and takes a bite of the cronut, while my gaze follows her every move.

Her throat bobbing as she swallows.

Her chest heaving when she moans.

She licks her lips, drawing my attention there. "You'll have to teach me."

I drop my voice. "I can teach you. I can show you many things. New York"—I kiss her neck—"pastries and bagels"—another kiss—"how to shower."

She giggles. "Now, I've had plenty of bagels, and I know how to shower."

"You still need me to reach those... *sensitive* spots." I kiss her lips, savoring the lingering sweet cream there.

She shifts on the bed, moving the box away from us, and kisses me back, her tongue eager to find and explore mine.

"Time for that shower yet, or what?" I grip her thigh that's draped over me.

She nods against me, and I waste no time standing up, scooping her into my arms, and taking her to the bathroom.

"The cronuts!" Her voice strains between laughs. "You knocked them to the floor."

"We'll get more." I set her on her feet in the bathroom and turn the water on. "Right now, we have more pressing matters."

I strip her shirt over her head, then cup her breasts over her bra, noticing how full they are. More than they were a month ago, and it drives me wild.

I tug on her bottom lip with my teeth, swallowing her moan, as she works on undoing my pants.

Once all our clothes are at our feet, I follow her into the shower, my gaze glued to the curve of her perfect ass.

Reaching out, I palm it and lick my lips.

I close the shower door behind us and let the water cascade down our naked bodies.

She rests the back of her head on my chest as my hard length presses against her lower back.

Steam rises around us as I slightly turn her head toward me, so I can nip at her ear, then her shoulder.

I worship her.

I will always worship her like she deserves. She's brought so much light into my life, and now a baby… I'll do whatever it takes to show her how special she is. How much I love her.

How much I'll love our family.

Bending at my knees, I let my length press between her cheeks, rubbing it up and down until her pants are audible over the rushing water.

Without exchanging words, with nothing but our bodies for communication, she places her hands on the tiled wall opposite us and arches her back.

And I'm certain I've died.

I've died, and this is heaven, where I get to have Sage spread out and eager for me anytime we want.

I use my foot to nudge her ankle to the side, so her legs are spread wider.

She's trembling with want.

Desire.

And I'm all too happy to oblige, especially when she glances back at me, her gaze hungry, her lips parted. Tiny droplets of water fall from her bottom lip, then chin.

Waiting.

I grip her hips with both my hands and bring her back to me, sliding into her tight heat in one smooth thrust.

She clenches around me.

I grind my teeth and reach around her to knead her nipple between my thumb and forefinger, making her jerk against me.

The water pelts against my shoulder as I pull out and thrust back in, looking down between us, licking the warm water off my lips as I disappear inside her.

Her moans echo against the tile, and each one fuels me to move faster, harder, deeper. I pump into her with vigor.

She slumps against the wall, her breasts pressed against the tile, her back curved as her ass hits my stomach with every thrust.

I rest my hand against the wall next to her cheek, and her slow cries grow louder the faster I move.

Until her body tenses and explodes in my arms.

I soon follow, tightening my hold around her limp and satisfied body as I empty my release deep inside her, marking her until my dying breath.

And when that happens, when it's time for me to go, I'll imagine Jersey's glowing smile, her feminine sounds, her sweet taste, and I'll die with a fucking smile on my face.

I pull out and turn her around to kiss her, pushing my body flush against hers as the water slowly cools. "We better hurry and use what's left of the hot water." I smooth her hair back, admiring her lazy eyes.

Her flushed cheeks.

"Then, you better get to work and show me how to properly bathe already. I'm filthy," she whispers, her voice low and seductive, then grabs the shampoo.

I cup my hands for her to pour some into my palm, then lather it in her hair. She does the same for me, and our gazes remain locked as we massage the shampoo onto one another's head.

It's simple, but with her, this is sensual. *Intimate.*

I've never been this intimate with anyone other than Sage. Never recited poetry I wrote for anyone. Never loved anyone as deeply as I do her—so deeply that I'll do anything to make her happy. Anything just for a small smile, even.

We take turns rinsing, then repeat.

Afterward, I rub every inch of her soft skin with soap—her shoulders, arms, and back. I take extra care when I get to her breasts, lathering them with circular motions.

We move in sync. In a relaxed rhythm like this is a normal Sunday. And suddenly I want this to be every morning for us, enjoying each other.

When I reach between her legs, rubbing along the swollen seam of her, her eyes flutter. I fight my urge to get lost there again.

I'll never get enough of her.

I then move out of the way and let her rinse off while the water is still at a bearable temperature.

Once we're both clean and rinsed off, all I want to do is dirty her up again.

To hear my name on her lips.

To consume her like she's consumed me.

We remain standing in the shower, both staring at each other like we're waiting for the other to make the next move.

So, I take the lead and run my hand down her stomach, past her belly button, between her legs again. I swallow her gasp as I kiss her lips without removing my fingers from her most sensitive spot.

I rub circles on the bundle of nerves that are tensing once again.

"I can't tell for sure, but you're wet again, aren't you?"

She nods, then gulps as her eyes slowly open.

"You're so perfect."

"And you—" She sharply inhales, digging her nails into my skin, when I sink two fingers inside of her.

"Yes?" I breathe against her jawline as I continue working her.

"How do you... do... that?" she asks between pants.

"What? Make you hot? Needy?" I run my nose along her cheek, breathing her in, wanting so badly to taste her.

Growling, I pull my fingers out, and her eyes widen when I reach for the door to the shower.

"What're you doing?" She grabs my arm.

"I'm freezing." I shrug, trying my best to hide my enjoyment at seeing her pout. I slide the door open and grab a towel from the hook.

She scoffs and pulls me back to her. "You better finish what you started, Baxter, or so help me... My hormones are not to be messed with right now."

Chuckling, I kiss her lips, then kneel, kissing between the valley of her breasts on my way down. I place another lingering kiss on her stomach, gazing up at her as I continue farther down until I'm on my knees and push her legs open.

I lift her leg over my shoulder and steal a glance at her as she braces herself on the bar outside the shower.

Her pupils dilate.

Filled with hunger.

My sexy firecracker.

I swipe my tongue along her heat, enjoying the

taste of her, already missing it when I pull back to lick my lips.

I continue my assault, licking every sweet inch of her.

Her hips buck.

The bathroom fills with more fog.

After a few more swipes of my tongue along the seam of her, she moves her hips, riding my face, seeking her pleasure.

It's sexy.

So fucking sexy when she comes alive like this, under my touch.

For me.

Gripping her ass with both my hands, I continue sucking her until she trembles with her climax rippling through her in waves.

She cries my name.

She falls apart in my arms.

She's mine—right where she belongs.

When she smiles down at me, a warm, sparkling smile, I know this is the beginning of the rest of our lives.

CHAPTER THIRTY-SIX

SAGE

Taylor: Are you almost here?

She's at the office already? She's early.

I type out a message to her, then glance up to make sure I'm not walking into oncoming traffic.

Me: Two blocks away. Everything okay?

Once I make it safely across the street, I check the new message from Taylor.

Taylor: Yeah. But you don't want to miss this.

Confused, I pick up my pace and race toward CJJ. I'm almost out of breath when I reach the double doors and head inside.

When I step off the elevator, Taylor stands outside her office, her arms crossed.

The whole suite is quiet. No clicking keys, ringing phones, or light chatter.

The few people, mostly assistants, pretend to look busy, but they keep stealing glances toward Mr. Cartright's office.

There are muffled voices coming from that direction, and all I can make out is Mr. Cartright's voice that someone isn't a team player and that they're causing more drama than they're worth.

I jump when Piper flings the door to his office open and rushes out, her hands balled into fists at her sides.

Once I reach Taylor, I set my things on my desk. "What's going on?"

"Piper *finally* got fired." She bites her nail, a slow grin spreading, and she claps. "Hot damn, it's the best wedding present I could've received."

"What?" I freeze.

"I knew all I had to do was wait for karma to bite her on the ass."

Frowning, I clutch my chest. *She got fired?* I mean, I didn't like the woman, but I didn't expect her to lose her job.

"Don't be sad." Taylor points at me. "You're not going to feel so bad for her when you find out what she did." Taylor leans her hip against the edge of my desk.

Bending toward where I sit in my seat, she says, "That snake is the one who fed Tank McAllister the garbage about Jock Stock. Evidently, she's friends with his girlfriend and whispered shit to her about the company."

"Are you kidding me?" My jaw drops.

"I wish." She grimaces. "She simply cannot stand for other people to be successful."

"Do you think…" I glance from her to Piper's office to my computer. "You don't think that's what she was doing on my computer, do you? Trying to get information on Jock Stock?"

"That's exactly what happened." She stands upright.

"But how did she know my password? I keep it locked at all times like they taught us in our cybersecurity training."

"I talked with Maya before all this, and Piper, the little minx, slept with the IT guy and sexed your password of out him. The little—"

There's a crash in Piper's office, drawing our attention there. After a moment, she emerges, her mascara-streaked face scrunched. She narrows her eyes at us like her dismissal is our fault and storms in our direction.

"I hope you're happy," she sneers at Taylor. "You've had it out for me since I got here just because I didn't like your stupid boss."

"Catherine did nothing wrong." Taylor's face

reddens. "Why do you insist on blaming everyone else? Why can't you see *you're* the problem?" Taylor steels herself in a challenge. "I didn't make you sabotage our client."

She scoffs, then squares her shoulders. "You didn't deserve them as clients to begin with. They're out of your league." Piper turns her scathing glare toward me. "And you. You come in here trying to act like you're better than everyone."

I shake my head, confused. "Piper—"

She points to both Taylor and me, her face red. "I don't know what game you're playing, but I'm going to figure it out. You'll pay for this. I—"

"Piper!" Mr. Cartright steps out of his office, his hands on his hips, as the security guard from downstairs enters the suite to escort her out.

I dip my head and turn my focus to my computer.

Piper's sobs echo as she rushes out of the office with the guard right behind her.

Once the coast is clear, I pop into Taylor's office. "How did you figure it all out?"

She leans back in her chair. "I had my suspicions, which were all but directly confirmed when I met with Tank's agent. He refused to give up her name, so I didn't have proof." She throws her finger up. "But then, Maya's client mentioned a dark-haired woman, who looked a lot like Piper, sniffing around trying to poach them. From there, I kept a close eye on her and found her getting real chummy with the IT guy in the break room. I asked him about her, and the rest came tumbling down."

"I can't believe it." I worry my bottom lip. "What do we do now? Can we reach out to Tank's people again?"

She taps her fingers on her desk. "I'm going to try Tank's agent and see if he can publicly retract his attack now. I couldn't convince him at the meeting. The evidence of Jock Stock's legitimacy wasn't enough for them, but I bet I know a new angle to try this time —discrediting Piper, for starters."

"I have an idea too," I say at the same time she snaps her fingers and says, "There's another tactic we can try."

I swallow the lump in my throat and wait for her to go on, but she stares at me expectantly. "You go ahead," I offer.

"No, no. What're you thinking?"

"What if Tank tries the app and sees for himself? I mean, they've completed countless beta tests. Since the numbers and feedback you gave McAllister didn't work, why not let him try the product?"

"That's exactly what I'm thinking!" She nods. "He can get a firsthand look at it and feel more assured that the app is legitimate."

"Definitely," I beam.

"It's perfect." She picks up her phone, then drops it

before I turn. "Don't be afraid to speak up, Sage. I want to hear your ideas."

I give her a small smile, agreeing to do so in the future, then walk back to my desk, feeling lighter.

It's almost lunch time when Taylor re-emerges from her office. She leans her hip against my desk again and grins—it's a victorious one. "I made a few calls and finally got through to Tank's agent, and I spoke with Westin too. We're going to all sit down tomorrow afternoon and arrange for Tank to try out the app."

"Fantastic. I can't wait to tell—"

"There's more." She rubs her hands together. "If all goes well from there, we're going to discuss Tank's public retraction and endorsement of the app, and there's a possibility Tank will make an appearance at the launch party."

I raise my eyebrows. "Seriously? That would all be huge."

"Bigger than huge." She bounces against my desk like we've discovered gold, which in a way, we have. "Dare I say Piper's meddling was a blessing?"

"I think it's fair to admit."

"We have a lot of work to do. Can you order us some lunch? We'll eat in my office."

"Will do."

My phone vibrates on the desk with a message from Aiden.

Aiden: Tank McAllister might come to our party? Are you kidding?

Me: Well, there are still a few moving parts, but aren't you glad you hired us?

I add a kissy emoji and sit back, a large weight lifted off my shoulders.

Aiden: Yes, for many reasons. Mainly because it brought you back to me.

I sink into my chair, melting like a bowl of ice cream during a hot summer afternoon.

"I assume Aiden put this blush on your cheeks?" Taylor appears next to me, and I jump in my seat. "Everything's going well, then?"

"Better than well." I smile, blushing harder as I think about our shower a few mornings ago.

"I'm glad to see you like this, Sage." She pats my shoulder and walks away toward the restrooms, leaving me with so much warmth in my chest.

It's good to feel this way—*happy*.

An hour later, my cell phone rings, and Aiden's face lights up my screen.

"Let's go out this weekend," he says as soon as I answer. "Somewhere romantic. Wear something sexy."

I picture the dress I already bought for this weekend, and I can imagine Aiden's drool.

I peer over my shoulder at Taylor behind her desk. Her ring shines when she switches the phone to her other ear. "What's more romantic than a wedding?" I ask him.

There's a pause on his end.

"Aiden?"

He clears his throat. "What do you mean?"

"Taylor's getting married this weekend, remember?"

"Oh, right. I forgot that was coming up so soon."

"What did you think I meant?" I giggle.

"When should we go?" He sidesteps my question altogether.

"The wedding is Saturday, but we should stay a few days. Make a mini-vacation out of it. What do you say?"

"I like the sound of that." He perks back up.

"Okay. I have to get back to work, so I can put all my focus on you this weekend."

"That's an even better idea. Get to it. And, Jersey?"

"Yeah?"

"Love you."

I hang up, feeling heat creep to my cheeks again, blushing like he screamed to the whole office that we'll be together this weekend.

Which will hopefully include a lot of naked time.

I take in the office—they've mostly resumed business as usual. People walk around with coffee mugs, papers in the crooks of their arms, Bluetooth headsets on.

But there's a special feeling in the air. The kind similar to Christmas.

When I first came to this city, when I first entered this office, I was optimistic. I was ready to start fresh and hoped for the best.

But now... my life is becoming so much more than I ever dreamed. More than the things on my bucket list. More than anything my imagination could've conjured.

I have a job that could launch my career and my future. Friends who keep me sane. A man who loves me.

A baby on the way.

The past is behind us, a new future lies ahead, and for the first time in a while, I'm moving forward with a mended heart.

There's something about weddings. The flowers, music, and people gushing. The love at their center.

When we first arrived at Taylor and Joe's ceremony earlier, my stomach sank. The white arch decorated in peonies and baby's breath with green accents. The sun shining through the windows. The soft piano music.

It reminded me of my wedding. Of what was supposed to be the best day of my life, but there was so much missing that day. It wasn't like Taylor's day, which has been filled with family, friends, and loud, joyous chaos as everyone dotes on the newlyweds.

Watching Taylor with her mother almost gutted me.

I haven't spoken with my mom since our phone call when I told her how disappointed I was, not that she's tried to contact me. I wish I could be close to her.

That I could go to my mother when I need advice or even a simple hug.

But I've never had that kind of relationship with her. I thought we could after I divorced Dave. All these years, I thought he was the problem, the one who put even more distance between my mother and me, but as it turns out, my mother and I are simply two different people with different values—to put it nicely, anyway.

I've vowed every day since I found out I'm having a baby that I wouldn't turn into her. That I'll be driven in my career, but I'll always put my child first.

I'll attend as many school plays and recitals as I can.

And I'll most certainly put my child's report cards up on the refrigerator and tell them how proud of them I am.

Aiden too.

He and I made it to the hotel last night in time to wash up and go to a candlelight dinner at a restaurant on the water. We held hands as we walked along the boardwalk afterward.

The sea breeze fanned my hair.

I could almost taste salt on his lips when I kissed him underneath the stars.

It was a quiet night, but when we got back to our hotel room, he made me scream. Tremble. Writhe.

He made me come so many times, it was like he

was trying to beat a record, which was more than fine by me. I'm crazy about him as it is, but these new hormones heighten my sensitivity.

I steal one more glance at Aiden from my spot on the dance floor, where I wait for Taylor to toss the bouquet.

He's had a funny look about him all evening. A bright glimmer in his eyes. A constant twitch of his lips like he has a secret.

He's extra sexy tonight too. His beard is trimmed to a mere scruff, and he got his hair cut before we left for the weekend, which makes him seem less rugged and chaotic but still as intense as usual.

This new peace about him makes the butterflies in my stomach run wild.

After Catherine catches the bouquet, holding it up like she won an Olympic trophy, I practically bounce to my seat next to Aiden. I kiss his lips, then pull back as a server asks if we'd like a glass of champagne.

Aiden grabs two and starts to hand me one, but stops himself. "When will you be able to drink again?" he whispers. "Because obviously, I'm having a hard time getting it through my brain."

I giggle, scooting closer to him. "If it makes you feel better, I have a hard time remembering too."

"How are you feeling?"

"Better after I got some carbs in me." I rub my stomach, recalling the numerous trips to the bathroom today. "They should call it all-day sickness instead of morning sickness."

He squeezes my hand, bringing it to his lips, and kisses my knuckles.

"Sage!" Catherine and Taylor wave me back to the dance floor.

"Be right back." I kiss Aiden's cheek and pull my dress up, so I don't step on it as I walk toward them.

"Catherine, it's great to see you again." I give her a hug. "How have you been? California still treating you well?"

"Always, especially with my assistant Tristan by my side. He's been a godsend." She holds her hand over her chest as the other with the bouquet drops to her side. "I thought I'd never recover when I lost Taylor, but Tristan has been amazing."

"He's not as great as me, but I'm glad you found someone." Taylor touches her shoulder with her free hand while the other holds her dress up. She's stunning in her floor-length ivory gown that hugs her slim curves. "And I too found someone perfect for me."

I dip my head, blushing.

"I would not have survived work and planning a wedding and remembering to eat without Sage." She turns to me. "You literally saved my life."

"You're very sweet." I hug her, squeezing my arms around her. "Thank you for everything."

"Taylor tells me you've been a great asset and do a lot of the social media marketing," Catherine says.

"Taylor's put a lot of her trust in me."

"Because she deserves it." Taylor hooks her thumb at me. "She's been kicking ass and will not be my assistant for long."

"Oh, I..." My throat goes dry as I glance between them.

Taylor turns her sly grin toward me. "With Piper gone, we're going to need a new publicist soon, and Catherine here still has a lot of pull with Cartwright and the other partners."

I blink between them. "Are you serious?"

Catherine smiles into her drink, then takes a sip.

Taylor squeezes my hand. "Honey, you're over-qualified to be an assistant, but we all have to start somewhere. It's New York, and CJJ is a premier company. It's the big league, so starting as an assistant was good for you to learn the ropes and climb, babe."

I try to swallow to wet my dry throat, but it's difficult. Being a publicist at CJJ would be a dream come true—everything I've worked for. "That would be amazing, Taylor," I manage, still stunned. "Thank you so much for believing in me."

"I knew you had it in you. It's why I hired you." She shrugs like it's no big deal. As if she's not making my heart so full it could burst.

A handsome man with blue-green eyes and dark

brown hair appears by Catherine's side. She closes her eyes when he kisses her cheek. Turning back to me, she says, "We'll talk soon." She wraps her arms around the man's waist and introduces him to me. "This is my boyfriend, Jackson. Jackson, this is Sage, Taylor's kick-ass assistant."

"Nice to meet you." I shake his large hand, taking note of the dimple in his left cheek when he smiles. It gives him a boyish quality, a contradiction to his commanding stance and deep, throaty voice.

"Great to meet you too, Sage." He nods as I feel a warm hand on my lower back. Aiden appears at my side, and I introduce him to the group as well.

"Aiden is a client too. Sound familiar?" Taylor eyes Catherine and Jackson, a teasing smile on her pale pink lips.

Catherine rolls her eyes and snuggles deeper into Jackson's side as he says, "Something about you CJJ women. You have some kind of magnet pulling us to you. We don't have a choice but to fall for you."

Catherine tosses her hair over her shoulder. "It's the competitive side you love."

"That's definitely it." Aiden squeezes my hip. "This one tried to fight me over a cronut. I knew I never should've introduced her to the best pastry in New York."

"You did this to yourself." I shrug, earning me laughs from the group.

Joe joins us as a server comes by with a tray of champagne, which they all accept. I shake my head when the server offers me one. I take a glass of water instead and raise it to meet theirs in a toast to the happy couple.

I sigh into Aiden's side as guests clink their silverware against their glasses, signaling for Taylor and Joe to kiss.

When they do, I place my hand over my chest, smiling widely for them. For their future together and their happily ever after.

Taylor deserves all the happiness in the world, and I'm fortunate to have run across her ad for a new assistant. Yet again, I count my blessings that she took a chance and saw potential in me.

Now, I might be promoted soon.

I always heard New York is fast-paced. A whirlwind. And they're right. I've only been here for almost five months, and my life has already drastically changed.

For the better.

CHAPTER THIRTY-EIGHT

AIDEN

"What were you thinking about all day?" she asks as we settle down from our high, pulling the covers over us. "You were smiling the way you do when you think about Pop-Tarts. Or my ass."

I kiss her temple. "I'm always thinking about your ass. It's too perfect not to."

She nudges me with her shoulder. "Seriously, what is it?"

"Just thinking about you."

"Oh," she breathes, shifting the covers to inch closer to me.

My mouth and hands were all over her the second we stepped inside our hotel room after the reception. We didn't even make it to the bed before I was inside her, pumping into her, bracing her against the wall.

All night, we danced and hung out with Catherine,

Taylor, and their guys. Sage's chest moved up and down when she laughed, making her breasts push up against her dress like they were about to spill over.

My hands itched to touch her.

And I snapped the second I got her alone.

She didn't mind, either. She was wet for me. Her hands were frantic. Her movements wild like she was feeling the exact same about me—she had to have me.

"What were you talking to Taylor and Catherine about? The trouble you got into when you were in Vegas?" I joke, recalling the lemon drop shots Taylor mentioned.

"What? No." She playfully smacks my chest. "I couldn't do much, anyway, since I was already pregnant at the time."

I rub her stomach. She's still not showing, but I know she's carrying our miracle. After a moment, I lie back. "You never did tell me about that trip. I've been wondering..."

"About the strippers we saw?"

"What?" I growl. "You went to see strippers?"

I feel her warm breaths against me as she laughs. "Don't worry. I was just hit on once, but I only have eyes for you."

I hug her tightly. "That helps a little, but the idea of some guy shaking his junk—"

"Aiden?" She brings my face to hers and kisses me, then whispers against my lips, "I love you."

I sigh. "I love you too. So damn much."

I kiss her softly, then lie back, closing my eyes, forgetting what we were talking about. All I can think about is some guy half-naked on stage hitting on my girl.

"You're shaking."

I open one eye and stare at the ceiling, but she comes into view, her hair mussed from where I ran my hands through it.

Her amusement is obvious. "You're hot when you're jealous."

"I'm not jealous."

"You are. Your whole body is tense, and you have this crease in your forehead." She rubs her thumb from my hairline down, between my eyebrows.

I sigh again. "I'm being ridiculous. Go ahead. Say it."

"You're ridiculous... but I like it." She kisses me, running her hands through my hair. "Can I tell you what Catherine and Taylor were talking to me about now?"

I sit up against the headboard, bringing her with me. "Yes, please, change the subject."

"You know how Piper was fired? Well, her position has yet to be filled."

"Right..."

"Taylor thinks I'd be perfect for it. She said Catherine has some pull and that we'd talk soon."

"Jersey..." I cup both her cheeks. "That's amazing."

"It is, isn't it?" Her eyes shine with wistful tears. "It was hard selling my business in North Carolina. I felt like I was really helping people, and I loved it. But I'm realizing that it was for the better. I mean, I could be a publicist here, in New York City. I could have clients like you. Dreamers of all kinds. I could help people's businesses be successful, but this would be on a much bigger stage. Like moving from high school theater to Broadway."

"That's great news." I place a firm kiss to her lips. "And you deserve it."

She dips her head.

I know it must've been hard to build her business, then to sell it, but it got her here. She's strong. She makes the difficult decisions in order to do better. To do more. To kick ass in a world like Manhattan that often chews the faint of heart up and spits them out.

I lift her chin and meet her gaze. "You fucking deserve this. All of it. You've worked hard and continue doing so every day. And you're not going to stop there, either. Big things are coming for you."

"For both of us." She leans into my hand on her cheek.

I swallow the lump in my throat. I love how much she cares about my success, like it's her own.

It's sexy.

And makes me love her more.

"For both of us," I repeat.

It feels like we're taking on the world together. Like we can do anything as long as we're a team.

It's what I've been missing. Someone to share successes with.

It feels good and right and even better that it's the woman my heart has waited for.

———

Sage steps out of the bathroom, running a comb through her wet hair. "You're still in bed?"

I sit up, exposed from the waist up.

Her hungry gaze lands on my bare abs, traveling farther south, and as much as I'd like to haul her back to bed with me, there's something I need to talk with her about. I stare out the window. At the sailboats in the distance. The clear day.

Being at the wedding yesterday, seeing Taylor and Joe with their families, made me miss my own more than usual. It's time I make visiting them a priority.

"What's wrong?" The bed dips where she sits next to me.

I tear my gaze from the window and face her. "After the launch, I want to visit my parents and sisters. Since I left, I've only gone back for Mia's and Avril's graduations, and I'm long overdue. I want you to come with me, if you can take a couple days off."

"Really?"

I intertwine my fingers through hers. "Yeah. I'd like for you to meet them."

She slides her other hand onto our joined hands. "I'd like that. I'll talk to Taylor first thing tomorrow morning."

"They're not going on a honeymoon?"

"They're going after Jock Stock launches. She wanted to wait for a honeymoon, anyway, and this works out."

I kiss her forehead. "Now, let's get something to eat because I know how angry you get when your stomach starts growling."

"Especially since I'm eating for two."

"Exactly. I noticed a little café along the boardwalk our first night here. I think you'd like it."

"You know me too well." She scoots to the edge of the bed, glancing over her shoulder at me. "You know what else I want to do at some point?"

I raise my eyebrow as her smile becomes wistful.

"How good are you at Frisbee still?"

I scoff. "Even better than when I was in college. Why?"

"I was thinking we could play, say, in Central Park sometime. I haven't been able to enjoy The Lawn yet, and Frisbee with you would be perfect. Especially now that the weather is so nice."

"Summers in New York always are."

"So, what do you say?"

I crawl toward her and kiss the back of her head. "I say, yes, and you're going down."

"We'll see." She goes to stand but whirls around again. "And maybe we can take a cooking class?"

I raise my eyebrows, my lips twitching. I'm not a cook—and I don't say that lightly. I'm the kind of monster who can't even make a peanut butter sandwich. I mean, I *can*, but I always smear too much of it in one corner instead of evenly spreading it.

But there's nothing I wouldn't do for my Jersey.

"Yeah. We'll take a cooking class." I nod. "But a basic one that shows us how to boil water or something."

She kisses my cheek, then pulls back, giggling. As she hops up to dry her hair, I'm left with my chest swelling.

We've been making so many plans for the future.

This is how we were always supposed to be, Sage and me.

The wedding, watching Taylor and Joe exchange vows, gave me a second idea, beyond visiting my family.

But I'm going to need to be patient—one thing at a time.

I need to do this right.

CHAPTER THIRTY-NINE

AIDEN

Soft wisps of hair fall from the bun on top of her head.

I take in the curves of her shoulders. Her naked torso. The sheet is bunched around her waist as she faces the window, and her breasts are on display for the city beyond.

Sage makes me weak in the knees.

She's spent almost every night for the last month here, and the more time we spend together, I'm a better man with her next to me.

She shows me a new world.

We've been crazed with the launch coming up next week, and we appointed a board. They've been on our asses. Every day is a new challenge, and it takes a lot of energy to stay on top of it all.

But at night—at night, it's Sage and me and the

moans between us as we get lost in each other. For those few hours, we think of nothing else.

Even in the chaos, we're each other's peace.

I clear my throat, but it doesn't faze her. "What're you doing?"

She scribbles something on her notepad, then says over her shoulder, "I'm writing."

I'm not surprised. She's been writing a lot lately, especially since she read one at open mic last week. Her face reddened as she bared her soul to the room. She was brave, like I always knew, and I felt insurmountable pride.

I kneel on the bed and lie beside her, running my fingertips down her bare back. "What's your inspiration this morning?"

She makes another note on her paper, shivering as I continue rubbing her back. "Tina."

"The woman who does hot yoga in the nude?" I blink, raising my eyebrows in confusion.

"Yeah." She smiles down at her paper, makes another note, then meets my gaze. "She was having another yoga session, sans bra, and it got me thinking."

"Tell me more," I whisper, waggling my eyebrows.

She rolls her eyes. "I was thinking that she's in her apartment, doing yoga alone. A tiny speck in this vast city that is so crowded it often feels like you're in the middle of the whole world. And she's there, in the living room of her small apartment, naked, even though many neighbors and people walking below on the sidewalk can clearly see her." She peers down at her notebook, scanning the words and crossed out lines, then frowns. "Like she's crying out for attention, desperate for someone to *see* her."

I grip her behind her neck, running my thumb across her cheek.

"We're a lot like her. All of us. Maybe we're not all trying to be seen by the world, but by someone. Someone special. It makes us feel loved, a rare sentiment, don't you think?"

"That's beautiful." I bring her down to kiss her lips. "Can I read the poem?"

She snatches the notebook up to her chest. "Not until it's ready."

I tilt my head to the side. "Duh."

She worries her bottom lip. "I'm going to submit it to hopefully be published."

"Really?" I prop myself on my elbow.

Her eyes are as bright as the sun this morning. "I want to try to put myself out there again, beyond reading in front of people only to hide afterward. I want something permanent." She dips her head. "And I don't want the last poems I submitted to be the ones from college. From when I was in a bad place."

"Hey..." I lean up, gripping her cheeks again. "We've come a long way since then. And I have no doubt your poems will forever be printed in a magazine. They'll be crazy not to want them."

She kisses me, crushing her lips to mine with sudden fervor, and I roll onto my back, pulling her with me until she straddles me.

I cup her swollen breast, kneading her hard nipple between my thumb and forefinger.

She moans into my mouth and arches her back into my touch. "We can't," she murmurs against my lips, but she doesn't stop kissing me. "You need to... you have to work."

"Maybe I'll skip today." I dip my head toward her breast and pull the bud into my mouth, between my teeth, sucking on the sweet taste of her.

She cups the back of my head to keep me there, but between pants, she stutters, "You... can't skip... They... need you."

"What about you?" I mumble as I move to her other breast. "What do you need?"

I love the weight of her breasts in each hand. They're full and perky and perfect.

And since the pregnancy, she's extra horny too —so hot.

"I... need this. God, that feels fucking good."

I hum against her as I continue sucking on her obviously sensitive nipples. She loves when I do this— and I'm always quick and willing to oblige—but this morning, she seems to be enjoying it even more.

Her moans are louder.

She's needier.

And I get lost in her, putting aside all the work I have to do today.

She tugs me back by my hair, blinking down at me.

"Ow," I groan, squeezing one eye closed as she loosens her grip on my hair.

She shakes her head, rapidly blinking like she's trying to remember where she is. "You need to go to work." She clears her throat. "I have to be at work in an hour too."

"Buzzkill." I kiss her lips, then jump up, adjusting my erection over my boxers. "I can't go to work with this."

She crawls to the edge of the bed and wraps her arms around my neck. "I'll make it up to you tonight."

"I'll hold you to it." I palm her ass as I give her one more kiss.

"I love you. Now, go." She smiles as she shoos me away.

"Okay, okay. I'm gone." I grin, enjoying the new routine we've settled into.

One I could definitely get used to—and plan to.

Just a few days to go now.

CHAPTER FORTY

SAGE

My hand trembles as I put the finishing touches on my makeup. This is it—the night. This is what we've been working so hard on for months, and I can't help but run through every detail in my head to think of something we might've missed.

Although Taylor and I thought of everything—or at least most of everything—I have this strange feeling we overlooked a crucial detail.

"It'll be great," I reassure myself.

Squaring my shoulders, I leave the bathroom and slip into my dress. It's long and flowy, which covers the early signs of my baby bump, and the way it pushes my breasts up makes me feel sexy. Naomi helped me pick it out, and I bought it solely for this occasion.

For Aiden's big night.

I pull my phone out to check in with Naomi. She took a change of clothes with her to the hospital, so she can meet us at the venue straight from work. She'll be tired, but it means a lot that she cares so much and wants to be there for the guys and me.

I poke my head out of Aiden's front door and find him pacing the hall as he talks into his phone. He's mumbling, so I can't make out what he's saying, but his deep laugh puts me at ease that everything's fine.

"We're going to be late if you don't hurry. For the first time in history, we're going to be late," I tell him, walking out into the hall.

He glances up with a mischievous gleam in his eye, then hangs up and stalks toward me.

His hair is styled to the side. He's in a crisp suit, much like the one he wore to Taylor's wedding last month, but this is a deeper navy color, and the pale blue shirt underneath works perfectly.

He looks good. Sexy and smart, and he's about to become an icon of the sports industry.

When he reaches me, I run my fingers through his hair and nibble on his bottom lip. "Your hair grows so fast."

"I love when you talk dirty to me," he teases, wrapping his arms around me.

I tilt my head, playing with the hair at the nape of his neck. "We really will be late if you want me to get—"

He groans, resting his head on mine. "I do want. I want very much for you to strip out of this stupid dress and get dirty."

"Stupid?" I pull out of his embrace and do a little spin, showing him my red dress that dips low in the back.

When I face him again, I smile with victory.

Rubbing his chin, his nostrils flare as he slowly narrows his gaze at me. "What do you say we show up fashionably late? I've heard people talk about how fun that is, although I've never understood it. But I can be on board."

I tsk at him, pulling him inside. "We'll save that for our celebratory, private after-party."

Once we're inside, he presses his front flush against my back, wrapping his arm around my stomach, splaying his fingers at my belly button. "I'll definitely hold you to that," he whispers in my ear, sending a shiver down to my toes.

I place my hand over his on my stomach, and warmth spreads throughout my entire body.

Aiden kisses my cheek, then whispers, "Are you sure you don't want to tell anyone yet? Because I'm dying here."

Keeping this secret has been hard on me too. I've wanted to tell Taylor, and Aiden's desperate to share with the guys and his family. But I keep insisting we wait. Last time, I miscarried at around eighteen weeks, and I could hardly stand having to tell people I lost her.

So, I'm being extra cautious now.

"I know." I sigh. "But we need to be certain before we share."

He nods against me. "I'm just... I'm happy, Jersey."

"Me too," I whisper, leaning into him, holding his arms around me.

Right where I want to be.

"Ready to do this?" I turn in his arms, splaying my fingers across his chest.

"With you by my side, I'm ready for anything." He kisses my temple, then pulls back. "Too cheesy?"

"Nah." I kiss his lips, smiling. "I like when you're cheesier than a cheese pizza for me."

He throws his head back and laughs. "Now, *that* was too much. Does pregnancy make us both outrageously dorky?"

"Dorky?" I scoff as we head toward the front door. "Speak for yourself."

His chuckle rumbles from deep in his throat, echoing around the walls of this loft.

When I turn around, I sharply inhale as I take him in. The top few buttons of his shirt remain open, revealing his smooth and tan chest.

I clear my throat and place my hand on his cheek, tracing his jawline with the tip of my forefinger as I bask in this world where Aiden and I have a second chance at love.

At a family.

I nod, giving him a watery smile. "Let's do this."

In the cab, I run my finger over the velvet box in my pockct. All month, I spent every spare moment looking at different styles and cuts. Several stores and jewelers. So many diamonds I feared growing cross-eyed.

Until I finally found the right one. One that's fitting for my Jersey. One she'll love.

She turns to me, threading her fingers through mine. "I want you to know I'm very proud of you, and I'm so lucky to be here to witness you and your glory. Taylor even told me she's got tonight under control and that I should join you for the fun. This is a big night, and she knows how much I want to be there for you."

I kiss the back of her hand, then her lips, thankful she's here too.

"You don't know what a first down is?" I stare at her.

She pops a french fry in her mouth. "No. Should I?"

"Yes. You should... I mean, how... how can you not know anything about football?" I sputter.

She shrugs, and her nose wrinkles like she smells something foul.

It's adorable.

It distracts me from what we're even talking about.

"So, explain it to me." She tosses a fry in my direction when I don't answer.

My friend Carter snorts beside me, and I kick him under the table.

After half an hour of me explaining the game to her, including drawing diagrams on napkins, she nods her head and says, "I think I'm ready to play now."

"To play football?" I raise my eyebrows.

"Yeah, why not? Because I'm a woman?" she challenges.

"No. Because it can be rough." I sip my drink.

"I can get rough."

I choke as my mind goes dark.

Dirty.

For my friend's girl.

"That sounded weird." She blushes. "What I mean is, I'm tougher than I look." She checks the time on her phone and groans as she stuffs her trash into a paper bag. "Have to get to history. See you guys later."

Once she's out of earshot, I turn to Carter. "It's only a crush."

"I didn't say anything."

"You didn't have to. Your snorts spoke volumes." I roll my eyes, leaning back in my chair in an attempt to seem unaffected. "I don't even know her that well. We just met. My crush will go away."

"You and Sage hang out more than you and I do, and I'm one of your closest friends." Carter leans forward. "You talk about her nonstop."

"She has a boyfriend, who's also my friend. My feelings will go away," I insist.

He shakes his head like he pities me. "You don't just get over love, not when it's dopey, out-of-your-mind love."

"And you're saying that's how I feel about Sage?" I laugh, shaking my head, but inside, my chest tightens.

My throat constricts.

These feelings... they're real. The kind I know won't go away.

When we reach the hotel venue, I hold the door open for her, then give her my arm, and she hooks hers through it. Her red dress dips low, her collarbone prominent, her shoulders rounded.

She glows more and more each day.

I stop her outside the revolving doors. "Do you remember when we were in college, and I tried explaining the rules of football to you?"

Her laugh echoes into the night. "What made you think of that?"

"It was the first time I realized I was in trouble."

Her expression sobers. "What do you mean?"

"It was the first time I realized I had feelings for you."

She gulps, then runs her hand from my cheek to my chest. "I remember... I remember when I first realized it, even though I couldn't admit it."

"Oh yeah?"

"You were showing me how to toss a Frisbee. You touched me, and..." She licks her lips, her eyes glistening. "And I knew."

"I'm sorry."

"For what?" She furrows her eyebrows.

"For ruining your lipstick." I cup her cheek and crush my lips to hers, swallowing her shock.

I fuse my mouth to hers and have to fight with myself to take her hand and walk inside instead of running back to the confines of my loft.

So, I continue holding her close, kissing her, loving her.

She hums when she stops our kiss, and her lips are indeed smudged and swollen.

Using my thumb, I swipe at the corners of her mouth.

"You're forgiven," she whispers.

I tuck her into my side and head toward the front entrance.

My crush on Sage happened almost immediately.

When we met, we connected, but I chalked it to be friendship. It's all we could have at the time.

We were at lunch a couple weeks after we met when I realized my crush was very real and very inappropriate. I always felt guilty having feelings for my friend's girl.

But Sage and I—we were always meant to be.

Hand in hand, we enter the doors and step into our future.

———

"Naomi's pulling up. I'm going to meet her outside." Sage kisses my cheek, then rubs it. She obviously got red lipstick on me, but I don't care.

I don't care to be marked by her.

"Dude, we're almost out of chips and queso, and the party hasn't even started." Jared waves his hand over the table full of food.

"If you would stop eating them, we'd have plenty," Westin scolds like a father would a child.

I chuckle, coming up behind them. "We should've known. I mean, chips are his weakness. That one's on us."

"Sadly, you're right," Westin agrees as Jared rolls his eyes, then crunches on another chip.

"Dude! What did we just say?"

I step back, sure that Westin is about to smack the plate out of his hand.

"You're very pissy tonight. Aren't we supposed to be having fun?" Jared scoffs.

Westin opens his jacket and places his hands on his hips, hanging his head. "You're right. I'm just nervous."

"Don't worry, man. Only the whole world is watching us tonight." I clap him on the shoulder, and Jared snorts on the other side of him.

"Is that your attempt to make me feel better? Because it sucks."

Jared sets his plate down. "At least you're not asking a very important question that will change your life. Does that make you feel better?"

I snap my head sideways to make sure Sage isn't within earshot, then jab Jared in the side. "Keep it down. It's a surprise."

"Everything's in order?" Westin asks, scanning the small gathering of people. It's mostly our team and their family and friends so far. Taylor's here too, running around behind the scenes.

"We're set. I'm keeping things simple, so there wasn't much to do, anyway." I scratch my chin. "But that's for later. Right now, we have guests arriving." I nod to the front door where people enter. Many are wearing a camera around their neck, small notebooks in hand, and they peer around the small space.

Journalists.

They're here to cover the launch—*us*.

Later tonight, Tank McAllister will also be joining us. Tank McAllister, a pro-athlete. He was a dick during that interview, but after I cooled down and we talked, I realized he brought up valid points. After trying out the app for himself, though, he admitted he was wrong about us.

And he'll be here tonight.

It's happening.

"We're ready, right? Everything's in place if the site crashes?" Westin looks between us.

"*When* the site crashes from too many users signing up and buying their stocks, yes. Ethan and Lila are at the office as we speak, holding down the fort until Jared and I get there after Taylor's speech and introductions. Everything's fine," I reassure him, my voice steady.

"You're very calm. Usually, you're the one with sweaty palms and shaking knees."

Jared eyes me too, wearing a matching suspicious expression.

Naomi walks in with Sage on her heel. They're laughing, and Sage's smile brightens her whole demeanor.

Her usually pale cheeks have color in them.

Her dress sways as she moves.

I can't take my eyes off her as she approaches us.

"Oh my God, it's because he's in love." Jared groans, and Westin rolls his eyes.

"That's exactly it." I smirk as Sage slips her hand inside my jacket and wraps her arm around my waist.

"What're we talking about over here?" Sage asks as Naomi greets us.

"You."

Westin wipes his brow, shaking his head, while I glare at Jared.

"Only good things, obviously." He picks his plate back up.

I kiss the top of Sage's head, peering over it as more people file in.

I grab two flutes of champagne from a server and offer Sage one, but she shakes her head. "Damn it, that's right."

"What's right?" Westin asks, confused.

"I, uh…" She waves her hand. "I'm dehydrated is all. I'll drink water."

I sip my champagne and change the subject. "Isn't that Walter Evans?"

"The sportswriter?" Jared follows my line of vision. "Yes," he hisses.

Jersey runs her hand down my arm. "Go dazzle people. Work the room. Sell them on your charm."

Jared scoffs. "Are you sure you want him going? Westin's a much better choice for that."

"Shut up." I smack Jared's arm, then kiss Sage on the lips and do as I'm told.

I tag along with Westin to greet the guests and thank them for their support. Westin does most of the talking, but he makes sure I'm by his side, while Jared wanders off every now and then like a curious toddler.

No matter whom we're talking to, I always find Sage in the growing crowd. Her eyes shine. She points at me occasionally when she talks to people, and her back straightens with pride.

It makes my chest swell.

When Westin and I pull away from our chat with an investor, Taylor appears by our side. "You guys ready? Where's Jared? It's almost time to address and wow the crowd. Introduce you guys. And then, the hard part of the night will be just beginning."

I chuckle as Westin groans.

Taylor glances between us, her eyebrow quirked. "What happened? Aiden's usually the broody one of you two. Did you pull a *Freaky Friday* and switch places or something?"

"He's got his panties in a twist because he hasn't had enough to drink." As I say it, I grab a full glass of champagne from a passing server and hand it to him.

He rolls his eyes but accepts it.

Sage comes up to us. "Good luck." She kisses my lips, lingering there, until Westin clears his throat.

"Good luck to you too, Westin." Giggling, she gives him a hug as well.

We make our way to stand by the stage, grabbing Jared along the way.

"Good evening, everyone," Taylor's greeting echoes throughout the room as she speaks into the microphone. "Thank you so much for coming out to celebrate the launch of Jock Stock." She pauses as the crowd applauds. "The app will go live in one hour, and we're all very excited for the future of this company." She shifts her gaze around the room full of reporters, podcasters, and more, a small smile playing on her lips. She's comfortable, like she belongs on stage. "When I first met Westin, Aiden, and Jared, I instantly saw the potential in them as entrepreneurs. When they told me about their company, I was impressed, and my respect for them only grew as we continued working together. They're hard workers. Intelligent. Determined. And tonight, we celebrate their accomplishments."

She glances over her shoulder and waves us on.

Once we're on stage, Taylor addresses the crowd again. "Now, I'll turn it over to Westin, Aiden, and Jared. Let's start with questions."

Hands go flying.

The crowd buzzes.

And my heart races.

The adrenaline makes me feel alive. Like something truly special is happening in this room. In my life. In this world.

Jock Stock will bring a whole new element to sports and beyond. I've believed in it with my whole being since day one when all it was comprised of was a few letters and numbers fueled by plenty of caffeine.

I instinctively stand off to the side with Jared as Westin takes most of the first few questions. They're simple, mostly regarding our future plans. "It depends on how much more money our investors are willing to give us," he jokes, earning him a resounding laugh. "Seriously speaking, we are grateful for how far we've come, and we don't plan on stopping here. We'll continue to grow. Adapt. And bring even more innovation to sports enthusiasts. There's plenty of potential, and I believe in our team."

Taylor points to a man with his hand raised. "Speaking of the team, there are still many disbelievers out there regarding Mr."—he checks his notes—"Baxter's credibility. Can you speak on that?"

"Of course." Westin points to me, and I stand tall, despite wanting to hide. Taylor warned us already that even though McAllister publicly apologized and endorsed our product, people would still be skeptical. "Over the last two years, we held several rounds of beta testing, both private and public, for each season. We've worked tirelessly as a team to offer the best possible product. A product we believe in. One that we're proud of. We have positive data to support our algorithm's reliability. I'm not only saying this because I've known Aiden for years, and I'm biased. Although those things are true, the fact is, we have a lot of hard evidence to support our work at Jock Stock."

The doors open behind the audience, and a small group of people walks in. They're all tall and built—athletes. I recognize the large-framed guy in front in a leather jacket and fight a smirk.

"What about Tank McAllister's accusations?" the same reporter asks. "Did you or a representative of the company coerce him into his retraction of his initial stance?"

Taylor nods to us, then looks behind the crowd at Tank. "Why don't we ask Mr. McAllister himself?"

Everyone turns, and there's a low hum among the journalists and reporters. Flashes of cameras go off as Tank swiftly walks to the front, his gait purposeful and commanding, probably because he's so used to the pressure of being in front of a crowd.

He waves to a few people and shakes our hands when he reaches the stage. "I won't take the spotlight from these guys right now, but I'm doing everything I can to set the record straight." He peers at the crowd, his jaw hard. "I was given bad information. It's hard for me to admit, but I acted impulsively and took this information to heart—that's on me. Don't punish them for it. I've tested the app myself, and it's legit."

He points at us when the reporter stands back up. "But what you said is true. Mr. Baxter has no formal training or experience with building algorithms. Is that not correct?"

I clench my fists at my side, fighting my instinct to feel shame. The instinct to let them bash me and my capability.

Instead, I step up to Tank, who nods and gives me the microphone.

All eyes are on me.

I'm the center of attention—a rare occasion—and I've put myself here.

"My name is Aiden Baxter." I search for Sage in the crowd, and when I find her, my whole body relaxes. My voice steadies, and my confidence grows. "I'm responsible for the algorithm, although I've had a lot of help from the team. Lila and Ethan are in the offices. Jared's here tonight." I point to him, and he waves. "This has certainly been a team effort. Westin and I might've dreamed up this company, but it's because we've all worked together that we've been able to reach this level."

"What about your—"

"I'm getting to that." I smile. "I'm not going to stand up here and tell you there's no other engineer or developer who could've done a better job than I have —because there are. But I'm done hiding because I sometimes feel like an imposter. I'm like many others out there. I wanted a change, and I went for it. I created my own destiny. I taught myself what I needed to know to help build the algorithm for Jock Stock because it made sense to me. It's part of me. But you don't have to take Tank's or our word for it. In an hour, the product will speak for itself."

I wave before anyone can ask anything else.

I meet Westin at the side, where he stands clapping for me. "Proud of you, man."

I shake his hand, then hug him, feeling a heavy weight lifted.

CHAPTER FORTY-TWO

SAGE

The music in the background picks back up. People shuffle to try to ask Tank and the guys more questions. But all I can focus on is Aiden. He stands tall, stepping off the stage a new man.

My man.

Watching him, I stand taller too, my heart full of pride and happiness for him.

I only tear my gaze from him when a quiet commotion sounds from behind me. When I turn around, I find Taylor nudging a dark-haired woman outside. She looks like...

Piper.

I rush to Taylor's side. *What the hell is she doing here?*

"I'm not going to let you come here, *drunk*, and make a scene." Taylor grabs Piper by the arm, but she jerks away.

"What're you—" Piper sneers when she lays eyes on me. "Oh, look who it is. Wonder Woman here to save the day."

"What're you doing here, Piper?" I steel myself, very aware there are reporters crawling out of the walls of this place right now. We can't afford another PR nightmare.

"*You*." Piper jabs her finger into my shoulder. "You come in here from *Nowhe*re, North Carolina, with your stupid flats and try to steal *my* job? By sleeping with clients, at that? I don't think so."

I hold my hands up. "I was never after *your* job."

"Oh, please. You're the one who got me fired. Or should I say, your little boy toy did, didn't he?" Piper presses as Taylor finally is able to pull her down the hall and outside, away from prying eyes and ears. "Let go of me." Piper shrugs out of Taylor's grasp.

I try to reason with her. "Piper, I know it's hard to lose your job, but you can't crash this launch. You're only making it worse."

She snickers, swaying to the side. "You slut, you got me fired!"

I hold my hands out to steady her. "I've always just done my job. You're the one who leaked information."

"I was going to pin it on you, you know?" She tilts her head back and laughs, the sound high-pitched and evil, and then she sneers at Taylor. "But you had to go and figure out what I was up to. You've always been a thorn in my side, and I refuse—"

Tank emerges from the hotel with a woman by his side. "What the hell are you doing, Piper?"

"Keep your voice down, babe." A woman tugs on his sleeve, glancing around to make sure no one recognizes him, I assume.

Tank peers down at her, his jaw clenched, then points to Piper. "You said she was only here to apologize for what went down. It's the only reason I agreed to let you bring her."

The woman buries her face in her hands.

"I *am* sorry... that my plan didn't work out as expected." Piper tries to walk but rolls her ankle.

"Are you drunk?" Tank puts his hands on his hips, shaking his head, muttering, "Unbelievable."

"You should go before anyone sees us." Taylor brushes past Piper and hails a cab. "Go." She nods toward it.

"I can't believe you're kicking me out. Why are you taking her side?" Piper crosses her arms, facing me, and grimaces like it's painful for her to talk about me.

"It was never about taking sides, Piper." Taylor shakes her head. "Sage is good at what she does and has earned her place at CJJ. You're the one who stooped low enough to get yourself fired."

"I wouldn't have had to if your assistant hadn't

been sleeping with your client, spreading rumors about me and trying to outdo me."

"Are you insane? I never spread anything about you." I blink, shocked that she's accusing me of such juvenile games.

Maybe it's the booze talking, but she's delusional.

"I thought the ladies asked you to leave." Tank steps forward. "You need to go before you embarrass yourself further."

He leads her toward the cab and helps her inside as if he's a cop, ducking her head into the back of the car. She mumbles the entire time, slurring her final attempts at more jabs against us all.

As the cab drives away, Aiden joins us, along with Westin and Jared. "What did we miss?"

"Just Cruella de Vil getting what she deserved." Taylor shrugs.

Aiden wraps his arm around my shoulder, looking down at me questioningly.

"Piper was here, wasted and..." I shake my head. "I'll explain the rest later."

Tank turns his large frame toward us, his eyebrows furrowed. "I'm so sorry. I swear, I did not bring her here to cause drama. I truly thought she only wanted to make amends." He looks past us at his girlfriend, his expression disappointed.

"I didn't know, either. I thought the same as you."

"Why are you even friends with someone like her?

Do you realize how stupid she made me look when I accused these guys of not knowing what they're doing? *Jesus*."

"I'm sorry, okay? I'm just as embarrassed," his girlfriend says, pleading with him. "She's gone now. Can we talk about this later? And enjoy the party in the meantime, please?"

Tank sighs, turning to us as if he's asking permission.

Taylor and I both smile as she says, "We've had plenty of run-ins with Piper. What was one more?" We laugh, and the tension slowly fades.

The thick air clears the rest of the way when another car pulls to a stop in front of us.

"The boys are here." Tank steps around us to meet the giants who jump from the vehicle. They all fist-bump and joke as Taylor and I fade to the background.

Aiden glances at me, his eyes wide.

From what I can tell, the guys are football players and maybe other athletes too, since they're Tank's friends.

I nod that way. "Go. Be awesome."

He kisses me, squeezing me tightly, then waves to everyone to go inside and enjoy the rest of the party.

Taylor and I hang back as they lead the way. She pulls me close as we follow them inside. "I can't believe Catherine was ever friends with Piper."

"They were *friends*?"

"Yeah, in college, but she's always been so hateful when others succeed. Jealousy, man, it makes people do crazy things."

"You can say that again."

"She's wrong, you know?"

"What do you mean?" I stop and face her.

She squeezes my arms. "You're not getting promoted because of your relationship with Aiden or anything other than your talent."

I gulp. "Did you say..."

"You're getting promoted. I confirmed it with Mr. Cartwright a few days ago."

I cover my mouth with a shaking hand.

"I was going to wait until Monday to let you know, but I can't keep it in any longer."

"Oh my... Taylor... this is amazing," I sputter as I pull her in for a hug.

"We'll work out the details on Monday, but for now... we party."

"There's a lot to celebrate." I smile.

Taylor and I continue down the hall until we reach the rest of the crowd.

I meet Aiden's gaze across the room.

He grins.

He and I had ups and downs and learned from each one. We came out the other side as better people.

A better couple.

And I'm confident we'll be better parents someday too.

There was a time when I would've given anything to turn back time and alter what happened between us.

But things are finally falling into place.

We're together now. We're stronger because of our messy past, and looking back, knowing how things are turning out for us, I wouldn't change a thing.

CHAPTER FORTY-THREE
AIDEN

I'm standing in the middle of a huddle of football and basketball players. Around Tank McAllister and his friends. They crowd us like we're the celebrities here. As if they're eager to meet us, when it's the other way around.

I don't freak out over celebrities. I don't squeal like a teenager when someone famous is close by.

But when these athletes shake our hands and congratulate us, I damn near faint.

"I'd love to stay and chat about that touchdown last season"—I point to one of the quarterbacks—"but I need to be at the office in less than thirty minutes. Great to meet you all, and we'll talk soon."

"We'll hold you to it." They point between the three of us. "All of you."

Westin and Jared walk next to me as we head

outside. We remain cool until the door closes behind us.

"Is this our life now, dude? Being friends with pro-athletes?" Jared's jaw drops.

"I mean, one of them invited me to dinner at their place next month. What the hell?" Westin's eyes are wide.

"This is it, man." I run my hands through my hair, squeezing my eyes closed, soaking it all in. I open them and find them staring at me. Clapping both their shoulders, I repeat, "This is it."

The doors burst open, and Sage and Naomi come out. They're both grinning, and Sage jumps into my arms. "That was amazing," she whispers against my lips before she crushes hers to mine. She keeps her gaze on me as she pulls back. "You all killed it. Like fucking rock stars."

"Seriously." Naomi crosses her arms and cracks a small smile.

I want to stay and celebrate some more.

But there's work to be done.

And a proposal to give afterward.

"Go." Sage nudges me. "Taylor and I will handle the rest of the party. Then, I'll meet you at your place later, okay?"

I nod and capture her lips one more time, then head off with Jared and Westin in the direction of our building.

More champagne awaits us at the office.

"Soon, we'll be able to afford crystal, but until then, plastic will do." Nikki laughs, pouring a round for everyone. "A toast to Jock Stock."

We raise our glasses, and Westin holds his hand out. "I'll keep this brief. Many people don't understand what it means to dedicate your time and energy to a dream. To have faith that it'll work out. It takes a special kind of person to keep going when you hit one roadblock after another like we have." He looks around the room at us. "I'm proud of each of us. We've had long nights. Very long days. We've poured our souls into this, and I want to thank each of you for your dedication, resilience, and excellent work. This company is here because of you. And it's only the beginning."

"Cheers." I hold up my cup to meet everyone else's as we whoop and holler.

We disperse to our desks, clicking on our keyboards and mouses. I dim the light in my office. Nikki plays music from her phone, but it's muffled by the blood rushing to my ears. I can't hear anyone as I zone in on my computer, waiting for the clock to run out.

"We're live," Westin announces, and the real party begins.

———

"Come to my office." Westin sneaks a bottle of champagne and cups on his way.

"Are we in trouble? Being called to the principal's office?" Jared snorts.

I roll my eyes, then clap him on the back as we follow Westin.

The launch is a success. The app crashed from the number of users logging on, but between Jared, Lila, and me, we got it back up in record time. Our research, tests, and team proved to be effective. The board is happy. The investors too.

Users have shared and tagged us across many social media sites—they're even more excited about football season than before. They can't wait to see how their stocks in the players do.

I had to sit back several times to take in the positive comments and feedback. How is this our life now? I've asked myself this many times during the night. I don't know that it's something I'll ever get used to.

It's humbling and surreal.

"A special toast." Westin hands Jared and me a small cup, then holds his in the air. "It's been years of stress and lack of sleep. Jared, you might not have been there from the beginning, but you've become a partner. An integral part of this company."

I nod, tapping my cup to Jared's in agreement.

"We've come a long way." Westin peers at us like we're his sons, and it gives me a new sense of pride that we've come together—three guys with different backgrounds, families, and personalities—to create something this unique on such a grand scale.

After we clink, we stick around in Westin's office. Jared takes a seat in the corner, and I sit on the edge of Westin's desk.

"I'm just glad Aiden lasted this long with one laptop. How many times did you unplug it, hold it over your head, and threaten to toss it out a window?" Jared jokes.

"Oh yeah?" I point to him. "How about the time you showed up to the new office in a beanie, hood over your head, and dark circles under your eyes like a raccoon? Scared the shit out of Nikki, who almost called security."

Westin chuckles into his champagne.

I turn to him, swallowing my sip of the bubbly liquid. "Don't think you'll get away so easily."

"What?" Westin holds his hand out.

"When you showed up to our first meeting with our first investor? You wore suspenders like you were going to a fifties costume party."

Jared spits champagne onto the floor, his face red from laughing.

"Dude, the mess!" Westin stands from his chair.

"I'm... not even... sorry," Jared manages through his

chuckles. Clearing his throat, he shakes his head. "I'll clean that up, but so worth it. I forgot all about that story."

"As IT supply salesmen, we didn't exactly need to dress up. How was I supposed to know what to wear?" Westin shrugs, cracking a smile.

"You sure showed us." I wave my hand over him, by far the best dressed of us three.

After half an hour of us reminiscing, I get up and toss my cup in the trash. "That's it for me. I have one more accomplishment for the night."

"Go get her," Westin says at the same time that Jared says, "Lucky bastard."

I take one last look at them, finding comfort in our friendship and working relationship. We'll get married, have children, grow up, but at our roots, we'll stay the same—three average guys who bonded over sports. We may be millionaires one day, but the money will never replace our core foundation. One of understanding, sympathy, and brotherhood.

I congratulate the team once more and grab the bouquet of roses from my office on my way out. My fingers tremble during the cab ride to make Sage mine. To make her my Jersey, once and for all.

When I told Jared and Westin I was proposing, I wanted to tell them about the baby on the way. To tell them I'm going to be a father and celebrate with them.

But she said we should wait. I know she's scared, and I am too, so for now, I'll bite my tongue.

I feel it in my bones, though—we'll be parents. It'll work this time.

I walk through the door to my loft, clutching the bouquet of roses to my chest as I lay eyes on her.

The ring's in my pocket. The words and emotions are caught in my throat as I take her in.

Sage stands from the bed—she's in one of my plaid shirts. The top few buttons are open, and it falls just below her ass.

My heart thunders as I admire her—she's magnificent and sexy, and soon, she'll be showing much more. Which will make her that much more beautiful, carrying our baby.

This is it.

"Hi," I breathe.

Her smile spreads slowly.

I hold the flowers out for her.

"What're these for?" Her lips curl, spreading into a smile around the petals as she breathes them in.

Emotions further clog my throat as I kneel in front of her, taking the small box out of my breast pocket.

Her hand flies to her mouth as she drops the roses to her side.

"Sage..." I start. "I've been in love with you since college. Since we had lunch, and you joked with me about football. You didn't know anything about first downs or field goals, but I fell for you. I fell for you then, and I fell for you again when you showed up to our first meeting all those months ago." My voice is a soft whisper when I say, "I fall for you every day."

"Oh my God," she says.

"I've made a lot of mistakes in my life. Many accomplishments too, tonight included. But you... being with you has been my greatest joy. Now, you and I are having a baby, and I already love him or her with every bone in my body. There's just one more thing I'd like."

She dips her head.

"Will you marry me?"

She nods, her tears streaming. "Aiden... you make me happier than I ever thought I could be. Happier than I thought I deserved. Every day with you is... an adventure, to say the least."

I laugh. "Is that a yes?"

"Yes," she whispers, then says more loudly, "Yes!"

I scoot closer to her and wrap my arms around her waist, pressing my ear to her stomach as she cradles my head.

I'll be here for her and all the big things—appointments, cravings, baby proofing this place, or looking for a new place—all of it.

But most importantly, I'm going to be there for her with nothing but love and support and adoration as we continue building our life together.

I stand and kiss her, swiping my tongue along the inside of her bottom lip. I fist my hand through her hair and tilt her head back, so I can kiss along her jawline. "I love you," I whisper.

"I love you too." She grips my shoulders, letting out a gasp as I continue placing kisses down her exposed throat.

I continue kissing her there as I unbutton the shirt she's wearing. "This shirt on you..." I mumble against her soft cheek. "You should wear more plaid."

"I was thinking the same." She grips my shoulders, her chest rising and falling as more of her skin is exposed.

I capture her lips as I reach the last button. Running my hands inside, I brush it off her shoulders and down her arms until it lands in a pool around our feet.

"Fuck," I growl—she's bare underneath.

Her perfect breasts are even fuller, and every touch sets her on fire—she's more sensitive to everything these days.

I can't get enough. Of the way she jerks at the slightest flick of my tongue against her lips, her nipples, between her thighs. She's sensational.

I place my hand above her hip and kiss my way down from her breasts to her stomach. Lingering there, I place kisses around her belly button, my overwhelming joy clogging my throat.

"This is just the beginning," I whisper, still in awe.

A few moments later, we fall into bed together, getting tangled in the sheets as we make love.

Slow.

Tender.

Love.

I revel in her touch. Her soft skin. Her low whimpers.

Her gasps mix with my groans as I slide into her, moving inside her with slow, deliberate thrusts—we get lost in this moment.

All my dreams have come true—all *our* dreams. We're finally home.

Our home.

She shifts on her feet next to me, smoothing her dress.

It's flowy, barely covering her bump. She's almost four months along and has started showing.

She's healthy, as is our baby. Her checkups have been good so far, and each time I hear the heartbeat—the swooshing sound of life inside her—I shed a tear. It's the most beautiful sound. I even asked the doctor if I can have a recording. She and Sage both laughed, but I was serious and waiting for the day that'll be possible.

Next week, we'll find out the sex. If we'll be buying pink tutus or football jerseys. Who am I kidding? Either way, they'll be wearing jerseys. I'll teach them everything about sports.

"Do I look okay?" she asks me.

"More than okay. You're perfect." I kiss her head,

then splay my fingers across her stomach, hoping to feel him or her kick. Each time is more of a rush than standing at the top of the Empire State Building. Better than the fucking Super Bowl.

Feeling my baby kick is the biggest high I've ever experienced.

"I can't wait for them to meet you and tell them our news."

"Me too." She gives me a sweet peck.

I knock on the door, and after a few seconds, it swings open. My mom stands there, blinking rapidly. "Oh my God, sweetheart. You're here." She wraps me in a hug that reminds me of my childhood.

Of the love I felt.

I never went a day without her hugs. Without her hair tickling my nose. Without her sweet perfume.

"I told you we were coming." I laugh under my breath as she lets go.

"Well, I've been waiting for this day for quite some time." She hangs on to my arm as her gaze falls to Sage, and recognition flashes across her expression, although she's still shocked. "Sage? My word, you're absolutely stunning."

"You're very sweet. Thank you." She leans forward to hug my mother.

"Come in, come in. Avril is upstairs, and I'll call Mia to head over, and your father—Harry!" She searches down the hall and in the home office like he's a lost dog. When she turns to us, she gushes, "You two... It brings me such joy seeing you two together, and I have to know everything. All the details of New York City. Your work. *Everything.*"

"What's wrong?" My dad emerges into the living room, his shirt untucked with grease stains on the front.

"Our son's home." My mom stands to the side.

"Already?" His gaze locks on mine. "Aiden! Let me get a good look at you, son, because I don't know if I recognize you anymore." My dad comes around the couch and holds my arms out in exaggeration. He always does this when I come around, joking as if it's the first time he's seeing me. He studies me up and down like the time he checked me for broken bones after I fell off my four-wheeler. It was a few months after I'd broken my nose, so he was still wary of my body's fragility.

"I can show you my ID if you want," I tease, and he yanks me into a firm hug. "Hey, Dad."

"It's good to see you, son." He pulls back and pats my shoulder. "It's been too long, but I see you on the Internet a lot. Mia makes sure to keep me up to date with the Facebook and the YouTubes. I'm new to Twitter, but I'm getting good at it too."

"I'm proud of you, especially since you didn't know how to connect to Wi-Fi the last time I was here."

"I'm changing with the times, I guess." He shrugs,

and his eyes shine. "I'm proud of you, Aiden. You've done us all proud with your new company."

"Even though I'm not a lawyer?"

"Especially since you're not a lawyer. I never wanted to tell you back then, but lawyers are a little too stiff for me. And their sense of humor? Nonexistent." He twists his lips as my mom comes up beside him.

"Oh, you're just saying that because you and Gerald had a fight on the golf course last week," my mom ribs him, referring to one of three lawyers in town. "Now, sit, sit, while I get us some drinks."

As she scurries to the kitchen, I turn to Sage, who's remained quiet. "Dad, this is Sage."

"Nice to finally meet you in person." He goes to shake her hand but stops himself. "I just realized I'm filthy. Been working on the car all afternoon. I meant to get cleaned up before you got here, but it seems I lost track of time." Holding his finger up, he backs away. "Let me get changed real fast, and then I want to hear everything. All the details. *Everything*," he says, sounding eerily similar to my mom.

"It's true what they say," I whisper to Sage as we sit on the couch.

"Hmm?"

"Married couples *do* start to act and sound like each other after a while." I nod toward the direction my dad disappeared.

She giggles, leaning into my side. "I already rock your plaid. Now, I just need to get the growls and curses down."

"Doesn't sound like me at all."

She nudges me with her shoulder, shaking her head.

"Mia's on her way, and Avril's changing." My mom re-enters the living room. "I hope you kids are hungry. I'm cooking a pot roast, and it's almost done."

"Sounds great. Do you need help with anything?" Sage offers.

"No, no." My mom waves her hand, then takes a seat across from us.

After a few minutes of small talk, there's a sound of a car pulling into the driveway, gravel crunching beneath the tires, followed by a door slamming shut.

"That was fast," my mom says when Mia steps inside.

"I was already almost here when you called. It's pot roast tonight." Her gaze falls to Sage and me as we stand. Covering her mouth, she squeals. "Oh my God. Finally!"

I grunt when she practically tackles me and hug her back. "Good to see you, sis."

"You too, big brother. It's been too long." She smacks my arm, then looks behind me. "Sage?"

My parents and sisters have seen Sage on FaceTime a few times since we got together, so they recognize her.

But I'm ready to finally tell them the big news. We've only told our closest friends about the engagement and the baby. We've been waiting to tell my family in person before we post it on our social media.

Before I can scream it to everyone I know—and even people I don't.

I wrap my arm around Sage's shoulders and watch my mom over Mia's head. She covers her mouth with shaking hands, and I nod. "I'd like you all to officially meet... my fiancée."

The next few minutes consist of a series of screeches, cheers, and congratulations—and that's before my dad and Avril join us.

"What? What did we miss?" Avril runs down the stairs.

"Our big brother's getting married!" Mia holds Sage's left hand up to show my little sister.

Over the next thirty minutes, they gush over Sage's ring and the proposal story. We leave out the part about the baby, so we can tell them all together after we settle down. Too much excitement at once might make Mom's heart burst, so I figured we could have dinner first.

As the sun sets, we finally sit at the dinner table. My stomach's growling.

Sage giggles. "Heard that."

"I need food."

"I have plenty of it," my mom chimes in, bringing a

basket of hot rolls to the table.

Avril follows with the pot roast, and Sage hops up to help bring the rest.

"Put your phone away, honey. We're eating." My mom points to Mia once we're all seated.

"I'm sorry. I had to tell Tanner about the wedding coming up."

"Tanner, who?" I raise my eyebrow.

"My boyfriend." Her eyes light up like she just remembered something. "We're moving in together. He asked me last week. We have so much to celebrate." She claps like she did as a cheerleader in high school.

Boyfriend?

Moving in?

What the hell?

I blink, the gears in my head turning. "You never said anything about this relationship being serious. Don't I get to meet this Tanner first?"

"You know Tanner. You were on the football team together." Mia waits for me to catch up.

And when I do, I wish I hadn't.

I set my glass down for fear I might throw it against the wall.

My eyes bug out of my head like the cartoons she and I used to watch. "Tanner *Gardner*? Are you fu—" I stop myself, remembering I'm in my parents' house. We're at the dinner table. My mother will cut my tongue out if I curse right now, no matter how justified it would be. "You are *not* moving in with Tanner Gardner," I warn my sister.

"Good thing I wasn't asking your permission." She cuts into her pot roast like the conversation is over.

"What's wrong with Tanner, sweetie? He's a nice young man," my mom says, her eyes too innocent.

She wouldn't say kind things about him if she knew Tanner slept with everything that walked when we were in high school. He broke as many hearts as he did rules, and I will not let my sister be added to his list.

"For starters, he's five years older than you." I scoff.

"So? Not like I'm fourteen anymore."

"He's no good for you. He's a..."

"A what?" Mia challenges.

"A player. He had several girlfriends in high school —often, at once."

She drops her fork, and the clink echoes as Sage rests her hand on my thigh. "I know who he *was*, but he's changed."

I scoff again, at a loss for words. I turn to my dad, hoping he'll see reason. "A little help here?"

He finishes chewing, calm like we're discussing the weather. "Listen, I shared your concerns too, son. But the more I got to know Tanner, I realized he's a fine young man. He owns a business. He's a hard worker with manners, and he cares a great deal about your sister."

I grit my teeth, and Sage squeezes her fingers around my thigh.

"This is not dinner table talk, anyway," my mom cuts in. "Let's change the subject. Like Avril's new major."

"You changed it again?" I ask her, but my glare is still locked onto Mia. *We're not done*, I mouth, but she rolls her eyes.

Avril wipes her mouth. "It's only my third time, and it's my last. I realized my heart wasn't in psychology, so I thought about it and decided on creative writing."

"Really?" Sage perks up, and I fight my smile. "I have a minor in it and write some poetry."

Avril rests her elbows on either side of her plate, seemingly forgetting her food. "That's amazing. I'd love to pick your brain and maybe read some of your poems?"

"Of course. I'll do my best to answer any questions you have, and I'd love to share my poems with you. Actually..." Sage blushes, and I wrap my arm around her shoulders, nudging her to share another bit of news—we obviously have a lot of catching up to do. Phone calls haven't been enough. I've missed a lot. "You'll be able to read one of my poems online soon. It's being published in an online magazine."

"Oh my gosh," Avril gushes, pulling on Sage's arm.

"Congratulations. I know how hard it is to get one accepted."

"Oh yes, I got plenty of rejections before this. But it's worth it not to give up." She grins at me. "And I have your brother to thank."

"I didn't do anything. It was all you." I stick my fork through a piece of meat and potato.

"He writes a little poetry himself."

I drop my fork. "What did you *just* do?"

"Poetry? Really?" Mom's eyes widen. "I couldn't even get you to read a paragraph from your school homework, let alone write anything yourself."

"I didn't know you had it in you." Mia looks at me with a suspicious twinkle in her eye.

Sage pats my leg. "He's really very good. If he lets you read his work, you'll see."

"It's hardly my 'work' when it's only one poem, which was written in desperation to win you back."

There's a collective *aww* from the women at the table, and my dad nods as he chews, watching me with pride and respect.

It does something to me.

This whole dinner does.

We continue talking while we eat, and although most of what we share is news, it doesn't feel like it's been years since I visited.

We're a family. One that immediately accepts Sage like she's their own because that's what the Baxters do

—they're welcoming. There's a ton of room in their big hearts.

It's special, and I'm proud to be one of them.

By the end of dinner, I already miss my family. Two more days with them won't be enough.

Once the plates are cleared, Mom sets a peach cobbler in the middle of the table, and Avril brings a tub of vanilla ice cream to go with it.

"Wow, this smells heavenly." Sage rubs her stomach, and I can practically see drool falling from her lips.

I lean down to whisper, "Let's tell them."

"Now?" she asks, and her gaze never leaves the dessert.

"I can't wait anymore."

"What're you two whispering about?" Mia eyes us.

"Oh, honey, let them be. They're in love." Mom smiles as she places a big helping of pie onto a plate and sets it in front of Sage, then does the same for me.

Once everyone has a piece and is settled, I push my cobbler around as the ice cream melts on top of it. "We have one more piece of news to share."

Sage sets her fork down, waiting for me to go on.

I place my hand on her stomach and tell my family, "We're also expecting."

"Oh my God!"

"That's great news!"

"Oh my God!"

"Congratulations!"

More shrieks sound around the table as my mom throws her chair back and comes around the table to hug us both. "You've made me so happy."

She kisses the side of my head, then does the same to Sage.

Our dessert waits while we get in more rounds of hugs, and we resume as they ask us how far along Sage is and when we'll know the sex. What we'll name the baby.

At one point, I look to my dad, who beams. He has the same loving gleam in his eyes he gets when I do something he's proud of.

When I played football.

When I graduated college with honors.

When I moved to New York to take a chance on myself.

He always encourages me and makes sure I know he's proud of all my accomplishments.

I know I'll be a damn good father because of the example he's set.

When the time comes, when I'm in need of advice for fatherhood, I'll go to him. He'll be there for me, as will the rest of them.

As I sit back, my heart as full as my stomach, I feel at peace.

Whole.

Happy.

I interlock my trembling fingers around my belly and hold him.

He brings me calm and peace. Like he's saying everything will be okay.

Aiden and I found out we're having a baby boy. In the doctor's office, Aiden held my hand and kissed my lips and provided unwavering support as we went for our checkup.

Aiden's been strong these last few months.

When I was constantly throwing up, he was there to bring me water and rub my back.

When my feet hurt, he massages them.

And when he tells me he loves me, my world brightens.

"How's it going in there?" Naomi's voice rings out.

I open the bathroom door and step into the dressing room.

She brings her hands to her mouth. "You look amazing. Absolutely radiant."

"That's the sweat from being seven months pregnant." I laugh and smooth my ivory chiffon dress that brushes across my bare toes along the floor. I hold it up as I move to stand in front of the mirror and straighten the flower crown on my head, feeling like a boho princess.

I'm swollen all over, and I've never felt more beautiful. More blessed.

I rub my stomach, imagining a day when this sweet boy will be grown up. How I'll tell him about his baby sister who's an angel now, watching over him.

That she'll be in our hearts forever.

"You're the most beautiful bride I've ever seen." Naomi wipes at the corner of her eye.

When Aiden and I discussed our wedding, he wanted something for us to remember, and I couldn't agree more. When we were at Taylor's, we enjoyed our time in Long Island so much, we decided to find a place by the beach in the area.

And I'm thankful for this day.

Our wedding.

One with our closest friends and family. A wedding to Aiden, my true love. It's what I always dreamed of.

"I can't believe today's finally come." I watch

Naomi in the mirror as she rests her chin on my shoulder. "I can't tell you how many times I imagined this moment. The stars finally aligned."

"As they usually do when something's meant to be. Like you and Aiden."

I place my hand on hers. "Thank you for everything."

"I didn't do anything but order flowers, book the venue, put together the menu, and some little things."

"Yes, totally *nothing*." I roll my eyes, then turn to hug her. "Have you been okay living alone?"

"Of course. I've been so busy planning your wedding during my free time that I haven't noticed I even live alone."

"Ouch," I tease.

We both laugh, but my smile falls, concerned for her.

"I'm really fine." She squeezes my hands. "I work so much I'm hardly there, anyway. I'm even thinking of getting a smaller place."

I nod.

"How's it been living with Aiden?"

"Perfect." I sigh.

"Bitch." She nudges my shoulder with hers. "Kidding. I'm really happy for you."

"I hope..." I look down at our joined hands. "This day will come for you too, you know. You'll find your person too and have your own happy ending. When I first moved to New York, I stopped believing in love, but it's out there. It really is," I whisper.

"I hope you're right, but let's not talk about me. It's your day."

The door cracks open, and Naomi's mom, my aunt Ginger, steps inside. "I'm sorry to interrupt, but it's time."

I take deep breaths as excitement makes my body hum. "Let's do this."

I put my sandals on, and Naomi grabs my bouquet from the loveseat. She hands it to me, then leads the way out.

Guests of the hotel turn their heads toward me and smile as we walk toward the ceremony. I feel like a celebrity.

Once we reach the room where the wedding is being held, Westin and Jared stand by the double doors, as does Taylor. She's wearing a matching dusty blue dress like Naomi's. Taylor and I have grown even closer the last few months. She's helped me transition into my new role as a publicist for CJJ.

I inherited most of Piper's clients, but Taylor and Maya agreed to take over some as well, since I'll be off for maternity leave in a few months. I'll work from home a lot, but I'll have my hands full with a newborn, so we agreed to keep my workload relatively light for the time being.

Which I'm more than happy with. I want to spend every minute I can with my son.

Westin, Jared, and Taylor turn toward us when Naomi and I approach them. Westin comes to me first and kisses my cheek. "You're stunning. Aiden's a lucky man."

"That guy makes me want to kick his ass for being so lucky." Jared smiles. "I'm happy for you two." He wraps his arms around me, and I hug him back, laughing softly into his shoulder.

"You guys look great." I grip their arms.

"I told you I look good in anything, but this gray suit was an excellent choice." Jared tugs his jacket.

Westin throws his head back, groaning. "I swear, you get more and more arrogant and annoying every day."

"Should've known Jock Stock's success would do that to him." Taylor laughs, giving me a hug. "You're gorgeous, honey."

"Thank you."

Aiden's parents come around the corner, and his mom covers her mouth. "Sage, my goodness, I'll say it again—you're an angel."

I blush as she hugs me. "Thank you. And thank you for all your help and support during the planning and just... it means a lot." Tears well in my eyes as I pull back.

She rubs my shoulders, her smile widening. "Sage, it's my greatest joy to welcome you into our family, and this family?" She glances at her husband, then focuses again on me. "We're there for each other, no matter what."

A single tear falls, but it's a happy one.

She was there to help me put my dress on, as were Mia and Avril. They turned music on, and Naomi and Taylor kept things light and fun.

My mom may not be here today, but it's okay, because I have all the family I'll ever need here with me. A family who accepts me as more than their son's bride, but a welcomed daughter and sister too. Something I've never known and don't take lightly.

The outpouring of love from the Baxters is something I know our son will grow up secure and happy because of.

When we're in place, I stand to the side, and Westin opens the double doors. The soft melody starts slow. Taylor and Naomi both smile at me over their shoulders before they hook arms with the groomsmen.

Two-by-two, they walk down the aisle. I fight the urge to peek through the doors to find Aiden, but I wait. I wait for the big reveal.

When it's my turn, I step into the spotlight, so to speak, and the guests stand to face me. The floor-to-ceiling glass windows reveal the ocean beyond. Flowers decorate the small space. Everything is stunning— something out of a wedding magazine.

But all I see is him.

His mouth falls open.

His dark hazel eyes focus only on me, following every step I take.

He watches me like I'm all he sees too. Like we're the only two people in the room. His gaze is admiring. Proud. Loving.

And I know I'll write many poems based on his gaze alone.

My heart races as I hand my bouquet to Naomi and get into position across from him. He immediately grabs hold of both my hands and starts to step forward but stops himself.

I smile because I have the urge to do the same—to hug and kiss him—but we have a ceremony to get through first.

The officiant welcomes the guests and reads a Bible verse to get started.

We repeat after him.

We each say, "I do," and exchange rings.

My leg bounces as the anticipation grows until he says Aiden can finally kiss his bride.

And I kiss my husband like it's been years since our previous one, instead of last night. I mold my mouth to his, returning his obvious love and devotion through this one kiss, as cheers erupt around us. For a small crowd, they're loud, and it makes us both smile when we pull back to face them.

Aiden throws our joined hands in the air, which starts another round of cheers, and we make our way down the aisle.

Together, one hand in his and the other around my swollen belly, we pass our friends and family, our world.

When we reach the double doors, he stops us and cups my cheek with his free hand. His titanium wedding band is cold on my cheek, and it makes my heart skip a beat.

"Ready to do this, Mrs. Baxter?"

"If by *this*, you mean the rest of our lives together, then"—I stop less than an inch from his lips and whisper—"hell yeah."

I kiss him, then turn to walk with him.

As we make our way to the reception, our hands still joined at our sides, our bond is without a doubt... forever unbreakable.

THE END

Reconciled by Evan Grace

Deliverance by Kimberly Knight

Unbreakable by Georgia Coffman

Want to see what else is coming from The Salvation Society?
Click below for a complete list of titles:
https://www.thesalvationsociety.com/all-books/

ACKNOWLEDGMENTS

Readers—thank you again for picking up this book. It was emotional for me write. I smiled, shed tears, and clutched my chest in joy as I wrote. This story was my first real attempt at an angsty romance with all the tension, heartache, and happily ever after, and I hope it's one you found beauty in. I know this story will stay with me for a long time to come, and I hope it'll be the same for you.

Readers, bloggers, and bookstagrammers—an endless thank you for reading and reviewing early copies of *Unbreakable*. I'm grateful for all your shares, kind words, and amazing contributions to making the book community what it is—a fun and safe space full of support, love, and encouragement.

To Corinne and The Salvation Society team— thank you for taking a chance on me to write in this world. A big thank you goes to Corinne for opening this amazing world to authors like myself, who've been fans for years. This experience is one I'll always remember.

Bobbie Jo and Laurie—I appreciate you both so much for reading early drafts of this book and offering such helpful feedback. I'm so glad I was able to talk out plot points and characters with you both. You make this process so much easier.

Robby—thanks for always answering my questions and sending me insightful articles that offered me a glimpse of what it means to be in software development. It was vital when creating Aiden's character. I'm grateful for your patience, assistance, and on top of all that, your friendship too.

Marion—I love that you challenge me to be a better writer and storyteller. Your feedback has made a tremendous positive impact on me, and I'm so happy we've been able to work together.

Marla—thanks for catching the little things that go beyond proofreading. I'm so glad to have you on my team!

Kandi—I had trouble writing the poems, and you guided me to dig deeper. To sit back and consider the flow and direction of each poem. You gave me a lot to consider, and I'm so thankful.

Chelle—The Salvation Society brought us together, and I'm so ecstatic to have met you. You're there if I want to celebrate, to rant, to fantasize about beach vacations (we'll take one eventually!). Thank you for your generosity, your humor, and your friendship. You make this author life less lonely and a lot more fun.

My mom—where do I begin? You find the beauty in everyone and everything, and there's something significantly remarkable about that. I think it's because of you that I've come to have a special appreciation for poetry. For being creative in general. You're there when I need to talk. When I need to share my insecurities. You've cheered me on since day one, and for that... I'm eternally grateful.

To my husband, my number one fan—You believe in me. You're proud of me. You show me what love is every day, and it's the reason I can write about it. Being married to you has been my greatest joy, and I love and appreciate your faith in me. How you lift me up when I'm down. How you keep me moving forward so I don't sink into the dark hole of doubt for too long. I'm strong because of you. I'm chasing after this author thing—a lifelong dream—because of the push you gave me years ago. For that and so many other things, thank you. Oh, and kudos for thinking up Jock Stock and answering all my questions. I love you, forever and always.

www.ingramcontent.com/pod-product-compliance
Lightning Source LLC
Chambersburg PA
CBHW060609100726
47907CB00006B/1557